DJ

OF

INCAPACITY

~~ ~~

ANN M PRATLEY

BY ANN M PRATLEY

Power Moore Investigation Tales
Hoonigan
Resolution of Happiness
Home by the Sea
Tiger in Our House
Catch a Catfish Killer

Forbidden Conflicts Series
Amethyst of Youth
Ruby of Law
Diamond of War
Sapphire of Prejudice
Emerald of Wisdom

Freedom of Flight Series
Christian
Brandon
Trinity

Painful Deliverance Series
Painful Deliverance
Darkness of Heart
Friendship of Desire

Golden Desires Series
The Golden Desires
The Golden Supremacy
The Golden Unity

Chisholm Manor Series
Alessandra
Elizabeth

CHAPTER 1

Incapacity: the quality or state of being incapable; lack of physical or intellectual power.

When the news fully broke and the extent of what had happened was realized, the nation stood still with lack of understanding. What was being reported on was a truly horrific tragedy. Nobody had ever heard of anything like it happening in the history of their town, city, state or country. Surely it could have been avoided. What had gone so wrong, for something so unbelievable to have happened?

As the country woke up after the initial discovery, state by state the media reached the latest listeners and readers. Seaview. That was the name of the small town it had happened in. People actively had to go online to research where that was. It wasn't a town that had produced any talented musicians, famous actors, or world renowned authors. It didn't seem to be a place where some great business mogul had hailed from. There didn't appear to be any reason why anyone would have heard of Seaview. It was small and it was unnoticeable. When people drove through it, it captured them for a moment. It was quaint and pretty, they would say. Less than a mile out the other side of it, drivers had already forgotten it.

The first person to find a body was Molly Jenkins. When she woke, she moved to do the first thing she'd done every morning for the past fifteen years. Rolling over toward the centre of the large bed, she threw her arm across the chest of her husband, John. It was a cool morning, and his body was always reliably warm. Feeling his arms wrap around her in response to her movement each morning was one of the simplest but also most incredibly rewarding joys of their long marriage.

It took Molly only a sliver of time to realize that the usual warmth that emanated from John's body was missing. It just wasn't there. The discovery momentarily surprised her. *He* was there. He wasn't absent from their marital bed. No, what was missing was his usual heat. As Molly's mind sharpened, she realized it wasn't just his usual heat that wasn't present. With care and a gnawing thought in her mind, she moved her arm from over his chest, up toward his neck. As she did, a thought entered her head that she didn't even want to consider as a possible reality. When she touched his throat, she was stunned to find it was cold. There was no movement. There was no sound of him breathing. There was just nothing.

Inside her own chest, Molly could feel her heart begin to pound heavily. It was already telling her what she suspected. She fought to push her suspicion away and instead keep exploring. Her head and her heart were wrong. John couldn't be gone. He was only 35 years old. He ran almost every night. He ate healthily. He followed all the rules for living a long and healthy life. No, it just couldn't be true.

With terror etching deeper through her entire body, she shifted her hand once more. Up and over his neck it moved. Slowly and tentatively she let her fingers lightly glide over his chin until they found the lips she'd always loved to kiss. As she touched them, memories flooded over her. From the first moment those lips had sought out and found hers, she'd felt something she never had with previous boyfriends. John's kisses affected her in a different way. She'd always known that as long as they both lived, she would never tire of kissing those lips. They were full, soft, and always warm.

Except today.

Finally she felt tears come to her eyes, even as she fought to remain calm. There must be another explanation, she told herself in the silence of her mind. As soon as she turned on the bedside lamp, she would see that he was alright. All she had to do was reach over and flick that switch. Once she did that, she would have her truth.

With dread deepening inside of her, she lay still for a moment longer. She wanted the truth if he was in fact alright. If the truth lay in another direction, she wasn't sure she was ready to face that in the harshness of lamplight.

Taking one more deep breath, she moved her fingers up slightly. Under his nose there was no indication of any exhalation from him. Even though it was yet another sign of what she was beginning to believe, she ignored that and moved her fingers around and over his cheek. Slowly her fingers further explored, around the side of his eye and over his temple. Upward they moved toward his hairline. She smiled briefly at the feeling of his healthy hair. Often he'd made her giggle when talking about how yet another of his friends was starting to show signs of baldness. For as long as she could remember, it had been one of John's fears - that he would lose his hair young. As yet there was no indication that it was happening to him. His concern over it was something they'd often teased each other about.

Teasing. That, along with a great sense of humor, was something they'd always enjoyed sharing between them. It was rare that anything was ever taken to heart in a hurtful way. They were lucky in that. Both of them had always known it.

Molly's smile froze as she further fought the gush of tears that threatened to break free. She just had to hold herself together long enough to reassure herself that he was fine. As her fingers moved further into his hair, that was the first moment she felt an odd stickiness. It was liquid of some kind. She could feel it on her fingertips. In that moment, panic replaced the previous feeling of pending sadness.

Another slight movement of her fingers and she screamed inwardly. Where his scalp and skull should have continued … they didn't.

In shock, Molly moved with speed to throw back her side of the covers and jump off the bed. Although she made no outer sound, inside of her head she was screaming. She had to turn on the light. She didn't want to, but she knew she had to. She was having a nightmare. Someone was playing a joke. There had to be an explanation. It had to be *any* explanation other than what she really thought was happening.

For a long while, she stood unmoving. Naked and cold, her body felt like it had frozen still. In the darkness of the room, she could see nothing, but she knew she was facing the bed. Right in front of her was her beloved John. Only the two of them lived in the small cottage. Having kids was something they'd both wanted to put on hold. They'd only just had that conversation - the one where they had agreed they were finally both ready to move forward and prepare for parenthood. When they had made love the night before, it had been the first time they'd done so without any form of pregnancy prevention. For all she knew, she could now, right at that moment, have new life growing inside of her.

Pregnancy. Yes, that could be it. She'd heard about the strange ways it could play with a woman's mind. That was a perfectly plausible reason for the strangeness of what she was experiencing, she justified to herself. Their pregnancy attempt had been successful, she was pregnant, and her hormones were taking her through some weird nightmare.

Despite knowing she was just making up an excuse for reality to turn out to be fiction, Molly took a deep breath and reached toward the light switch. The journey of her finger from her side to the switch was short in distance. It seemed to take forever in duration.

Fearful of what she was about to see, she closed her eyes as she moved the switch from the off position to the on position. It was such a small action but in the moment, it felt incredibly big. Through her eyelids, she saw the brightness of the room change. For a long time, she stood still and listened. Whenever the light went on, John always affectionately told her to turn it off and give him some loving. She waited for his voice. He needed to speak. Before she opened her eyes, he needed to call out to her. He needed to reassure her he was awake and he needed her.

Molly waited to hear the comforting reassurance of his voice. As tears threatened, she clenched her eyelids down. She didn't want to face the truth that she was fighting so hard to not accept. Whatever lay before her, she wasn't ready to see it.

It must have been another five minutes or so before she finally knew she had to do something. She was naked and she was growing increasingly colder, standing as she was.

With fear and dread in her heart, Molly Jenkins finally opened her eyes. As she did, the sight before her made the internal scream she'd experienced earlier and had been holding back in silence, finally escape.

CHAPTER 2

Bryce Spring, the local sheriff in the small town of Seaview, felt comfortable after that first emergency call came in. There was no doubt it was a homicide. With his head half shot off, the physical form of John Jenkins was now only a dark shadow of what a good man he'd been. It wasn't a usual occurrence in their sleepy town, but coming to the decision that it was a murder seemed to be the easy bit. The hard bit would be finding whoever did it, but Bryce had been a big city detective in a former life. He could certainly handle a murder investigation, along with the assistance of his deputy and other staff members.

He'd maintained his confidence until a second emergency call had come in … and then a third … and then a fourth. Before the fifth call had even been made, he was in denial no more. Now there was something that had happened that needed far more resources than he and his tiny team at the sheriff's office could handle. Although proud of who he was and what he'd achieved in his forty-nine years of life, he wasn't too proud to ask for help when he needed it.

Seaview wasn't naturally in the jurisdiction of the Bureau of Investigation but when Sheriff Bryce Spring explained multiple separate and seemingly unrelated murders in one night, someone took notice. They were sending an investigative crew immediately. Almost as soon as he hung up from that phone call, he was handed notes. Five new calls had come in. Each call had been made by one person who had found one other person dead. All, so far, had suffered from being shot. Not only that, but they'd been shot in the head. Every single one of them had been subjected to a one bullet kill.

Bryce attended each of the scenes before he began to assign one of his crew to stand guard and secure each crime scene. When he ran out of crew to place as guards, he had no choice but to quickly locate a security firm in a neighboring town. After being satisfied that one scene was secure, he moved onto the next.

What he saw that morning would haunt him forever. People from his community - people he'd known - had all been shot in the same way, in the same part of their bodies. In some, bullets had passed through their skull neatly, leaving only a tidy hole. Others' skulls hadn't been left anywhere near as tidy. The shootings had happened in a diverse range of places. Most had been shot while asleep in their beds. A few seemed to have been shot in public places. One was still sitting behind the wheel of a car, her body left slumped over the steering wheel and a mass of blood and brain matter splattered the inner side of the windscreen.

The more he saw, the more Sheriff Spring began to question his initial thoughts. Perhaps the horrors he was seeing weren't due to homicide at all. Perhaps, instead, it had been some freak episode of mass suicide. That consideration was pushed aside briefly as the sheriff secured that scene so he could make his way to the next one. No, suicide wasn't possible. If that was the case, where were the guns that all the victims used? Although that might have been a tidier answer, it was inconceivable that the deaths could be anything other than murder.

At one point, Sheriff Bryce Spring thought he wouldn't be able to take any more. What he'd thought was a weird few-person shooting was escalating at an alarming rate. By midday, more than four hundred calls had come in. All were reports from someone having found a lifeless body - most often of a loved one dear to their heart - and the trend continued. Each had been killed by one gunshot to the head.

The sights just didn't seem to stop. In all of his decades in law enforcement roles, he'd never seen anything like it. Periodically he had to tell his deputy to take over. It didn't help. Even when he removed himself from the scenes, all he could see when he closed his eyes by then was body after body with such horrific images. Granted, those with a tidy and neat bullet hole were easier to look at than others, but even those were people he knew. The scale of destruction alone had left him feeling sick.

It was in that moment that he resolved it was time to give up law enforcement as a career. If something so horrific could happen in such a small and peaceful town like Seaview, he wasn't sure if he could take any more years of seeing such things. He'd see this investigation through, helping the Bureau as much as he could, but after this one was solved, he was going to retire. Many of the bodies he'd had to look at were people he had known to one degree or another. It was definitely time to stop seeing things like that.

CHAPTER 3

"Got your camping gear packed?" Special Agent Tim Moore joked to his work partner, Special Agent Ashley Power as they made their way out of the large Bureau of Investigation building that housed their offices. They were hardly ever in their offices but it was a central point they spent time in at the start and end of the many cases they were assigned to together. It was also where they were usually assigned cases from their superiors. Today was no exception.

"Oh, here we go. What are you talking about, Moore?" Ashley replied, grinning as they climbed into the dark Bureau-issued SUV. She had enjoyed three days of solitude in her home since they'd finished their last case. As always, by the fourth day off work, Ashley was itching to be given an investigation to go and work on. Her mind always needed rest after case completion, but even she believed there was such a thing as too much time off. After resting, her mind then needed to be active again, diving into the world of analysis and deduction. That was what she loved most about her job - the logical investigation that entailed working something out. Yes, there was the feel-good aspect of catching the bad guys and helping to put them away, but, for Ashley, it was the working things out that really inspired her. She loved problems that needed solving. She loved situations that needed resolving. In that way, her career with the Bureau suited her nature perfectly.

Tim and Ashley went out on jobs together a lot. They'd gotten well used to each other's humorous quips and teasing over their time as partners. Some might have looked at them on occasion and thought they were flirting with each other, but it wasn't like that between them. They got on well, just like long time friends. When Tim looked at Ashley, he knew she was a beautiful woman. That was forgotten day to day when he saw her on the job. She was a professional and she knew her stuff. Together they'd worked on some high profile serial killer investigations. No matter how they were when away from crime scenes, how they acted when on the job was serious. There were psychos out there in the world. Tim and Ashley both felt passionately about taking those freaks down and ensuring they'd never have another opportunity to hurt anyone else.

"I heard this 'lil town that we're going to has werewolves and vampires who have a particular thing for beautiful women in law enforcement," Tim said, almost giggling.

Ashley secured her seatbelt and started the engine as she looked at him and rolled her eyes. She couldn't help but smile at his immature and somewhat sick sense of humor that showed itself on occasion. Then she got serious. Rather than respond to his remark, she resolved to shift his focus back to business.

"Come on," she said, reversing out of the parking space. "Give me all you got about what we're heading into this time."

The tone of her spoken words settled Tim. He knew when it was time to stop trying to be funny. Pulling from his pocket a wad of paper and opening it out, he attempted to flatten it to make it easier to read.

Ashley said nothing about the state of the paper in Tim's hands. He was hopeless with paper, treating it as if it were something archaic from the dark ages. Sometimes when she watched him, she wondered if he'd ever actually gone to school, he seemed so weird around the stuff. Initially she'd given him more than a few stern words about it, then she'd gone through a phase of teasing him about it. Finally she'd learned there was just no point in trying to make him treat notes with more respect. Now she just remained quiet on that particular subject.

"Okay!" he started. "Seaview. Small town. Woman gets up this morning and finds her husband dead in their bed. His head wasn't all there."

"Shot?" Ashley asked.

"Yes," Tim replied. "The sheriff reported he believed it was, without any doubt, from a gunshot. He also believed it wasn't self-inflicted."

"Okay," Ashley said, nodding. "I take it we're not going to this town just because of one shot to the head though, are we?"

"Someone didn't read the brief," Tim teased her in a singsong voice. The look he received in return silenced him in teasing her further. "No, it was only the first of hundreds of the same kind of calls that came in before lunchtime."

Ashley was stupefied, assuming she couldn't have heard him correctly.

"What?" she asked in disbelief.

"I mean just what I said. By lunchtime, they had received around four hundred calls, all from one person or another reporting they'd found someone shot in the head..." Tim said. His words were cut short as the vehicle halted sharply, the brakes having been heavily applied unexpectedly. As he fought to get over the shock of what had just happened, he saw his partner turn to look at him.

"You're telling me that *four hundred* people were shot in the head in one place this morning?" Ashley asked, sure she must have interpreted his words incorrectly.

"Apparently," Tim replied, nodding. "Well, it's not known yet *when* they were shot, and it's not exactly in 'one place' - just the same town. From this, it sounds like the sheriff wasn't too precise in details, which isn't at all surprising. He's doing what he can to run around and make sure each scene is secure and untouched until we get there but he must be manic, to say the least."

Ashley sat still for a long while, absorbing what she'd been told. Hearing the news had left her mind rushing. It was hard enough solving one homicide, or even one that had several victims. The thought of four hundred victims was overwhelming, even for her.

"I guess we're going to need far more resources than just you and me then, huh," she said as she looked at Tim. "Holy cow!"

Straight away she pulled out her phone and called her supervisor, Sarah, at the Bureau office. Ashley was relieved to find that she and Tim weren't the only ones going to the tiny town. Fifty agents in total were on their way, along with an extensive array of forensic professionals. That number would have seemed excessive on any other case they'd worked on. Knowing that there were more than four hundred victims, Ashley wondered if even fifty or so could possibly be enough.

"Definitely not our average day, huh?" Tim muttered as the car started once more. The look on his partner's face told him she was equally in disbelief about what had been reported to have happened, and excited to be assigned to the case.

"Buckle up, Timmy Boy," Ashley said as she pulled out onto the road again. "Sounds like this is going to be one hell of a ride."

CHAPTER 4

Sheriff Bryce Spring felt like he was at the end of his tether. He'd never before been so rattled in his long career. Earlier on in his life, he'd attended quite a few scenes where there were multiple fatalities. This was different. Something about driving from scene to scene and seeing body after body made the situation increasingly more than he felt he could handle. It only added to the pain, knowing that so many of those killed were people he actually knew. That made it all that little bit harder for him to distance himself in the way that he knew he should in his role as the town sheriff.

It was 4pm when he sat in his office, looking out the window, and saw the first SUV drive in. Letting himself experience one funny thought for the day, he shook his head. Why did the Bureau of Investigation always seem to use black SUV cars as a way of being unidentifiable? It only made them *very* identifiable! He let a small sound of amusement escape his lips before he felt his eyes water. Until that moment, he hadn't realized quite how much the horror of the day was affecting him. Seeing two agents get out of that SUV and begin to walk toward his building, he felt relief. He was no longer going to have to handle the horrors alone.

Quickly he got himself together and walked out to greet them in the station foyer.

"Welcome, and thank you for coming so quickly. I'm Bryce Spring, the sheriff," he said as he held out his hand to both of them upon their entry to the building.

"Hello, Sheriff, I am Special Agent Power and this is

my partner, Special Agent Moore. We understand you have a rather strange situation here today," she said, wondering how she could possibly even address what had happened in the small town.

Bryce chuckled sarcastically even though it wasn't anything to laugh about.

"You cannot believe. Even *I'm* finding it hard to believe! But please come into my office," he said as he turned and led them through the station.

"We were told there have been around four hundred people killed," Tim said as he sat down.

"There *were* around four hundred," the sheriff replied, looking as defeated as he felt.

"Were?" Ashley asked. "Has the number gone down? Have some of those turned out to be survivors?"

Bryce shook his head as he looked at her.

"Unfortunately, no," he replied grimly. "When I called the Bureau at lunchtime, it was just over four hundred. At last count, we are now looking at," he said as he pointed to a whiteboard on the wall. On it was one large number, written in red marker. "Six hundred and seventy five."

The room was silent as all three looked at that number. It was incredibly difficult to comprehend. Finally Ashley spoke.

"I don't understand. Are you saying that all of these people have been found today?" she asked and saw the sheriff nod. "And … they've all be shot?"

Once again the sheriff nodded.

"They have," he replied. "Every one of them has been shot once, in the head. From the destruction, I don't think they've all been shot by the same weapon. Some heads are … well, let's just say that some victims look different from others."

Ashley and Tim didn't question what he was really saying. They both suspected they knew what he meant. Different kinds of bullets and different kinds of guns resulted in far different ways that the human head suffered when it was shot.

"Were they all in one place? Was it some kind of gathering?" Tim asked, intrigued.

"Nope," the sheriff said, his voice continuing to clearly demonstrate the depth of his despair. "Some of them are in vehicles. A few are in the local park. Most are in their beds."

"Did any reports come in last night through the emergency line?" Tim asked and saw the sheriff shake his head in response. "No calls to say someone had heard gunshot, or had seen anyone new or strange in the neighborhood?"

"Nothing," the sheriff replied.

"Do you think they were all shot in the night?" Ashley asked. "*Last* night?"

Bryce nodded again.

"So far almost everyone who is deceased, has been reported as having been seen somewhere or other, yesterday or last night," he said. "Whatever happened, it looks like it all went down between a normal bed time last night, and normal wake time this morning."

The door opening broke into each of their thoughts.

"Sorry, Sheriff. I just need to update this," the department office manager said as she pointed to the board. Everyone watched as the number was changed to 689.

"Another fourteen have been found since last update?" Bryce asked her.

"Yeah, I just got more calls," she said as she handed him yet another folder. "Eight are in homes in Lewis Lane, and another six have been found in other public places. I've got the full details here."

"Jesus," the sheriff muttered to himself as he opened the file. Again, more names that he recognized appeared on the lists before his eyes. In disbelief, he refocused on the two agents sitting across from him. "I've never seen anything like this before. Is the whole frigging *town* going to be killed?"

Ashley and Tim looked on, continuing to observe the extent of dismay on the face of the man in front of them.

"Not if we can help it," Ashley said quietly. "Have you attended all scenes found prior to now, Sheriff?" she asked and saw him nod. His mental and physical exhaustion was obvious. "We can attend these fourteen then," she said as she held out her hand.

Bryce didn't hesitate in passing the file to her.

"I…" he started to say.

"You're overwhelmed, as any of us would be. Take a breather. We'll check out these ones. Here's my number. Call me if more get reported," Ashley said as she stood. "Don't worry, Sheriff. Many of our best forensic scene examiners are on the way. We'll get to the bottom of this. We are going to catch whoever did this."

Bryce looked up at her.

"You can't think this is one person?!" he exclaimed. "Killing so many in one night? It would have to be a whole frigging *tribe* of people to kill like this, and if it is, where the hell are they right now?"

Both agents heard the frustration in the sheriff's voice. They could relate. They'd seen the best forensic and law enforcement professionals lose it before, especially over serial killers who seemed to have a knack for killing right in front of the world and then getting away with it.

"Are you married, Sheriff?" Ashley asked and saw him nod. "May I suggest you call your wife, tell her you love her, and then tell her to come here to be with you? You need her and, right now, this might be the safest and most secure place for her to be."

Bryce realized then that since the first phone call had come in earlier that morning, he hadn't even thought about Tracy. He felt panicked as he pulled his phone out of his pocket. After dialing her number and waiting, his panic increased. He was just about to hang up and run out of the building when she answered.

"Tracy!" he said, relieved. "You're okay…"

"Yes, I'm alright, but I've heard some news, Bryce…"

"Get in your car and come here now."

"I'm fine…"

"For God's sake, Tracy. I have never *ever* tried to tell you what to do but please come here," he said, almost begging.

"Alright," she replied quietly. "Alright, Bryce. I'm leaving now. I'll be there soon."

"And please … be careful," he said, feeling tears come to his eyes. "I love you. I don't know what I'd…"

"I'm leaving now. See you shortly," he heard her reply before she hung up. She was always curt in her responses to him. That had been going on for years, even though they did have what he considered a healthy marriage. He didn't usually mind that after he told her he loved her, she hardly ever said the same to him in response. With all that he'd seen that morning, today was a rare occasion when he did wish she'd said those three simple words. They took so little effort to say, but meant so much to hear.

After the call disconnected, he let the tears flow heavily. Nothing had ever affected him like that particular day was. Who would kill so many people? And why? What could the people responsible possibly gain from delivering so much destruction on the lives of others?

As the questions settled in his mind, finally his emotions dulled once more. They were valid questions. Who? Why? Resolved that it had to be done, he began opening the numerous files that had been piling up on his desk, and started looking through them. He knew he had to distance himself from knowing so many of the people who'd been killed. They were familiar faces and names, but they were also victims.

What stood out to him was that not *everyone* was being killed. Why not? John Jenkins had been killed in his bed. His wife, Molly, who slept right beside him, hadn't. That pattern seemed to have been repeated over and over. Why?

He was glad the agents from the Bureau had arrived, especially if they had arrived in the numbers the agents had indicated they expected. They would be the best at dealing with the high number of crime scenes, but Bryce was the one who knew the people of the town - those who were dead and those who'd been left alive.

CHAPTER 5

"What's the first address?" Ashley asked Tim in the SUV after they'd walked out of the station. She was slightly rattled from having seen how affected the local sheriff had been. She had already perceived upon meeting him that he'd been in law enforcement probably his entire life. The way he carried himself and the way he spoke said that he knew his stuff. It also suggested he had many years of investigative experience behind him. His accent told her he was from the big city, and not born and bred into Seaview. Knowing all that made it doubly concerning that he had been affected like he obviously was.

"Lewis Lane ... number 41," Tim responded to the question she'd just asked.

The address was entered into the GPS that sat on the dashboard. The town was so small that Ashley had no doubt it would only be a day or two before she and Tim would develop such a familiarity with the town that GPS wouldn't later be needed. With the feeling of urgency they both felt, it was a necessary tool for the immediate moment. Not that time would make any difference to the victims, of course. No, the urgency Ashley and Tim felt driven by was the time it might take to find a clue that would enable them to get on with finding the killers.

As they drove away from the sheriff's department, their minds were busy.

"How would someone even kill such a huge number of people?" Tim mumbled, mostly to himself. "I mean, think about those numbers. Six hundred and eighty nine people shot and killed, in just one night. They aren't all in one place..."

"It *is* a small town..." Ashley justified, also trying to make some sense out of what had happened, and *how* it could have happened.

"Yeah, but the killer still had to get from house to house, and so far we haven't heard of any reports of anyone hearing gunshots. Why is that? How can 689 bullets be fired in such a tight community, and nobody hear and report even one of them?"

"Silencer?" Ashley asked.

"Maybe," Tim conceded, nodding. "But then there's the issue of ammo."

"We don't know what kind of guns were used yet. All we know is what the sheriff said - that different weapons and bullets must have been used due to the differences in wounds inflicted in the victims."

"True," Tim responded, nodding. "But no matter what kind of weapons were used, almost 700 rounds is a lot to carry around and to take time to load." He paused for a moment, his mind rushing through possibilities. "No one person could do this. It must be numerous people. Perhaps a group of criminals ... except, in a small town like this, surely if a group of rough-looking guys appeared, looking like they were likely to hurt people, that would be reported. But again, no report. Whoever did this has acted with a surprisingly high degree of stealth."

"I agree," Ashley replied, nodding. "Whoever it is, at the very least they must have a military background - maybe even special forces. They'd have to have tactical knowledge and incredible skills in strategy. And why do it this way? I mean, they could have just planted bombs around the town if they wanted to kill everyone..."

"But they haven't killed everyone, have they," Tim replied, his voice and facial expression grim.

Ashley turned toward him and their eyes met. Both

could see concern in the other's eyes. Both knew that whoever it was that had delivered such destruction, might not be finished yet.

CHAPTER 6

As they pulled up to the home at 41 Lewis Lane, both agents took a moment to extend their view from the home in front of them, to further down the street. They were used to seeing the establishment of the crime scene tape that was secured around the scene directly in front of them. They weren't used to seeing it duplicated several times along the same road. It was a surreal thing to see. They weren't in the area of just one crime scene. They were in an area of a number of different and individual crime scenes. That was something that neither had ever experienced in their combined careers in law enforcement.

After Tim and Ashley got out of the car, they moved quickly to where they saw a law enforcement officer standing. Both agents held up their badges and introduced themselves.

"Thank you. The sheriff called to say you were on your way," the officer said, his face dismal.

"Can you show us in and tell us anything you've already found out?" Ashley asked.

"Yes, Ma'am," the officer said as he lifted the tape to allow the agents to move underneath. "Inside is one deceased - Mrs Joan Clancy. She was found by her son, David, when he came home for an arranged visit today."

"Is he still here?" Tim asked as they entered the home.

"Yes, but he's in a bad way," the officer said. "It's not surprising after seeing his mother like that but, so far, it has made it hard to try and get anything out of him.

Hopefully you guys will have more luck."

When they reached a small living area, the agents saw a young man in his mid-twenties, sitting still as if in shock.

Ashley moved to sit beside him.

"Hello, David," she said quietly. "I'm Special Agent Power. May I ask you some questions?"

The young man turned to her slowly and nodded.

"My mother … she's … she's … her…" he started to say as his hand moved up to point at the top of his head. "Who would do this? Why would anyone want to hurt my mom?"

"That is what we're here to find out, David," Ashley said. "Can you tell me about your movements today?"

"Yeah," he replied as he nodded. "I woke up at normal time, around eight. After breakfast, I went to the gym and then, after I showered, I drove here. Mom cooks lunch every Sunday. Well, she calls it lunch but it's more like a real late lunch or early dinner. She always expects me around two. I always come over and have it with her. She gets lonely…" he said before beginning to break down. "I should have spent more time with her. I didn't spend enough time with her!"

When Ashley saw him look up at her with intense grief in his eyes, the sight tested even her in not giving in to emotion.

"When did you last see your mother alive?" Tim asked gently, sensing from experience that his partner was already finding something about the interview very difficult.

"Last Sunday," David said. "We didn't talk on the phone much. We just always spend Sunday afternoons together. We've been doing it for years - ever since I left home. Every time I come home, she's here, waiting and happy. Nothing has ever been wrong before, but now…" he said before breaking down again.

"So you haven't spoken to her at all since last

weekend?" Ashley asked, having gotten her emotions in check.

"No," David replied. "I should have. I should have called her during the week."

"When you last saw her, did she say she was having any problems with anyone? Anyone at all?" Tim asked.

"No!" David exclaimed. "My mom was nice. She went to church and she volunteered for charities. People liked her."

"And your father?"

David visibly showed distaste on his face.

"He's never been around," he said. "He got her pregnant and then didn't want to know. It was always just me and Mom. I'd hoped when I moved out that she'd find someone to love - a new guy - but she never did. Well, not that I know of anyway, but … is that it? Do you know something? Was she seeing someone? Did he do this to her?"

Ashley watched as the young man before her appeared to get worked up by his hypothetical questions.

"We don't know why this has happened," she replied, trying to calm him once again. "But we will be looking into all possibilities."

Outside they could hear another vehicle pull up. Tim rose and looked out the window.

"Crime scene investigators are here," he said quietly, directing his words toward Ashley. In reply, he saw her nod at him.

"Do you own a gun, David?"

"No. Mom never wanted one in our house and I don't want one either."

"So you don't think she had one here?"

David shook his head.

"No, she was pretty anti-guns, and verbal about it too," he said. "She wasn't afraid to share her views on people owning them, or about the laws that she reckoned make it too easy for anybody to have one." He paused for a moment. "If she had a gun, I'd be pretty surprised."

"Thank you," Ashley said quietly as a familiar member of the forensic team approached. By use of hand signals, Ashley could see that she was being asked if they needed to check David's hands for traces of gun residue. "David, this is Damien. With your permission, I'd like him to do a short examination of you, including your hands."

There was no argument to what they wanted to do. Ashley left the room with Tim, leaving David to be subjected to anything that might help find his mother's killer.

After leaving the living room, the agents walked further into the home and entered the bedroom of Joan Clancy with the forensic scene investigators. It certainly wasn't the first time any of them had seen a human body with the head in such a condition. That still didn't make it any easier. The victim was definitely one that hadn't experienced a tidy bullet hole. Ashley found herself deeply affected by the thought that the victim's son had found her in such a state, looking like she was.

Tim moved forward, careful to not disturb anything.

"She looks like she was in bed sleeping," he said. "There's no sign of her making any effort to get out of bed. Maybe she was shot in her sleep?"

"Maybe," Ashley agreed, nodding.

"We're not going with any suicide suggestion, are we?" a scene investigator asked tentatively. "Because even looking at that from here, I am pretty sure that isn't likely."

"No, with more than six hundred people having suffered the same fate, I am expecting this to be mass murder rather than mass suicide," Ashley replied. "Not that I can even guess how mass murder could be carried out on a scale like this. You'll let us know your findings?"

"Yep," the scene investigator replied. "This isn't like any job I ever worked on before, but there's enough of us in town now to get around the scenes and prepare reports, hopefully within twenty-four hours. Sorry I can't give you any specific time or promise it any sooner."

"No, that's perfectly understandable," said Ashley. "I don't think this is going to be a normal case for any of us."

After indicating to Tim to follow her, they left the room so the forensic team could get on with doing their job.

"One down, thirteen to go," Tim said. The thought wasn't a nice one. Every now and then throughout his career he'd had to look at multiple bodies on the same day, sometimes even at the same time. The extreme was completely different. Having always had an interest in cases of mass murder, particularly centered around serial killers, he was pretty sure that nowhere in recorded history was there anything like the current situation having happened before.

CHAPTER 7

"I don't think I ever want to see the result of a head shot again," Tim said when they finally finished visiting crime scenes later that night. They hadn't stopped at the fourteen they'd told the sheriff they'd visit. Somehow it seemed like so little when there were literally hundreds of bodies scattered throughout the small town. "I actually feel nauseous now. Even the victims who have tidy head wounds are making me feel sick."

"You don't usually get so affected," Ashley replied as she looked at him. Over their time of working cases together, she'd gotten to know his body language and facial expressions pretty well. He was definitely more pale and serious than usual.

"I know," Tim replied. "This one has really got to me, and we only saw a small percentage of the bodies. I can't imagine how the sheriff is handling it, having seen hundreds of them, including people he knows. I mean, how screwed up is that, having to see so many people you know, dead. Most people wouldn't see that in their entire lifetime, let alone in one day. I couldn't do that without expecting a fair few nightmares to come."

"Hmm," Ashley responded. Her head was processing thoughts quickly, having been provided with so many facts and so many unknowns all in one day.

Since joining the Bureau, she'd found herself caught up in a diverse range of cases. She'd even seen some scenes that had caused nausea and nightmares for months afterwards whenever she'd thought about them. It wasn't the type of killing that was the hardest to accept in the current case. It was the magnitude of *destruction* that it had delivered to such a small town. From what she could tell, a large chunk of the small township's adult population had been slaughtered. The other half had survived. Why? In so many homes, one person had been killed while the person lying next to them hadn't. Why was that? What was it about one person in a household that made the killer feel it necessary to take that person's life, but not the life of the person who was so close by? There were just so many questions. The hardest thing about that was that it was impossible to even know who to contact to come and help out on the case. She and Tim were good in their jobs and they worked incredibly well together but if they needed help, who in the whole world might have already experienced such a case?

"You're thoughtful," she heard Tim say, his voice edging through the busy thought processes Ashley was indulging in. She loved the analytical side of working on cases. She'd always been the type of person who asked all those necessary questions about life. Who? Why? When? How? Where? From a very early age, she'd asked those questions about anything and everything. Sometimes the questions were easier to answer. She suspected they definitely weren't going to be easy to answer on the current case.

In response to his words, she smiled sadly.

"Yeah, this one's getting to me too, and we haven't even been here one full day," she said. "My mind just keeps going back to 'why'. *Why* would someone want to hurt so many people? Is there something all these victims have in common, to have made them the target? I mean, let's look at some common motives. Affairs - not impossible but probably unlikely that so many people in this community were sleeping with each other. On top of that, the ages are 20 to 89. It's unlikely the people in the higher end of that age span are having affairs or sleeping around. Again, not impossible, but seems pretty unlikely. So what else? Money? This isn't a rich town. There's hardly any employment and the houses are just ordinary. I doubt that whatever someone might be able to get their hands on around here would be worth the risk of going to jail for life over. And besides, why kill so many? Even if it was someone on a rampage of theft, why kill so many when they could have just tied them up or knocked them out?" She paused, thinking. "No, this killer had a definite motivation - and motive, I'm guessing - and was intent on the actual killing. Otherwise there wouldn't be so much consistency in their *method* of killing. But why? And how did they know they would so easily walk away? They must have known that the town would be descended upon by law enforcement from all over. It's a huge risk to take."

"Criminals never weigh up the risk, and you know it, Ash," Tim said, feeling a sliver of concern growing about the morose vibe emanating from his partner. "They always think they'll get away with it, no matter what they've done or how bad it is."

"Yeah, I know, but still, what is around here worth stealing?" Ashley pondered. "We'll look into the wealth of everyone who was shot, but I just don't think that will lead us to anything in solving this one."

"Well, history has shown that there are always the good old assholes who simply love killing," he responded. "For them, there's no other motive behind it except the killing itself. They get off on it. They love the feeling of power they get from it - or whatever reason it is that the psychologists reckon."

Ashley nodded.

"In that, I am inclined to agree," she said. "Whoever has done this, has possibly done it because they just wanted to murder people … lots of people. But then, why pick Seaview? What is it about this particular town that made it such a huge target for such a horrible series of actions?" she asked, still trying to work things through in her head. "And how did they coordinate it without anybody being aware of something out of the ordinary going on?"

"I don't know, but we can't do anything more tonight," Tim replied, determined to at least attempt to get her to let her mind begin to rest. He knew it was a pretty futile thing to try with Ashley. Her mind always seemed to be active, probably even when she slept. It was one of the reasons he'd learned she found it so difficult to take holidays. If there wasn't something to work out, she didn't feel like her usual self at all. "All we can do now is wait for all the test results and crime scene reports to come in. Once we have all of those details, we'll know more and we'll have a better place to start working from. Get some sleep. I think tomorrow's going to be a really long day."

They said their goodnights and went into their separate rooms at the motel they'd been checked into.

Once in her room, Ashley looked around and sighed. She was used to staying in such places - and worse.

"For once I'd love to stay in luxury!" she whispered out loud to nobody. That was before she lay down fully clothed on the bed and let herself drift off into a deep sleep. The hours of slumber were her best thinking time, ironically. She hoped that trend would continue over the night to come, and that the morning would bring new chains of thought and insight.

CHAPTER 8

Interviewing even the small remaining population of Seaview was intense on time, heavy on resources, and severe on the emotional state of everyone working the case. After the first night of tossing and turning, Sheriff Bryce Spring bravely faced the second and third days of it in his role of sheriff. He was thankful that his job of seeing the bodies had at least ended. It had taken time and quite a logistical exercise but finally they had all been moved to the large morgue in a nearby city. It pushed resources there too, but at least it provided one central location for examinations of the bodies to be carried out. It was the general expectation that autopsies would show nothing that would have any bearing on the case, but given the fact that the entire situation had never been heard of before, they were carried out anyway.

Once the wide range of reports started to roll in from forensic teams and experts, startling and unexpected facts began to appear. After working through them himself, Bryce sat in his office with the two agents he'd seen the first day, plus a diverse range of other investigation staff.

"So, wait," he heard Tim say, querying what they'd all just learned from the report summaries that had been explained. "Let me make sure I've got this right. John Jenkins was shot and killed in his bed. His wife, Molly, owned a gun and had gun residue on her hand but she isn't the one who shot him?"

"Correct," the guest coroner said, nodding. Even in her long career of more than three decades, she was surprised by the degree of killing that had taken place at the one time, in the one town. While a part of her had been excited at the prospect of something new in her job, the amount of bodies she'd been presented with in her small part of the investigation had taken a small toll. She wasn't the only coroner working on the case, of course. There were over a dozen who had been flown in to provide support on various aspects of analysis about the bodies and scene forensics. She'd had to work with new people, but as they were all in the same situation, having never experienced anything like it, everything about it had ensured a lively conversation and sense of excitement in the formation of possible theories about everything to do with the case.

"Molly does own a gun. That gun, and the residue on her hand, puts her as the main suspect in the murder of Joan Clancy. John Jenkins, on the other hand, appears to have been shot by," she said as she approached and pointed to the large whiteboard. "Tony Stiles."

Three whiteboards, lining one wall side by side, were swiftly becoming the location for a large chain image. Following through whose gun shot who, and which hand appeared to hold which gun, the image was a mystery but incredibly intriguing to all who looked at it. There were so many names on the board that it had necessitated finding someone on the team who could tidily write small enough to get everything in, but big enough for everyone to see.

Bryce could hardly comprehend what he was hearing.

"All 689 people were each shot by one person?" he asked in disbelief.

"Yes, if you mean that each of the 689 people was shot by one person *each*. You don't have one suspect in this case, or five, or ten. For the 689 people who were shot and killed on Saturday night, you have 689 suspects - one for each murder."

"But the guns? Where did 689 guns come from?"

Ashley asked, intrigued despite the level of horror presented by the case.

On hearing her questions, another investigator spoke up.

"They already had them," he said, standing and walking up to the whiteboard. "Every person who fired one of these guns, owned that gun. All weapons were registered and in the ownership of the correct person who had them in possession in their home," he continued. "Every weapon has been located in the residence of the killer who owned it. No attempt appears to have been made to hide even one of the guns used."

There was stillness for a long while as everyone in the room processed the information.

"So these 689 people got together and planned to use their own guns to massacre 689 other people in their own town?" Tim finally asked, breaking the silence. Even with having seen and heard all that he had, it was hard to actually believe that what had happened, *had* happened. "Why would they do that?"

"Obviously, that is the unknown," Sheriff Spring said. "After questioning them, the killers' stories all seem to be the same, though, and this is where things get even weirder," he continued as he looked at each face before him. "Every one of these suspects believes that on Saturday night, they went for a walk to the local beach. Every single one of them says that they walked along it, enjoying the full moon that night, and then went home. Not one of them has strayed from that story."

"And, is it true?" Ashley asked. "*Were* they at the beach?"

"No," the sheriff replied as he shook his head slowly, the stress of the entire situation showing on him. "We have CCTV pointing at the vehicle and pedestrian entranceways to the beach. Not only that, but one of the larger houses that fronts onto the beach has its own security camera. As far as we can tell, not one of those people who say they were there, actually were."

"Has anyone been down there? Maybe further along the beach, or higher up, above the water line…"

"There are no tracks or any visual indicators to suggest that anywhere near six hundred people were at the beach, together and at one time recently," Bryce said. "If that had happened, there would be something to show it. I mean, six hundred people? I don't think that many could even *fit* comfortably along that beach."

"What about further along the coast though?" Tim asked. "If it's a beach, it's on an entire coastline…"

"Officers have been sent out to check a few miles up and down the coast in each direction," the sheriff replied. "Not all of it has a camera pointed at it, of course, but given the state of the sand and the places where people could enter onto it, we just can't see any evidence that anywhere near six hundred people were anywhere on our beach areas - not that night, and not anytime recently."

"And yet, each of them swears they were there," the coroner said. "They saw each other there. Some of them have actually cross referenced what they saw. They could remember who was wearing what, and who was walking and talking with who. If it's a hoax, it's a pretty elaborate one."

Bryce absorbed everything that everyone had said, combined with all that he'd read of notes presented to him. The question on his mind glared at him. It had also crossed the minds of every other person working the case. When he spoke it, everyone appreciated him asking.

"I think the biggest issue right now is what do we do with these 689 suspects?"

No-one answered.

CHAPTER 9

Six Months Later

In the small inland town of Leefton, Chad Rogers received a note in his mailbox. It surprised him. He'd been on the run from the law for almost a year. While he could concede it wasn't really any way to live, the alternative of going to prison was something he'd been pretty determined to not let happen. Some days, he did question that belief. Some days, he felt like giving up and just being himself rather than having to be someone else all the time.

It wasn't easy living the life he lived. Constantly pretending to be someone else meant he could never be who he really was. As he'd traveled from town to town, he'd also taken on and used different identities. It was a tough life but somehow he was making it work. The downside was that he always had to make sure that he never got too close to anyone.

The year before, he'd met and gotten involved with one guy. When things had felt like they were getting too serious, and Chad had acknowledged to himself that he was starting to have feelings for that person, he'd stopped it. That was the point when he'd packed everything up and run away to set up a new life as a new person in another new town. Sometimes he still thought about that partner, wondering how heartbroken he might have been after Chad had turned away and left. It felt heartless in so many ways, just disappearing like that while knowing how serious both sides had felt about each other. In other ways, it seemed like the right thing to do. Maybe there would be residual heartbreak for a short time but, in the long run, things would have been far worse if Chad had been caught and sent to prison, leaving a lover behind, knowing Chad was a killer.

Day to day, he was lonely. He missed sex, yes, but it was more than that. Living with so many lies meant he could hardly have a normal conversation with anyone anymore. That was something he missed even more than physical closeness. Some people were meant to be alone. He didn't believe he was one of them. He'd always loved being around people.

In his early adult years, he'd had lots of friends. He'd been the guy who would happily begin a random conversation with a random stranger, whether it was just in a queue at a supermarket, or out in a bar. No matter where he'd been in those years, he'd always felt an eagerness to turn to the person closest to him in proximity and begin talking. He loved hearing about other people's lives. Equally, he loved seeing people smile when they realized someone was interested in their life. Life could be so lonely for so many. He hated that about humanity. Too many people were surrounded by so many people that they chose to ignore and never speak to. In Chad's opinion, that just wasn't right. Now he lived that life too.

Oh, he was polite when he *had* to talk to someone. These days, when he bought groceries, he always said hello to the checkout operator, but he never took it any further. Conversation had to be kept in check, otherwise it was too easy to get caught in a lie. From town to town, his identity changed. With every new name, he had to have a new background, and a new past life. Everything had to be calculated. Then it had to be remembered.

Picking up the note out of his mailbox, Chad noticed several things about it. First, there was no stamp. Whoever had felt the need to deliver that particular note to him might have actually gone to his tiny home and personally placed it in his mailbox. If they hadn't done it themselves, they must have found someone else to go to his home to deliver it. He couldn't remember seeing or hearing anyone approach the property. The thought of someone so easily having been so close to him in his own place made him uneasy.

The second thing that caught his attention was the name on it. It wasn't his current name of identification. It was the previous one he'd used. That alarmed him greatly. Who in his current town knew anything about his previous identity? No-one he interacted with day to day appeared to know anything about him. The thought made him nervous. At the same time, he'd been aware for quite a while that, at some point, his luck was going to run out. It was highly likely that, eventually, he was going to be approached and he was going to be arrested. Maybe it was time to just accept that and live out his last days of freedom however he could.

That resolution made him study the remainder of the note. It was an invitation. While most invitations would be pretty simple in content, this one was extensive. It came with conditions - lots of them. Usually he wouldn't be interested. His nervousness would normally make him toss something aside that he wasn't sure of the intention of. Whatever it was, and wherever it had come from, it had been formulated by someone who understood people and psychology. Even Chad Rogers couldn't easily turn away from wanting to explore and read it.

Once inside his house, he sat on the old sofa and began to read the invitation properly. It greeted him personally by name and invited him to a hidden and secret dance party that was being hosted by an 'internationally renowned' DJ. To get in, he would have to bring the invitation with him. To maintain the integrity of such an event, he would have his phone confiscated upon arrival at the meeting point. No phones or other technical devices would be allowed into the event. It was also vital that nobody else know about the party, or the invitation.

Each invite had a secret code on it. Each code would only be used once. If he shared it with anyone, or attempted to make a copy, there would be consequences. The invitation didn't say what the consequences would be, but the tone of the wording made Chad think it was a pretty solid threat that wasn't to be taken lightly. There was no lightheartedness in the extensive wording. Although the event was described as something fun - a dance party - everything about how the invitation was structured made Chad think it was something far more serious.

In no hurry to move from the comfort of his spot, Chad read it all through once, then once more. The card intrigued him. In his paranoia, he considered that it could be a trap. He could be reading an attempt to draw him out to arrest him. That didn't really make any sense. If law enforcement knew where he was - enough to be able to deliver an invitation - they knew where he was in order to arrest him. No, that made no sense at all.

On the other hand, it could be a fun way to go out if there was an actual dance party. In all his pretending to be a good law abiding citizen of all the communities he'd passed through over the past few years, he hadn't really let loose and had much fun at all. Who knew when his last moment of freedom would be. Sure. It sounded fun. He could go along and check it out, even with all those rules. Why not?

For the remaining four days until the night of the dance party, Chad said nothing to anyone about the invitation he'd received. He was a criminal but, at the heart of his core, he did believe in integrity. He also knew how important it was to keep some things secret. That was something he was pretty good at, even though he sometimes wished he didn't have to be. He maintained the possibility that it might be a trap and, if it was, that was okay. The idea of going to prison was becoming so tiring that he was almost resigned to it actually happening. He would be careful. He had the meeting point for the dance party. He would go there earlier and suss the area out first to see what was actually going on.

CHAPTER 10

On that Tuesday evening, Chad prepared to go to the event that continued to hold his curiosity. It might be his last night of freedom. He was prepared for that. Whatever went down, he was accepting of. In the instance where the dance party might actually be legitimate, he'd have a good time. Plain and simple.

For a moment, he considered grabbing his gun. He took a long while to consider whether that was a good idea or not. That was what had gotten him into trouble in the first place. On that night, he'd only wanted to threaten someone. He hadn't counted on it being quite so easy to pull the trigger while pointing a gun. Seeing the damage that bullet had caused on the other guy's body had resulted in Chad having nightmares for months. Still, now and then, he had a brief vision of memory about that night. It wasn't a nice one.

After lengthy consideration, he left his gun where it lay hidden. After another read of the invitation, he also put down his phone. They were going to confiscate it anyway. There was no way he wanted anyone else having access to the information inside of it. The best place for it on that night was safely hidden in his home as well.

As he made his way out of his home, he questioned if he was doing something that was wise. Despite the high level of concern he felt, his curiosity was intense. Someone had singled him out when they'd sent that invitation to him. In all honesty, that kind of made him feel sort of special. He hadn't felt that way in a very long time.

Although apprehensive, he continued his slow journey to the meeting point. The invitation had coordinates on it, which would be useless without a phone, but he'd checked it out earlier in the week. It wasn't a place anyone ventured near, he supposed. Certainly in the couple of hours he'd sat and watched it from a quiet distance earlier that week, only a handful of other single individuals had visited it. He'd suspected they were also invited and wanting to know where they'd be going if they attended the event. One by one, he saw them walk there, heads down as they studied the device in their hands. Once certain they knew where to come on the night of the party, they'd turned and walked back the way they came.

Now Chad walked the same route again. He couldn't deny it was an odd place to meet. Well back from the road, it was on a private property that couldn't be easily seen from anywhere public, and it sure couldn't be seen from the township. It was also far enough away from the general population for Chad to suspect any noise made wouldn't be heard by those at home that night.

Although the meeting point appeared to be in the middle of nowhere, he suspected the party itself was being held inside an old factory that had been abandoned decades earlier. It was within walking distance of the meeting point and he knew the site. He'd explored it as an option for hiding out when he'd first arrived in the sleepy town. The buildings were unused but still standing in good order. If the night really was going to play out with people dancing the night away to whoever this 'internationally renowned DJ' was, it was feeling pretty well organized. Despite the risks he'd assessed and accepted, he started to feel a buzz happening about the possibilities that the night could bring. Who knew - he might even meet a sexy guy there and get lucky. At that thought, he smiled.

At the assigned meeting time and place, Chad was surprised by how many people were there. It seemed to be well in excess of a couple of hundred. Curious about the whole thing, he stood back and watched the processes for a while. Three men, all dressed in black with balaclavas on, were scanning the invitations and throwing them in a small fire, then frisking each individual as they passed through a makeshift entry point. Now and then a phone would be found and taken, but as far as Chad could see, most people seemed to have done as he'd done and left their phones at home.

As he approached, his anxiety heightened. He tried hard to push it aside. If law enforcement was doing it all just to capture him, it seemed a bit too elaborate. Finally he let himself fully believe that perhaps the event was exactly as it appeared. It was just a secret dance party. It had absolutely nothing to do with him personally. He was just one of the lucky ones who'd been selected to attend.

While he found the hands of security personnel moving over him, he stood still with his own hands held up high. He held back the smile that naturally wanted to burst forth. It had been a long while since he'd touched someone, or been touched. He couldn't help but enjoy the large rough hands as they ran over his body.

"You're done. Keep walking," the gruff voice finally said in its dismissal of Chad.

As he followed the person in front, who in turn followed the person in front of them, Chad imagined that from a distance they would look like a row of ants. Each one was doing exactly as the one in front was doing. Nobody spoke. Nobody dared walk beside anyone else. Everyone was quiet as they trudged forward in single formation. They could have been being led anywhere, to do anything. Perhaps he was the only person to consider that. Everyone else seemed to be keeping to themselves, but on most faces he could see excitement and the odd smile.

It was a good ploy, he had to admit. Sending out exclusive, personalized invitations made people feel special. It made them feel important, like they knew something that no-one else knew. Of course they'd all keep quiet about it. He had no doubt that tomorrow, each and every one of them would break the rule of silence and go spouting to their friends about the amazing exclusive dance party they went to. That would be the intention of almost all of the people he could see. How easy it was to manipulate people when one catered to their pride and ego, he thought to himself.

After a long, silent, and mostly uneventful walk, the destination was in sight. He'd been right. The event, however elaborate, was being held in the abandoned cheese factory buildings. Upon approach, there was no sign of lights and there was no sound to be heard. In single file, people seemed to disappear around the back of one of the buildings. When it was his turn to reach that point, Chad saw the dark door and stepped through it himself.

At first, he couldn't see anything. From the sounds around him, several people were finding the same problem. Despite that, no-one attempted to walk back out the way they came in. Like sheep, they kept walking forward, sometimes reaching out with their hands to touch the back of the person in front of them.

Through his steps, Chad could feel they were gradually walking down a slight incline. It went on for a long while. Finally he found himself entering through another door. Beyond it was a small room. It fitted only five or so people in it and had another door on the other side. Between the two doors, another frisking happened. There was just enough light in the room for it to be possible to see, even though it still was not bright.

Chad happily raised his arms again as yet another large and very buff man in black ran his hands all over Chad's body. Not surprising, Chad found himself in no hurry at all to pull away.

"Move along," yet another gruff voice said. There was no amusement present in it.

Smiling in happiness and apprehension, Chad stepped through the final door. On the other side, he was greeted by a huge open area. It was lit up with a wide array of lights in different colors. A small makeshift stage was set up in the centre of the room. All around, people were finally relaxing and talking to one another. It did actually look like a proper music venue. Chad was more than a little impressed.

As he waited for something to happen, he walked around. His eyes cast over the crowd of people. Some of them he recognized from different roles they played in the town. Generally he kept to himself but he did identify a couple of checkout operators from the supermarket, and a few other people from different places he'd had to visit. Everyone was smiling and their excitement was evident.

"Oh, excuse me," he heard a deep voice say from behind him as he felt a nudge against his back. When he turned around, he definitely liked what he saw.

"No problem," he said, grinning. No more words were needed.

Someone appearing on the centre stage was so discreet that hardly anyone noticed until he stood up and called out.

"How are y'all doing tonight?" a silky voice yelled over the buzz of the crowd. Straight away, people whistled and cheered. "Thank you, my friends. Let's get this party started!"

It was a short speech but it was all that was needed.

Finally, after so much anticipation, music started and it was good. The noise level went up immensely. As Chad looked around, he saw there were smiles everywhere. He was even further impressed. In addition to no cell phones, there was also a no liquor rule. A few people had lost drugs or bottles of booze along the journey from the meeting place to where they currently were. From the smiles all around, Chad suspected no-one was missing that.

"Man, this is wild!" he heard the deep voice say beside him. "Wanna get closer to the stage?"

Chad smiled and nodded. He didn't know if he was getting hit on. Despite having come to grips with his sexuality years earlier, he still found he hadn't honed his 'gay radar'. Because it was an ongoing fear, responding to someone in a way that wouldn't be welcome, he'd resolved long ago that he'd never come onto another guy. He definitely would welcome it if someone was blatant in their approach toward him, though.

Together, the two men moved inwards and around the other side of the stage. The darkened area was getting more and more packed but that didn't seem to stop anyone's enthusiasm. Once the two of them decided on what seemed to be a suitable spot, Chad found himself enjoying the company of his mystery man. If he'd worried he might be off the mark about being hit on, that concern was dismissed fairly soon into the evening. Not only was the dream guy moving against him with his body and his hands, but he also wasn't pulling away when Chad reciprocated. With every minute that passed, Chad's smile grew.

It seemed like hours passed, with people grinning as though they were euphoric. Some were sweaty and others were breathless. In parts of the room, it seemed as if unlikely people were coupling up. As Chad looked around, no matter where he looked he could see it was a wild night, with the people attending being of all ages. Even a fair few oldies were in the mix. That only added to the smiles that Chad indulged in throughout the evening.

As if to indicate the event was beginning to shut down, the music changed. Once the beat slowed, the DJ began speaking. It was almost hypnotic, the tone of his voice.

As the voice spoke over the sound system, Chad moved with his dream guy. With their arms around each other's hips, he looked into the dark eyes before him.

"Do you feel like *weird* all of a sudden?" Chad asked as he became aware of his mind becoming distinctively cloudy. He almost felt like he'd taken drugs. He knew that couldn't be the case. No-one had consumed anything since arriving. Not even water had been made available. There was literally nothing he could have induced, and he couldn't smell anything in the air. Whatever was doing it, it was rapidly making him lose accurate awareness of what was happening inside and outside of him.

"No, way! I feel great!" he heard his dream boy reply as he continued to grin.

Chad studied the face of his partner. The guy was so beautiful, right down to the lengthy scar on his left cheek. The scar didn't take away from the man's beauty. Instead, it enhanced it, making him so unique.

When Chad saw lips move towards his, he welcomed them. When they pulled away, he grinned.

'I want this guy', he thought to himself. 'I want him forever.'

That was the last honestly independent thought Chad Rogers had for the next ten days.

CHAPTER 11

The country couldn't believe it had happened again. Yet another shooting spree had been reported upon. This time it was in Leefton - another small town that was so unknown that people who saw the report on the media then rushed to search the Internet to find out where exactly it was.

Pretty much everyone knew what had happened in Seaview six months earlier. No resolution had come out of that, as far as anyone had heard. No news channel had reported on *what* had driven more than six hundred people to shoot an equal number of other people in their town, even though the shooting had been well reported upon countrywide, as had the news that the multitudes of shooters had been moved into custody in a secure military environment. It wasn't usually the place for murderers to be housed but it was the only place that was secure enough for so many, in an investigation that seemed far from regular. That so many people had been shot by people that many of the victims knew was something that still stumped even the highest ranking crime investigators.

As soon as the first ten calls came into the Leefton emergency call line between 6:00am and 6:30am, the local police department was on high alert. They, too, knew what had happened in Seaview six months earlier, and that it was still a mess of an investigation going on.

Receiving so many calls in such a short period of time made Chief Shane Brown's heart begin to pound. He immediately called the number that was associated with the Seaview incident, not hesitating even for a moment. If the Leefton death toll stopped at ten, that was fine. Maybe it was an overreaction to call the Bureau of Investigation just for that and, if so, that was okay. He'd happily face the telling off he'd probably receive from above. Still, in his view, it was better to be over cautious than under.

When he got off the call to them, he was informed of another twelve calls that had come in only while he was on the phone. On hearing that news, he hung his head in disbelief. Shit. Not only had it happened again, but it had happened in his town. What were the chances?

CHAPTER 12

Across country, Special Agent Ashley Power was summoned into her supervisor's office. She'd been on forced annual leave for the previous two weeks. It had been long enough to almost drive her stir crazy. Even though she did enjoy taking a couple of days off after finishing a case, she was a hard worker and she loved that. She wasn't meant to be idle - not for too long anyway.

"Take a seat, Power," her supervisor, Sarah, said.

Hearing the seriousness in Sarah's voice, Ashley prepared herself for some kind of reprimand - or worse, that she still hadn't used up enough annual leave. She couldn't have been more surprised by the words that next came out of her supervisor's mouth.

"It's happened again," Sarah went on to say.

Even though there was no real information provided in those words, Ashley immediately felt her heart begin to beat more loudly.

"What has?" she asked, but in her gut she knew.

"I suspect I don't need to detail it. I can tell from your face that you've already guessed correctly," said Sarah, assessing her agent's demeanor. "This time it's in a town called Leefton. I know the Seaview case shook you up..."

"I'm on it. When do I leave?" Ashley asked as she stood up. She hadn't been given any real information but her gut feeling had escalated.

"Sit down," Sarah said and waited for Ashley to take her seat again before she continued. "I need to know you're up for this. The Seaview mass shooting has never been closed."

Unsure if that was a question or a statement, Ashley shook her head.

"Well, we know *who* did the shooting," she said. "*Why* is the one aspect that we haven't uncovered yet. All of the shooters are still telling the same story. They've all been put through extensive polygraph testing. As far as all of them seem to know, they were at a friendly gathering at the local beach. Unless they all have secrets for fooling the polygraph, they really do seem to believe that none of them used their guns that night."

Sarah nodded. She'd read everything on the case and already knew the extent of uncertainty around Seaview. It was a scenario she'd never been associated with, or even heard of during her long career with the Bureau. And even though she had a decade more experience than Ashley, Sarah wasn't sure she'd have been able to handle the sights that Ashley and Tim had seen in Seaview.

"We'll uncover that," she said. "In the meantime, this new case has happened. The numbers weren't as high when the Leefton Chief of Police called, but there were enough bodies by then for me to think that a visit is justified."

Ashley waited in silence during the long pause before her supervisor spoke again.

"Do you really think you're up for this, Ashley?" Sarah asked. "It's more bodies, again with bullet wounds in the head…"

"I'm up for it," said Ashley. "I know … I know we haven't quite gotten to the complete bottom of the Seaview case, but maybe, this time, whoever is behind this will have left a clue. This could be just what we need to put the final piece into the Seaview puzzle."

"I agree," Sarah said, nodding. "I'll assemble a team…"

"The same one, please," said Ashley.

"I'll be sending a mix," her supervisor said sternly. "Some of those who worked at Seaview will be assigned, but I'm also going to throw in new people too. They'll see things with fresh eyes. I think that's essential."

"Yes," Ashley replied, nodding. Her heart was pumping quickly. She'd moved on with other cases in previous months. No matter what else was thrown at her, Seaview was never far from her mind or her heart. "And Special Agent Moore?"

She watched as she saw her supervisor smile. It was a rare thing to see.

"Yes, your partner will be going with you," Sarah replied. "Now, go get prepared to leave. The two of you need to be at the airport in ninety minutes for your flight."

"Thank you," said Ashley as she stood and prepared to leave.

Before she reached the door, she heard her supervisor call out to her.

"We're going to figure this out and stop whoever is behind this, Power."

Ashley nodded once more, smiled sadly, and walked out. She could only hope that the words she'd just heard would, indeed, prove true.

"Want me to pick you up?" she said into her phone as she ran to her car.

On the other end of the call was her work partner, Special Agent Tim Moore.

"Yep, I just got the call," Tim said. "I'll be ready and waiting out front by the time you get here."

As she drove over to Tim's apartment, Ashley's mind was active, and her emotions were intense. Even though they had solved who had shot who in Seaview, it just didn't feel like the case was actually closed. It was out of character for every single shooter in Seaview to hurt anyone. Why did they do it, and how had it come to happen that every one of them fired a bullet from their own gun at almost the same time? It must have been a coordinated attack, but how? *How* did that occur?

Of further confusion in the Seaview case was the mystery of some victims having been killed in their own beds, but their partners - the people who loved them and slept beside them - didn't seem to have any idea of the death in their beds until the next morning. Whether those victims had been shot while their loved ones were beside them, or they'd been shot while their partners were killing someone else, how was it that none of the living partners had perceived the death of their loved ones at the time it had happened? Still there were too many unanswered questions - just too many!

When she pulled up to the curb outside Tim's apartment block, he was already standing there, waiting. Ashley only had to slow down. They had been through the same action too many times to count. She hadn't even completely stopped the car when Tim opened the passenger door and jumped in with his small carry on bag on his lap. The car was already moving off again as he closed the door and put on his seatbelt.

"Unbelievable, right?" he asked as he finally turned to look at her. "Do you think it's the same thing?"

Just as he asked, both of their cell phones sounded. Looking at the screens, one word came out of both of their mouths at the same time.

"Shit."

On the screens both read the text clearly - and the figure. 'Leefton: 389 dead so far. All headshot wounds'.

The words were so few but they packed a punch.

"I can't believe this," Ashley muttered as she pressed her foot a little more down on the accelerator. "Are you ready to go another round of this?" she asked, finally giving her partner a thought. When she turned to look at him, she suspected the expression on his face pretty much mirrored her own.

"Whatever is making this happen, we have to stop it," Tim said quietly. The sadness evident in his eyes showed his compassionate side. "What a mess. Okay!" he then said, sitting up straighter while trying hard to switch off his emotion and switch on his analytical mind. "Let's look at this. Seaview. Six-eighty-nine fatalities caused by 689 people. Leefton. Three-eighty-nine…"

"So far," Ashley added into his conversation.

"So far," Tim agreed. "Where is Leefton? Could the same people or person who initiated the Seaview shootings, also spend time in Leefton?"

"I don't think so," said Ashley. "I mean, one's on the east coast and the other's in the central midwest. I suppose it could be someone who's traveling around. Lots of people travel for work these days. Maybe a truck driver?"

"Maybe. It has been six months," Tim said. "Do we know that there definitely hasn't been anything like this in the interim between these two points? Maybe it wasn't something on such a large scale so it hasn't been associated."

Ashley churned the idea over in her mind.

"You mean like maybe there've been some mass shootings on a smaller scale?" she asked.

"Yeah," Tim replied, nodding. "Whoever is doing this might have still been killing, but maybe they've been playing all this time with only individual shootings or only a handful of people at a time."

"Well, we know that all shooters in Seaview believed they were somewhere else, doing something else, rather than going and shooting who they each shot," Ashley said. "I guess if we put the feelers out for any instances where the killer was identified but didn't seem to have any recollection of it…"

"I think so too," Tim agreed. "It's a long shot, but it's

something. Plus if we can connect a few more dots around location, maybe we can identify someone who was in each of these places at the time these shootings happened."

"But, Tim, do you really think one person is orchestrating these killings?" Ashley asked. "I mean, how could someone even do that?"

Tim shrugged his shoulders.

"I have no idea, but this definitely isn't a normal case," he replied. "I think we have to be open to anything."

Ashley nodded but didn't say anything more. She'd heard stories of brainwashing and telepathy. She wasn't sure she believed in anything out of the ordinary, but she knew that in her job she had to at least consider all options. The easiest thing to believe was that all of the shooters in Seaview simply made up and stuck to the same story. That was possible. How they'd all managed to fool more than one polygraph test was uncertain. That test seemed to show that they all at least *believed* they were where they actually weren't. They'd have to have all been very good liars to fool the tests that were run. Was that even possible? Could part of the shooting spree have been receiving training in fooling a polygraph test as well?

As active as her mind was, Ashley knew there were no answers yet. All they could do in the present moment was get to Leefton and begin all over again.

With that in mind, her foot pushed down even harder on the accelerator.

CHAPTER 13

"Do you really think this is the same as the Seaview massacre?" Shane Brown, the Chief of Police in Leefton, asked when two Bureau of Investigation agents sat opposite him in his office. He'd been much faster to call in the Bureau than the sheriff of Seaview had been. Of course he had. Anybody in the entire country would have acted quickly after learning about the first few victims. They'd all suffered the same fate that those in Seaview had. It couldn't be just a coincidence. Somehow it all had to be related. How, it was impossible to guess, but it had to be.

"Do *you* think it's the same?" Tim asked the police chief in reply.

"I don't know what to believe," Shane replied. "The number of identified dead is now 743. It seems to be rising by the minute. There are bodies all over the place."

Ashley watched his face as he spoke. With Leefton being another small town but still larger than Seaview, it at least had a healthy sized police department. Looking at the police chief she faced, Ashley suspected he hadn't yet seen anything like Sheriff Bryce Spring had seen in his tiny town. Now and then, she still thought of Bryce Spring and the way he'd been psychologically affected by the mass shooting in Seaview. She'd heard he'd retired straight after that. He hadn't wanted to wait to see the case through to completion. Ashley hoped he'd found peace and some way to relax his mind after the masses of bodies he'd seen that first day after the Seaview shootings. Briefly she wondered if the Leefton Chief of Police personally knew the same percentage of victims and killers in his town as Sheriff Spring had. Despite her curiosity, it wasn't a question she particularly wanted to ask.

"Our crews of investigators are still arriving but those that are here have already begun visiting crime scenes, Chief," she heard Tim say, breaking her out of her thoughts. "Have the victims all been killed in the same manner?"

Chief Brown nodded, his face reflecting the gravity of the situation.

"All have been shot in the head," he said. "As far as we can tell, they're all one-shot kills."

Tim nodded in reply.

"It is looking like the same kind of mass murder, then, isn't it," he said quietly. He felt a combination of frustration, sadness, and determination to hunt down whoever was making such horrible things happen. "As Seaview, I mean."

As Ashley saw the chief nod, she also felt mixed emotions inside.

"Well, Chief Brown..." she started to say as she stood in preparation to leave.

"Shane, please," the Chief said, cutting her words short. "I don't think I can handle formality with this case."

"Of course. Shane," Ashley said, nodding. "We have details of the first scenes to visit. During the day, more of our agents and forensic staff will be turning up here as well. Please keep us informed as you receive more calls."

"You think calls will keep coming in?" Shane asked, feeling nauseous at the thought. "*More* of them?"

"Calls were coming in all day in Seaview," Tim replied. "I think you have to be open to more bodies being found yet, yes."

Chief Shane Brown said nothing as the agents left his office. The number of bodies was already in to the hundreds. Leefton was hardly a metropolis. Just how high could the body count go?

CHAPTER 14

When Chad Rogers first heard about the shootings, he was surprised. For almost a year, he'd made a point of never watching or listening to the news, and he didn't follow social media. He did all that he could to avoid interaction with anyone in any way. His first clue about the shootings came when he went to the grocery store and overheard people talking about what had happened. He didn't question anyone about any of it. To do so would have meant bringing attention to himself. He had no intention of doing that.

It was a curious thing, so many people having been killed in one night. He hadn't even heard any guns going off. Not that *that* meant anything he supposed. His house was a fair distance away from the main town, which was just how he liked to live. It was handy enough to be able to go and buy food or whatever else he needed. It was far enough away to be private.

As he entered his home, his mind was cast back to the night before. He'd gone for a long walk along the top walking track on the cliffs. It had been a great walk. He couldn't even remember what had inspired him to do it. He'd just found himself alone at home, and then suddenly needing to walk. The air up there had been amazing. He'd never been any kind of nature lover in the past. It just wasn't the way he was raised or the way he had lived. When he'd walked up to and along the cliff top, he'd wondered why he didn't do it more often. The air had been so fresh, and the breeze incredibly invigorating to feel on his face.

He smiled at the memory. Yes, he should do that more often. In fact, he should do it today. It felt good and it cost nothing to do. Why not? It had been many months since he'd interacted with any human beings other than those who served him at the grocery store. He worked hard to convince himself that he didn't need to see anyone else - that he was a loner. Walking and enjoying fresh air was something that fitted well with that lifestyle choice. Deep inside, he still wished that one day he could meet someone great to share his life with. In such a small town, or any other small town, how likely was that? Not at all really.

In the early evening, he ventured off for the walk he'd been thinking about all day. It was a beautiful night - calm and quiet - just as the night before had been. Once he was at the top of the long walkway, he could feel the breeze on his face. It was incredible.

For a moment, he wondered why he felt so euphoric being there. Having never been into appreciating the beauty of the planet, he laughed that thought away. Maybe the change in him was something to do with getting older.

As he walked along, he saw a couple walking toward him. He felt friendly. He said hello. Even that surprised him. When he heard them call out to him after they'd passed and smiled, he turned to them.

"Yes?" he asked. His happy mood was quickly replaced by paranoia and then resignation when he saw the Bureau of Investigation badges being presented to him. Shit. After almost a year, finally they'd caught up with him. He should have made time for some fun. He really should have.

"We'd like to ask you some questions," the female officer said. She probably would have been considered a looker by some guys. Chad preferred the male officer standing beside her. He hadn't met any attractive men in months. He really needed to do something about that.

"Of course," Chad said quietly while he wondered why they weren't already putting cuffs on him.

"We are following up some shootings that have occurred in town," Ashley said. "Where were you last night?"

Chad felt a sliver of relief. Perhaps they weren't chasing him because of his past after all.

"Right here," he replied.

"Right … here?" Tim asked, pointing at the ground but not at all surprised at the answer.

"Yeah, well, by here I mean this walkway right along here," said Chad. "Last night, I came up here. I liked it so much that I've come back today. Look at these views. I mean, shit, have you ever seen anything like it?"

Ashley and Tim followed the line of sight indicated by the hand of the guy they were talking to. On his face, they could actually see almost a level of joy that looked like euphoria. Given that the guy looked like the kind of hardened criminal they usually put away, it was a weird contrast to see.

"It is beautiful," Ashley said to bide time while she considered what to say next. "Do you have any identification with you, Mr …"

"Rogers. Chad Rogers. Sure," he said, pulling out his latest personal identification.

Ashley, honed to assessing how different people reacted to different people, could see that Tim was somehow affecting the guy in front of them.

"I'll be right back. I'm just going to call your ID in, Mr Rogers," she said as she turned and walked away. In that instance, she suspected Tim was definitely the one who would get information.

Tim watched his partner leave. He, too, could see something in the eyes of Chad Rogers that said he liked how Tim looked. That was always something that could be used to advantage in questioning.

"How long have you lived here, Chad?" he asked.

"Only a few months," Chad replied. "I move around a lot."

"Don't like to sit still?" Tim asked. For a moment, he wondered if he was looking at the actual organizer of the mass murders.

Chad considered how to take the conversation. He didn't much like being questioned but he was right in front of law enforcement. He knew he had to not look like he was a criminal on the run.

"I like exploring new places," he answered. "Now and then, I stumble on places like this and I stay there till I'm ready to see something new."

"Fair enough. Well, we have to investigate every person in this town, due to the high number of shootings," Tim said, gauging the response that would come. "Would you give consent to us taking a DNA sample?"

Chad lowered his face. The time had come. He had two choices. He had the right to say no to a DNA sample. In the time it would take for them to get a warrant to force it, he could probably be long gone. Or he could just save everyone time and admit who he was. His life wasn't changing. Really, he should just get on and go to prison for the accidental shooting the year before. What else was left for him? He couldn't meet or get involved with anyone new. He just didn't trust anyone.

"Sure," he said, thinking it could take a few days at least for them to run the sample. He could enjoy that time. Somehow.

Tim was surprised at how easily the guy had given in to the DNA request. He was about to speak when Ashley came back.

"Mr Rogers. It seems that until four months ago, you didn't exist. We'd very much like for you to come with us to the station," she said simply.

There was no resistance from Chad at all.

In interrogation, Chad answered only what he had to. He'd thought they would find out about his being wanted by the law for the shooting he'd taken part in by mistake. The more they questioned him, the more he didn't think they even knew about his past. They were just focused on the shooting that had just happened in his current town. That relaxed him. He didn't know anything about that, and he sure didn't take any part in it.

For hours into the night, Tim and Ashley questioned Chad Rogers. He was convincing in saying he'd been walking along the cliff walk the night before. The only problem was, so was every other person they'd interviewed so far. The repeating story told the agents that Chad more than likely did fit into the shooting somewhere. They just had to find out where.

A warrant was quickly rushed through to enable the search of his home. There, law enforcement officers found a gun. Once that was in their hands, they could fit him right into a gap in the same kind of chain drawing they'd created in Seaview.

Back in the interrogation room, Ashley presented him with a photo. It was a photo of the only person who had been shot and killed, for which the gun that killed him hadn't previously been identified through ballistics testing.

"Have you ever met this man, Chad?" she asked.

Chad looked at the photo. It was of a truly stunning man - just the kind he would definitely be attracted to. Although the person in the picture had a very visible scar on his left cheek, it didn't take away from the guy's beauty.

"I wish," he replied quietly.

"You've never seen him before?" asked Tim.

"No way," said Chad. "Man, I'd remember a guy like that. No, Sir. Never seen him in my life."

Tim sat back and looked at the guy. The tone of his voice and the relaxed stance of his body told Tim there was a high probability that Chad truly believed what he was saying. Tim and Ashley already knew that Chad was the one who'd killed Tony - the guy in the photo. The gun found at his residence had been rushed through testing with incredible speed, leaving no doubt. How could he have done that but so easily look like he'd never even seen the guy before?

"Perhaps you might have passed him in the supermarket or perhaps out at a bar…"

"Maybe in the supermarket, but I'm pretty sure I'd have noticed and remembered a face like *that*," Chad said, glancing at the photo again.

"Or a bar?" Ashley prompted him.

"No, Ma'am," said Chad. "I like privacy. I really don't hardly ever leave my house. Over the past couple of weeks, I've only been to the supermarket, and to the walk along the cliffs. That's it. I haven't done bars for years."

Tim and Ashley looked at each other.

"Would you be willing to give us DNA and take a polygraph test?" Ashley asked.

Chad looked straight at her, and then straight at Tim. He nodded, resigned.

"Yeah, like I already said earlier, sure."

When the results came back from Chad's DNA test and a sweep of his home, the detectives were surprised by other developments.

Tim looked up at Ashley as she handed pages to him.

"Tony was in Chad's house?" he asked and saw her nod. "They were lovers?"

"We think so," Ashley replied. "There were traces of Tony's semen in Chad's bed. Not only that, but Chad's

DNA was found in Tony's home too. "

"And Tony was … found in his own home, right?" Tim asked for clarity.

"He was," said Ashley.

"But Chad Rogers looks like he honestly doesn't even remember this guy," Tim said in disbelief. "Even the polygraph test he took confirmed that he's never met him!"

"I know," Ashley said as she nodded. "These people are really good at lying, aren't they."

Tim looked at her with his open expression of skepticism.

"Maybe one or two might be good at lying," he said. "You can't tell me that, between two towns, we now have what … one and a half *thousand* people who have all passed a polygraph test in these two cases, that are *all* that good at lying!"

Ashley agreed with him. Something just did not add up, and not just in a small way.

"Well, that is what we have to prove, don't we."

CHAPTER 15

"I can't believe this," Ashley exclaimed when she began to work through the last of the test results and reports that had been prepared about the Leefton shootings. Although she and Tim had already read enough to see the similarities, it was still difficult to hear just how similar the two cases were. "It's definitely all the same as Seaview? Again?"

Mandy Smith, the same forensic investigator Ashley had worked alongside in the Seaview case, nodded.

"Just as we previously suspected. Same thing, just on a larger scale," she said. "This time, 856 killed."

"And 856 different killers, who all used their own guns to shoot someone?"

"Yep," Mandy confirmed. "It's almost identical to Seaview. Shooter A uses Shooter A's own gun to shoot victim 1. Shooter B uses Shooter's B own gun to shoot victim 2. It's exactly the same thing, Ashley."

"And the time of death?"

"We believe that is also the same again," said Mandy. "All 856 were shot at pretty much the same time, most likely between 11pm and 1am."

Tim remained quiet as he listened to the conversation. The demeanor of his partner was evident. She was frustrated. She'd also wanted at least *something* about the event to be different from what had happened in Seaview. It was disheartening for everyone investigating, that somehow the same chain of events had happened, but this time with even more bodies being the result.

"And the shooters?" Ashley asked. "Once again, they've all shared the same story?"

"As you know, all shooters reckon they went for a walk along some walking track up near the cliff side," Mandy replied.

"And they've definitely all gone through polygraph too?"

"All of them agreed and were put through it," Mandy said, nodding.

"And just to be sure I've got this right," Tim said from the side. "*All* passed? Every one of them?"

"Yep," Mandy replied. "They all said they were taking the same walk, and the polygraph confirms it. If they didn't actually *do* the walk, they do all actually *believe* they did. I know you were hoping for the possibility that Leefton wouldn't turn out to be the same as Seaview, but sorry, Ashley. All of our tests indicate it is *exactly* the same."

"And no sign of any hypnotic or hallucinogenic drugs in their bodies?" Ashley asked.

"Nope," said Mandy. "Just like with Seaview, none of these shooters had any levels of drugs in their system at all."

Ashley sat her head on her hands on the desk. She'd expected the same result. That didn't mean she hadn't hoped it would be different.

"This is just so unbelievable. Is it possible that our whole frigging *country* is going to be eliminated like this?" she asked, muttering to herself.

Neither Mandy nor Tim answered. They both had silently been asking themselves the same question.

Later, a large group of Bureau agents and forensic experts sat in a hotel conference room.

"What are we missing, people?" Ashley asked to the crowd. "We know this has happened in two towns that aren't located close to one another. The killers are everyday people. We know that they haven't killed their own loved ones. Instead they go off and kill someone else. Why? *Why* are they killing those that they're killing? Has anyone found any links of any kind between any killer and their victim?"

"No," one investigator spoke up. "In each town, most of the killers and victims do know each other, but just like in Seaview, there doesn't seem to be any motive for the killings. These towns live pretty quietly. They both had low instances of crime until these shootings."

"Alright," Ashley said, nodding. "Then let's look at this differently. Let's say someone is out there who wants mass numbers of people to die. He or she doesn't want to do it themselves so they get others to do it. Why do it this way, and why pick these people?"

"He or she doesn't have to do the work themselves," one voice said.

"Right. In each instance the killer uses their own gun," another said.

On hearing that statement, Tim's thought processes gained momentum.

"Right!" he exclaimed as he moved forward toward the wall-sized white board and then turned to face the crowd. "That's one thing we *do* know. Every single killer used their own gun."

"Yes..." Ashley said. She'd been thinking about the two cases so much that her mind was starting to feel fuzzy.

"Were all of the guns registered?" he asked the crowd.

"Yes!" a voice called out from the crowd. "That's how we found the owners, who in turn turned out to be the killers. Apart from one, which was unregistered but was later found to belong to a criminal on the run, all were registered to the right owner."

Tim's face showed enthusiasm.

"What about those that were killed?" When he saw

only blank faces looking at him, he expanded. "Did anyone investigate if those who were *killed* also had a gun registered to them?"

"No," both agents heard a sea of voices call out.

"Go back," Ashley instructed. "Everyone, with the groups of victims assigned to you, go back and investigate their gun ownership history."

The room became noisy as people shuffled out. When it was quiet again, Ashley turned to Tim.

"What's your thinking?" she asked, relieved at his level of renewed energy.

"I'm not sure," Tim said. "It just occurred to me though - how did the manipulator of all of this know each of those killers had their own gun? It's like he or she didn't choose them to kill because of who they were as people, or whatever they did in their lives…"

Ashley considered what he was saying.

"He chose them because of their guns," she said.

Tim nodded. It was a fair assumption, but what did it *mean*?

"I can't believe that in a town this size, at least 856 people even own guns," Ashley said. "I mean, isn't that ludicrous? This is a small town. It's such a small population and there's hardly any crime, and yet 856 people feel the need to have a gun in their house? What the hell is this world coming to when that percentage of a town feel so scared that they go out and buy a weapon?"

Tim considered what his partner had just asked. He had no answer for the moment, but he definitely felt like they were getting closer. They'd overlooked something of significance in both towns. He could almost taste the edge of realization that was coming. Once they passed that, it was going to become infinitely easier to find out who was behind it all.

CHAPTER 16

Four Months Later

Jaz McMenamin relaxed back on the large bed in the back of his RV. His year so far had been incredible. He could hardly hold back the grin that graced his face whenever he thought over the preceding months.

When Jaz had been only four years old, he'd realized something special about himself. Being a kid who never got much attention from either of his parents, he'd gotten used to playing alone. The only living thing that seemed to like him was their pet cat, Georgie. Even now, Jaz remembered Georgie with fondness. That cat had been so fat that its tummy had almost dragged along the ground. It had been a lazy thing but, even so, Jaz had loved it. It had never so much as scratched Jaz, it was so docile and friendly.

One day, Jaz's grandmother gave him a small toy musical keyboard to play with. He hadn't even known he had a grandmother till that day. He never saw her again after that either. The keyboard, however, stayed with him. To this day, he still had it. At the time, it had seemed like a magical gift that a fairy godmother had given him. Jaz laughed at the memory of thinking that. Of course she was no fairy godmother. Such people didn't exist. They were an invention of fairytale writers and movie makers. The keyboard wasn't magical either, but at the time, something had happened that had made him think it was.

Their family home had a huge backyard that Jaz had always loved. In summer, it was a great place to run and lie around, often with Georgie following him. Even as fat as that cat was, when a piece of string was trailing along the ground behind Jaz, Georgie found enough energy to chase it. The sight always made Jaz laugh.

After receiving his keyboard as a gift, Jaz had loved playing it. His mother and father had equally hated it. They fairly quickly told him that if he wanted to use it, he'd have to use it outside. Jaz didn't even consider disobeying that rule. By that time, he'd already learned that when he went against the wishes of his parents, he had to pay for that in so many ways. Without complaint or objection, he gladly ventured outside with the small red keyboard in hand and Georgie slowly following behind.

Thinking back now, with his musical ability having extended as far as it had, the memory of that keyboard's tone was grating on him. At the time, though, he'd loved it. The most incredible day - the day that seemed to wake Jaz up to a different way to live - was a day when he and Georgie had relaxed together under a large oak tree in the yard. Jaz had played an unknown tune on the keyboard. At that point, he'd had no piano playing experience, and that keyboard was hardly any kind of actual musical representation of melody. Even so, he still loved to flutter his fingers over the keys, enjoying the sound. The fact that Georgie didn't run away told Jaz that he didn't mind the sound either.

On that particular day, at the end of the yard, Jaz saw a tennis ball appear under the hedge. Shortly afterward, he saw a small hand reach through the hedge in an attempt to grab it. Jaz stayed where he was, wondering how anyone would have the nerve to try and come onto his land. As he sat and watched the hand groping around, trying to reach that ball, a thought went through Jaz's mind. In the silence of his thoughts, he could almost visualize Georgie becoming strong, running toward the end of the yard, and clamping his sharp teeth down on one of those fingers. It was an odd thought and completely unrealistic. Georgie was dozing in the sun. He never moved anywhere very quickly.

Jaz rested his head back against the tree trunk. He could have jumped up, retrieved the ball, and passed it through the hedge back to its rightful owner. The thought of staying where he was, closing his eyes and letting his fingers dance over the musical keys won out. He closed his eyes and cut everything out of his head except the sound he was making. A short time later, when he heard a small scream of pain, his eyes opened quickly. It took a moment to adjust and see what had happened. When he saw Georgie down the end of the yard, Jaz put his keyboard aside and walked swiftly to the hedge. Upon arrival, he looked down. There he saw his cat with its jaw tightly clenched around an index finger. That fat cat looked like he had no intention of ever letting that finger go.

The sight shocked Jaz. The coincidence of what Georgie was doing, compared to what Jaz had visualized minutes earlier, stunned him for a moment.

"Help!" he heard the voice on the other side of the hedge call out. That was enough to make Jaz jump into action, kneeling down and prying Georgie away.

"Georgie! Let go!" he yelled at the cat. Finally the grip was lessened. When it was, Jaz edged the cat away. "I'm sorry. I'll get your ball. Hang on," he said as the hand finally retreated. "Here you go."

Once he'd passed the ball back under the hedge, he heard a quiet, 'Thanks', intermingled with definite sobs, and then a shuffle of footsteps moving away. The kid on the other side of the hedge was gone.

In hindsight, Jaz considered that the boy on the other side of the hedge might have become a friend if only Jaz had been friendly in the first place. Instead, Jaz had ignored him and the kid had just left. Jaz's thinking only went in one direction, and that was knowing he was alone again. What was new. He wasn't meant to have friends. He really wasn't meant to have anyone who liked him. Even his mother and father didn't like him. With those thoughts, he turned, walked back and sat by the tree once again. As Georgie settled beside him, Jaz picked up his keyboard. It was a long time before he again considered the coincidence between a thought he'd had, and an action his cat had taken.

Through the years that followed, Jaz's keyboard was upgraded by another unknown relative. As he ventured into life at 'big boy school', he still kept going out into his yard and playing around with musical tunes. Georgie was older so he hardly ever moved, and Jaz had heard his parents talking and arguing about putting Georgie down. Initially, Jaz didn't want that to happen. Before he'd gone to school and finally learned how to make friends with other kids, Georgie had been his only friend and supporter.

Eventually the decision was made. Jaz was ten by then. At that age, he could see that Georgie was too old to really enjoy life. The fat cat actually looked like it wanted to go to sleep and never wake up. When Jaz heard his parents arguing about what to do about it, he went to his room and pulled out his keyboard. The latest one had a volume control and a slot for headphones to be plugged into it. That was a blessing. It meant he could play inside without any possibility of his parents hearing it and doing something drastic either to the keyboard or to him.

That evening, as he sat on his bed, with his fingers playing a new melody, he wondered what it would be like, just for once, to be asked what *he* thought should be done about Georgie. He then wondered what it would be like to be asked what he thought about *anything*. No matter what he did, he was still treated like an inconvenience by his parents. While he thought that, he naturally played notes that matched his mood. As he did, he saw his bedroom door open. Expecting a reprimand, he quickly yanked his headphones out of his ears and faced his mother.

"We can't decide, Jaz. What do you think we should do with Georgie?" she asked. "He's more your cat than ours. You know him best."

Jaz was so surprised that he was silent for quite some time, not sure if maybe his mother had learned how to joke.

"Well?" his mother pressed.

"I think…" Jaz started to say, still surprised by being asked anything at all. "I think that Georgie wants to die. I think he's actually ready for it," he said quietly.

He watched as his mother nodded, retreated and closed the door behind her. It was another moment in his life that Jaz knew he'd never forget, and he hadn't. Georgie was put down the next day. It was sad but it was right. Jaz knew that. His lifelong friend was finally in peace. He couldn't regret that.

It wasn't until he started high school that Jaz truly began to believe that there was some kind of weird correlation between his thoughts when he played music, and the actions of others. He didn't want to trial it too often but, now and then, he'd see something that he would test it out on.

One time, the school bully was hurting someone, punching them until they went down on the ground, and then sinking a boot into their gut, over and over. Jaz sat off to the side, just tinkering with the keys of the small portable keyboard he carried with him everywhere. He looked at that bully and wondered how funny it would look if he were to punch himself for a change. Within minutes, it happened. The crowd gathered around laughed harder and harder as the bully began punching his own face with his own fist. That was one of the moments that secured the belief in Jaz. For whatever reason, when he thought something and played music, he could make other people do things they wouldn't have otherwise. He had to test it out quite a lot to be absolutely certain but it always worked, without fail. The downside was that he had to be careful. Whenever he just wanted to play music for the simple pleasure of it, he had to make sure he wasn't thinking anything bad unintentionally. He had no desire to see anyone he actually liked get hurt in any way.

By the time he was seventeen, he'd already trialed his gift in various different ways. He hardly ever used it, but when it was worth it, he definitely tried it on. Getting the most popular girl in school - someone who would never have looked at him otherwise - to give her virginity to him had been a classic use of his ability. He'd learned a great deal that night. But even more than coaxing her in the idea of being with him sexually, he'd gone one step further with her. That was the first time he'd tried afterward to see if he could get someone to forget what they'd done. When she went back to ignoring him the next day, he couldn't be sure if that was his doing or she did remember and just didn't want to acknowledge it. By the end of that week, he was pretty sure she'd just forgotten. Girls talked, and after they talked, they usually told their boyfriends things. Jaz was pretty sure that if she'd remembered, he would have had a punch in the face from one person or another before the week was out. Instead, there was nothing. Nobody punched him. Nobody even said anything to him. Even so, it was still only a suspicion it had worked. He needed to try something out with some other person to be sure.

He went on a series of other experiments in the months after that. Through one event after another, it became evident that he did in fact have the power to make someone do something, and then forget they'd done it. His mind opened up to the many ways he could use that.

The third stage of testing his skills involved putting an idea into someone's head ahead of time. That took some advance thinking, planning and effort. He initially tried with the popular girl again. He didn't engage with her at all day to day. As far as he knew, not one other person knew they'd had sex - including the girl herself. For his next experiment, he put an advance thought in her head that on the upcoming Friday, during their PE session, she should run up to his best friend and say hello. That was all - just a simple hello. It was something she'd never done before and would never do by choice. She was popular, and Jaz's best friend was a total geek. It was innocent enough that it wouldn't be harmful. It was unlikely enough that it would serve as truth. Could he plant a seed of an idea in someone's mind three days before it was to happen?

He did, and it worked. Although he rejoiced, he was also wary. He could use the odd power he had to his advantage in any number of ways, but he didn't want to. He was a good person. He really didn't want to hurt anyone. No matter how much he could gain from making other people do things unknowingly and then forget about it, he wouldn't use it all the time. He considered it like winning the lottery. With millions of dollars in the bank you could either go out and blow the whole lot, buying anything and everything just because you could, or you could let it sit there and really only dive into it when you truly needed something. One thing he'd truly learned as he'd waited for the day to be free from his parents, was patience. That was something he had lots of. Life hadn't started out great, but it was going to get better. He'd always truly believed that. With enough patience, anything was possible.

Generally he was happy in his life. Things progressed

normally, for the most part. His musical talent grew. That was his passion - making music. He became recognized by friends as the guy who should run music at parties and functions. During those times, he started dating Christie. She was the same age as him. She wasn't someone who was regarded as beautiful on the outside. What Jaz loved about her was her inside. Her mind and her heart were always blooming, like she was brimming and overflowing with the joy of life. He had loved so much about her, simply because there was so much about her to love.

Then she'd been taken away.

CHAPTER 17

Four Years Ago

"Hey, handsome," Jaz McMenamin heard his sweet Christie say to him in her early morning voice.

Jaz had woken up to the feel of his back warmly embraced by Christie's front. One of her arms wrapped over his and settled over his tummy. That in itself was enough for him to begin to feel his normal early morning happiness. They'd been sleeping together for four months, either at her place or his. As much as he loved everything about what they did together, there was something about going to sleep with Christie and then waking up with her that made everything feel that little bit more special.

As he felt her hand move downwards, he smiled to himself. It wasn't the reason he'd grown to love her so much, but it was still enjoyable knowing she loved their love making as much as he did.

"Whatcha doing there, beautiful?" he whispered, grinning.

The first response was the feeling of her hand wrapping around him, just as firm as she knew he liked.

The second response was her voice speaking again.

"I'm warming my hand on my hand warmer," she said, her tone sounding suggestive even though her words were silly. It was another trait she excelled in and he loved - being silly while sounding serious. "You don't mind do you? It seems available for me to use at the moment."

"Oh, I see. Do you think there could be some other

use for it right now?" Jaz asked, chuckling as he teased her.

He felt her hand begin to move along his length, firmly but slowly. It was difficult for him to concentrate on anything else when she did that.

"I do, but as far as hand warmers go, I do quite like this one," Christie said.

Jaz laughed as he subtly turned, demanding both of them rearrange their bodies so that he could face her. He was already hard and could have just plunged straight inside her. He'd learned a long time earlier that she loved that first thing in the morning. She'd told him early on that she felt different sensations when she wasn't as wet, such as after orgasm. She'd stressed enough times in the mornings that she sometimes wanted to be taken without any attention beforehand that would make her too moist. She was never completely dry, of course, he'd come to realize over time, but she did sometimes want the feeling of being filled up in a less wet state.

As he looked at her face and kissed her softly, he felt her upper leg raise and fold over his hip. He could tell it just might be one of those mornings when she wanted him straight away. Despite sensing that, he held back, making her wait. It was one of the many ways that he loved to tease her.

Kissing her soft lips, he felt her respond with passion. Her lips and tongue were always eager and active when they met his. Sometimes Jaz found himself so hungry for her mouth that he felt like he was starving. He knew other guys seemed to want a woman's mouth to always be elsewhere, but he knew he'd rather share a long, passionate kiss with her any day, than care about the alternative. Sure, it was nice when she kissed him down there, but that was nothing compared to how he felt when they indulged in their lips and tongues moving together. He could do that for hours. In that regard, Christie was the same. It was one thing that made them a great match as lovers.

As he made her wait for what she continued to imply she wanted, he enjoyed the sounds coming from her. She moaned when they kissed and she moaned when they groped. The sound of those moans made it increasingly difficult for Jaz to deny the both of them any longer.

Eventually, he lowered the hand that had been cupping her head as he kissed her. Gripping her butt tightly, he pulled her closer until he felt himself sink into her warmth. Yes, morning sex with only the very slightest of wetness. He had to admit - he was a bit of a fan of it too.

He heard her moan deeply as he pushed fully into her. The sensation was incredible, just as it always was. Together they moved while kissing and holding each other close, still lying on their sides.

"Don't you dare hold back," he heard her say close to his ear as she pulled away from his lips. "I'm so close. I want to hear you."

The words pushed him over the edge as he felt all the incredible sensations that came with orgasm. As he let out the ultimate sound that she knew was him climaxing, he felt her muscles clench tightly around him as she let go too. He'd been surprised the first time she'd had an orgasm from their joining. No previous lovers or girlfriends had been able to reach climax without direct stimulation of their clit. It had taken some getting used to at first. Now he just believed that whatever worked for her, he could very happily live with.

For a long time, they lay together in silence, still connected and once again kissing. It wasn't just the orgasm that Jaz loved. It was the closeness. After growing up in a family where he was constantly made to feel like he was just an annoyance to his parents, he'd since grown to love closeness with other people. Starved of the simple joy of cuddles as a child, he absolutely reveled in them as an adult.

Before he'd met Christie, he'd had a few women pass through his life, some as one-off or regular part-time lovers, and others as girlfriends who were more involved in his life. He'd liked them all well enough but there was always that lingering uncertainty if they really liked him for who he was as a person, or they viewed his skills as a musician and DJ as some kind of reason to admire him as a celebrity. He wasn't a celebrity, of course, so that made no sense, but there had been times when he'd been chatting to a woman and she'd implied she considered him one. That was about the time that he walked away from whoever the latest girl was. He was glad he could make people happy with his skills but he'd rather be without people who stood beside him because they could look cool in front of their friends for doing so.

CHAPTER 18

Present Day

As Jaz lay on the large bed in his RV, he remembered the day that had changed not only his life, but also the way he viewed the world. He and Christie had arranged to meet up that afternoon. All morning, he'd been happy with his decision that he was going to propose to her that very day. He was sure she'd accept, and they'd go on to plan an amazing wedding day, become husband and wife, and start a family, just like they'd talked about together.

Then he'd heard the news. Someone had run into her college and fired a semi-automatic machine gun at the hoards of students in a lecture room. When the gunfire had begun, some students had tried to run. They didn't get far. Every single student in that large lecture space had been killed.

Including Christie.

Despite how much time had passed since then, tears still came to his eyes each time he remembered that day. Hearing the news of what had happened, and finding out what had happened to the woman he'd so much wanted to marry and have beside him for the rest of his life, had resulted in him feeling a rage like nothing he'd ever felt before. Before that day, he'd rarely felt hatred or anger, but he suspected that if the gunman hadn't turned the gun on himself, Jaz would have hunted him down and killed him. Again, the one living being who loved him had gone forever. There was so much pain in that.

Yes, he'd changed that day. Seriously. At first, he'd felt sadness and then the anger had begun, and festered, and grown and intensified. Now, from that unbelievable pain, he felt power. It seemed like an eternity since that day that Christie had been taken from him. After that, he'd gone back to experimenting with playing with people. He'd held back prior to that, knowing it could backfire and people could get hurt. Now he *wanted* to hurt people. No, that wasn't quite right. He didn't want to hurt anyone really. He *did,* however, want people to stop hurting each other. Enough was enough.

As Jaz wiped his eyes and sat up, he yet again determined to switch his thinking from the past to the present. There was no bringing Christie back. He suspected he would find someone else to love eventually. He wasn't anywhere near ready for that yet, but he trusted that the healing would come over time. For now, he had his music, and that was important.

He'd developed a system of secret dance parties. They always made him laugh. People went to them, excited. They stayed through them, happy. Then they forgot them. Any other DJ wouldn't have liked that. For Jaz, it was essential. That was part of the magic. His dance parties had to be forgotten, just like everything those people did in their lives from before receiving their special invitation, until after they'd done what they were going to subconsciously do.

Finally moving from his bed, he stepped outside. He was currently at a coastal location. He didn't know where. He'd left his previous location and had just drove for the past three days. Soon he would find roots again. Not that he stayed for long. Really, he spent more time on the road, stopping near free wi-fi spots to do research when he could, to prevent always having to use his phone.

There were things he wanted to find out before

approaching a town. There were certain considerations to be taken into account about the population. Once he found what he was looking for, he would make his way there and begin planning another dance party. He only had to stay somewhere for 48 hours. That was long enough to put into place the plan, set up, and successful execution of a dance party. It was also long enough to plant a seed in the minds of those who attended - a seed that would grow into fruition long after he'd left town.

In that, he'd been experimenting. He knew that planting seeds of thought a month out didn't come to bear fruit. No matter what kind of idea he tried to deliver, one month seemed to be outside of his power. He also knew that ten days was *within* his power. It was an exciting thing, testing to see where the boundary of time lay. In the next town that fitted his needs, he was going to try for twenty one days.

He took in a deep breath of the fresh sea air and smiled as he turned his face to the sun. Yes, there were sad things about his life, but there were also good things to look forward to. He needed to appreciate those.

CHAPTER 19

"How's the mass shooting case going?" Ashley's supervisor, Sarah, asked her, surprising Ashley. She'd expected she'd been called into the office to talk about either of the more recent cases she'd been assigned to since returning from Leefton.

"Are you counting both as one?" Ashley asked.

"I am," Sarah replied, nodding. "Aren't you?"

"From our research, the towns aren't in any way related."

"Perhaps not, but I think there are plenty of indicators to suggest that it is one person who's somehow managing the planning of these attacks," said Sarah. "Even though we don't know how or why, I don't think it would be possible for a copycat to make this happen. I can hardly believe that *any* person - or group of people - has made it happen!"

Ashley hung her head as she looked down at her hands resting on her lap. She'd been on other cases since, but Seaview and Leefton were never far from her mind.

"I know," she said. "I … I don't know. I don't want us to give up but I just don't know what else we can do."

"Well, whoever masterminded this has to strike again," Sarah said. "They must get something out of it. That means that sooner or later they'll need that something to happen again. It might be a feeling - a buzz or some kind of gratification from knowing they caused destruction. You and I both know that serial killers don't rest until they're caught or they die. They might go quiet for a while. They might keep killing but use a different

MO so that we aren't onto them as a suspect for the odd murder, but they always come back to their same old ways. With some of them, part of the entire attraction is their addiction to taunting law enforcement agencies."

"I just don't think that's it with this person or group of people," Ashley said. "They haven't done anything to suggest they want to be famous, like so many serial killers do. I have no idea what they want to happen from this, but I don't think it's fame. I also don't think they like killing. If they did, they'd be doing it themselves. So far, there's nothing to suggest there's another person missing who might have done any of the shootings in either crime."

"You certainly could be right, Ashley," said Sarah. "Everyone's keeping their eyes and ears open. All law enforcement agencies around the country, particularly in smaller towns, know to contact us if they have any kind of multiple shooting, no matter how small in number." She watched as Ashley nodded and stood to leave. "Don't let this get you down, Power. The fact that we haven't gotten to the bottom of this isn't on you. Something out of the ordinary is happening, and how it's happening isn't evident to anyone. You're a fine agent. Don't let this one shake you."

Ashley smiled and nodded.

"Thank you," she said, knowing that she wouldn't be successful in not continuing to be shaken up by the shootings. Not all crimes were solved, and plenty of murderers throughout history had remained free and never been charged for what they'd done, but the thought of anyone else dying because the particular person behind all of this hadn't yet been caught, was truly horrifying.

CHAPTER 20

Kane Garmin did his usual assessment of himself as he stood in front of his bathroom mirror, ready for the night ahead. Why he'd been chosen to go to an 'invite-only dance party', he had no idea, but having lived what he considered an entire previous life in the military, he certainly understood and appreciated the words 'secret' and 'confidential'.

After reading through the lengthy list of strict terms printed on the invitation that had appeared in his mailbox, he'd first grinned to himself. Surely it must be a scam - something so common in today's world, he knew. He wasn't stupid. That old saying - 'if something seems too good to be true, it usually is' - still played in his mind as he studied his reflection. Even so, he couldn't deny that there was something about that invitation that had made him very curious. Sure, his decision to go to the dance party had changed from a strict 'yes' to a strict 'no' and then back again, the more he'd considered it. After all the to and fro of indecision, he'd finally settled on 'yes'. If nothing else, it could prove interesting, and that was something he'd been missing since he'd retired from the military.

Settling his eyes on the lines that were well established and visible around his eyes and mouth, he knew that most of them were natural and due to him quickly approaching the grand old age of fifty. It wouldn't be long and he'd be able to say that he'd already survived half a century. It wasn't old really, and he did know that, but couldn't deny that he felt old. He was pretty sure it was having been in war zones that had helped that along. For him, it had been a bittersweet life, all in all. Along with the excitement of being in places that only select personnel of the military were sent, there were plenty of sights that he wished he'd never seen. How people could do such things to each other, he had never been able to understand. That was what had prompted him to finally leave the military and try to find peace in his life again. Humans could treat each other so badly, and often for no good reason. He supposed he'd known that when he'd been younger, and before he'd even thought about joining the army, but war - that was the sadness of humanity on a whole other level.

Since getting out and returning to his hometown, life hadn't been anywhere near as stressful. Unfortunately, it also hadn't been anywhere near as exciting, or as full of the type of camaraderie he'd experienced when on away missions. There were plenty of people he knew in the town he'd resettled in. Sure, there were nice people, and not so nice people, but almost every time he walked through the quiet streets, he had to acknowledge to himself that something was missing in his life.

Desperate to at least try and slow the aging process, he'd recently taken up daily trail running. Day to day, as he laced up his running shoes, he told himself he was doing it for fitness. Inside, he suspected it was more that he was running in a useless attempt to get away from memories that consistently continued to plague him.

Memories. Unfortunately they never went away. In some ways, he sometimes hoped he would get dementia, and sooner rather than later. As soon as he caught himself thinking such a thing, he had to chastise himself. He was healthy in body, even if not entirely in mind. To wish the health of either away wasn't intelligent or good.

Inhaling deeply, his focus fell on the two large scars that were visible on his face. Some days, he could almost pretend they weren't really there, and he certainly did like to pretend that what had happened to him in the moments when he'd received those scars, hadn't happened at all. The only problem was that the pretend could only last a moment before the memory would hit him all over again.

No, the scars that plagued various parts of his body were as permanent as the memories he'd brought back from war. There was no real way to get rid of either - not permanently at least. But, for just one night, could he push the memories aside? Yes, for one night he could go to some random dance party and see what would happen. If it was good, upbeat music, he might have a great time, even if he did look like an old man - and an idiot - to the majority of the people there.

Plastering on a grin and touching up his spiky blond hair once more, he forced himself to at least consider that a good night might lie ahead for him. In truth, he doubted it, but he could at least pretend. Nothing wrong with that, and he knew it was something he was quietly becoming pretty good at.

CHAPTER 21

As he was moved through what appeared to be an almost military-like system to get people into the dance party, Kane felt his intrigue grow and intensify. He'd been a part of some major military operations, and he knew exactly how precise things sometimes had to run. While, on occasion, he'd met some young people who dared to challenge authority and go against the grain, choosing the path to do what they wanted rather than what they were told, generally he knew that life was always easier when one just followed the rules. It was the general way of society that for a few years, at least, when humans hit puberty, the need to challenge everything and everyone was paramount. After that time, Kane thought that everybody should just relax and take more time to breathe in the air that they could, and simply be kind to one another. As logical as it seemed, he knew that was a dream of utopia; not a reflection of reality.

Throughout his long journey from the dance party meeting spot to inside the venue, he saw several people suffer some consequences for not having followed the instructions that had been detailed fully on the invitation. A few had their phones taken off them, and a few more had bottles of alcohol or bags of drugs taken off them. Kane smiled to himself as he watched the tantrums that had taken place following that. To those reactions, he could only shake his head. Instructions were given, and they were clear. Why some people thought they could go against instruction and have no consequence, he'd never understood. Why make life harder than it needed to be?

After he handed over his invitation and watched it get scanned and then thrown into a fire at the final checkpoint, he noticed another one lying on the ground. Despite his commitment to always following rules, it took only a moment of hesitation before he realized that one hadn't quite made it to the fire after all. As discretely and swiftly as possible he picked it up and shoved it into his jacket pocket, hopeful he wouldn't live to regret the decision later. Why not. It was only a card, and he'd done as he'd been told he'd have to - handed over his invitation so it could be destroyed. Besides, it would serve as a great reminder of possibly the one night he might end up having so much fun that, for once, his memory might be left behind when it came to the horrors of war.

With the lengthy journey of security checks over and, pretty much, the blind leading the blind, he finally reached an open area. Although mostly dark, there was just enough light provided to enable people to see each other. It was also light enough for a small stage in the centre of the room to be visible. It wasn't anything like Kane had seen before - certainly not big enough to house musicians like he'd seen at the various concerts he'd attended since he'd returned home. But then the invitation had spoken of a 'world-renowned DJ', so he guessed that musicians wouldn't be needed for this particular kind of dance party anyway.

Glancing around the room, he was pleased to see that there weren't only young people present. That realization relaxed him. He wouldn't be 'the oldie' after all, especially with how many elderly people he could see. It was an odd mix to see, but kind of refreshing as well.

When he saw someone grow visible from the back of the room, then step up onto the small stage, he felt his excitement grow. Nothing about what was happening was familiar to him, and that was the greatest form of excitement of all. There was no way to predict how the night would go, or how it would end. That went against everything he'd ever had to learn, know, and carry out in the military. Even though he'd always loved structure, he couldn't deny there was something incredibly empowering about *not* knowing what lay ahead.

As he heard the DJ introduce himself, and the crowd go wild in their cheers as the music began to play through the large loudspeakers set up on either end of the small stage, Kane's eyes met those of a woman on the other side of the room. She was around his age, and rather beautiful in his eyes. At first, he looked away, diverting his eyes from her gaze in case he read her interest incorrectly. When he glanced back, she was gone from her spot. For a moment, he felt deflated. Since he'd returned home, he hadn't met anyone around his age who he felt in the least bit attracted to. In his heart, he knew it would be nice to.

Resolved to focus on the music and not let any negative thoughts or doubts plague him, he started to move his body. Who cared if he was old and making a fool of himself. There was something therapeutic and universally pleasing in music. It didn't matter who you were, or what you thought about anything else in the world. If you could hear music, there was a good chance that it could light up your day, or even your life if you let it.

After a few minutes of enjoying the feeling of moving his body to the beat, reveling in the combination of physical movement with the tune that he knew so well, he forgot everyone else, and everything else. All around him, people were dancing - young and old. Nobody was self-conscious, and nobody was being unkind. That was how he thought humanity should always have been. Everything he heard and saw in that moment made him smile.

"You move well," he heard a voice say from behind him. Uncertain who the person was talking to, he tentatively turned toward the voice and saw it was the woman he'd noticed earlier.

"Me?" Kane asked, grinning at her while feeling a slight blush move over his face. With all that he'd been through in his life, very little now made him uncomfortable, but when a woman he found extremely attractive gave him some attention, it was easy for him to revert to the timid, shy boy he'd once been, before the horrific sights of war had changed him.

He watched as the woman threw back her head and laughed out loud.

"You!" she said as she nodded and grinned at him. "I like your moves."

Kane felt his smile grow to the point where his cheeks began to ache. For a fleeting moment he tried to remember when he'd last smiled that much. He couldn't.

CHAPTER 22

As Jaz McMenamin stood on the same small makeshift stage that he took with him everywhere, he smiled. To others, it might have seemed like a friendly grin, representing a confident and true joy that might have come from seeing people enjoy themselves. A part of him wished that were the case. Before he'd lost the love of his life to a gunman who seemed to care nothing for life at all, Jaz had been happy. He never would have wanted to hurt anyone. Oh, how things had changed.

On the faces of the people dancing, chatting and laughing before him, he could see happiness. Should he have been fulfilled from seeing that? As his fingers danced across the keys of his keyboard, he pondered that question. He supposed a portion of the DJs in the world would gain happiness purely from seeing their audience enjoying themselves so much. He also supposed that another portion of DJs in the world wouldn't gain happiness at all from that, but they would from the money they made from playing to audiences. He fitted into neither group.

The recipe he'd formulated, perfected, and delivered in his dance parties wasn't centered around the happiness of people, and money was something he never made from the experiences. No, the only thing he wanted to get from the secret dance parties that seemed, so far, to be perfectly successful in accordance with Jaz's plans, was the opportunity to control people's minds.

No matter how old he got, the questions about how it all worked, and why it worked for him but didn't seem to work for everyone (he assumed), he still had no answers for. Was he crazy in thinking that his thoughts truly could control other people? It seemed far too ridiculous to be true, and yet it also seemed to be a truth that kept being proven again and again. With so many years of experience in testing behind him, Jaz couldn't deny the possibility that he did, somehow, have the power to control others. He could have used that power for so much good in the world. Once upon a time, he'd have loved to have done that, but now he didn't want to. Now, years on from the death of the woman he'd wanted to marry and spend the rest of his life with, he still wanted to use his powers to make a point. Since her death, he'd seen even more mass shootings on the news, but nothing had changed. Still, not only wasn't it discouraged to have a gun for personal use, but it was strongly *en*couraged. In his opinion, that was crazy. Over and over, people watched how much damage guns could cause, but still the problem with overuse of them only got worse; never better.

He knew his thinking wasn't entirely sound. It made no rational sense that having *more* people shoot each other could contribute to helping gun laws be changed and tightened. None of the people who'd died through his mind control had done anything wrong, that he knew of. He didn't look that closely into victims' lives, so knew he could be completely wrong about that, but he didn't care. Someone he'd loved had been taken from him, by a gunman who didn't care about any of the people he'd killed, so why should Jaz care either?

As was always the case, he let his focus lie with the questioning about what he was doing, and why he was doing it. For a short while, it was acceptable that he think things through, and convince himself that it was all for the greater good.

Then it was time to focus on the music, focus on the crowd, and begin to put into the minds of everyone in

the room, just what he wanted each one of them to do …
and then forget.

CHAPTER 23

Holding a woman in his arms again had left Kane Garmin feeling elated for the first time in years. He'd never been confident about how he looked, even though plenty of people had indicated to him, throughout his lifetime, that he was attractive. No matter how he felt day to day when he looked in the mirror, the way he was feeling as he held the warm body close to his, was pretty darned good.

"I don't even know your name," he heard the woman say against his ear as she lifted up onto her tiptoes to match his height.

"Kane," he told her as he pulled away slightly and looked at her face. "And you are?"

"Nancy," the woman replied before reaching up again and, this time, placing her lips on his. "I am very pleased to meet you, Kane."

Feeling the brief but sweet excitement of having been kissed, Kane's smile grew wider. He was an almost-50 year old man who was rugged and scarred. It was hard to know exactly how old the woman he was holding was, but he guessed she was at least in the over-40 age bracket, and maybe even closer to the same age as him. All that really mattered was that she was mature enough to know her own mind, and that meant she was mature enough to go after what she wanted, and know how to say no to what she didn't. In Kane's opinion, that made for the perfect woman.

As the dancing progressed, he watched her face. If he'd seen her eat or drink anything, he might have wondered if she was beginning to be under the influence of something, but he knew she hadn't eaten or drunk anything since they'd arrived. One thing the military had instilled in him were in-depth skills in always being aware of what was happening around him, and not letting any detail slide past him. Despite the room having a darkness to it, he was 99.9% sure that there was no way the woman in his arms could have snuck any food, alcohol or drugs into her system while she was in his arms - or even into the venue, given how strict the security had been.

Why then, did her facial expression seem to be rapidly changing from one of simple happiness, to a level of ecstasy that people generally didn't reach without assistance of some kind?

Silently telling himself to stop worrying about it, Kane pulled her close against him once again. If she was that happy to be in his arms, why would he want to question what was making her that way? He was a man who'd missed the company of a woman, and he was very attracted to her. When she wanted to be away from him, he would thank her for a lovely evening, bid her farewell, and see her on her merry way. Until then, he was quite happy to remain just where he was.

CHAPTER 24

"No!" Special Agent Ashley Power exclaimed when she received the news that yet another small town had begun to report large numbers of people having been shot and killed. "Sarah, no! Please…"

"I'm sorry, Ashley, but it is true, and this *is* happening," Sarah Johnson said to her agent. "Tim is on his way here now…"

"Here, Boss," Special Agent Tim Moore said as he entered the office in the Bureau of Investigation headquarters. It was normal for him to walk in with a smile on his face and an eagerness to tease both his boss and his work partner. It was easy to understand that neither would be appreciated at that moment. "You okay, Ash?" he went on to ask as he sat down beside Ashley and noted the expression of horror on her face.

"It's happened again, hasn't it," Ashley said, addressing both of the people in the room with her, with her words sounding far more like a statement than a question. "The exact same thing?"

"I'm afraid so," said Sarah. "I wish I could tell you differently."

Tim forced himself to tear his focus away from Ashley's face, and redirect it to his boss.

"Another small town?" he asked and saw Sarah nod in reply. "Multiple fatalities?"

"So far, there are just over a hundred, so not quite as big scale as Seaview and Leefton," Sarah said.

"Not *yet*, you mean," said Ashley. "We've seen this twice before now. The number starts a little high and then…"

As her words drifted off, Tim felt a pang of sadness at seeing her distress. He knew it wasn't where the sadness needed to be directed - that was with the people of the small town it had happened to that would need sympathy, support and answers - but he couldn't help it. He hated to see his partner upset, even though he shared the same frustration at them not having yet found out who was making so many people die in the same manner, or why they were doing it … or even *how* they were doing it.

"I know this is upsetting, but come on, Power," said Sarah, knowing a stern tone was always more effective with her agent than a soft one. "For each one of those people who've been killed, there's someone who found them…"

"And someone who killed them," Tim said. "I think this is the hardest thing about this case. We know that for each person killed, there's been one person who did the shooting, but all of those people who've been proven to pull the trigger don't even seem to know that they *did*."

"I know," Sarah said. "But as disheartening as it is that we haven't made much headway into finding out how this is all happening, we now have a new town that is suffering and needs our help. Now, are you two up for this, or do you want me to leave you off…"

"We're doing it!" Ashley insisted as she sat up taller in her chair and felt a new determination flow over her. "Send whoever else you want to, but I'm going," she added before turning to face Tim. "You in?"

"Yeah, of course," Tim replied, glad to at least see his partner's facial expression of defeat leave her face. "We haven't finished with all of this yet, and we won't be until we find out who is behind it, and why they're so set on hurting so many."

"Good!" said Sarah. "Then take this file - everything

I have so far - and go and get organized. I can get you on..." she added before she turned her focus to her computer screen for a couple of minutes. "Yep, I've just booked you on a 12.30 flight, so best you both hustle and get moving."

"Okay," Ashley said as she stood, silently preparing herself to see even more head gunshot wounds than she was already sure she'd seen enough of to last a lifetime.

"And listen, you two, if any of this gets too much..." Sarah started to say as her two agents began to walk towards the door.

"If that happens, we will definitely let you know, Boss," Tim said as he ushered Ashley out. Although she still looked like she was in shock from the news of the horrific happenings occurring yet again, he was hopeful that once they got on the road and were on their way to see whatever it was that they were going to see, she would bounce back to be her normal self again.

"Can you believe it, Tim?" he heard her ask quietly as they began their walk toward the large exterior doors of the building.

"Unfortunately, yes," Tim replied. The look he received from her as she stopped walking and turned to face him, he wasn't sure he'd ever seen on her before. "Ash, whoever is behind this is obviously enjoying something about it - the planning, the killing, and possibly even the fact that they've been evading our notice. Whether the mastermind behind this is someone who is actually killing, or just likes to get others to do it all for them, I think it's safe to put them into the category of serial killer, and it's a fact that serial killers don't stop doing what they do, until they're either caught or they're dead."

"You really think we can put this down to a serial killer?" Ashley asked as they began to walk again.

Having the question forced upon her instantly woke Ashley up from the small level of shock she'd been in since hearing the latest news. She hadn't previously thought about the person or people behind the horrors in such a way but she supposed Tim was right. Whoever was the driving force behind what had been happening, had ensured hundreds of people were killed.

"I guess it depends on what your definition of a serial killer *is*," Tim replied, glad to hear his partner's tone return to normal. "Sure, it's someone who kills multiple people, but where does the line for *that* lie? Do they have to have killed those people with their own hands?"

"People are convicted for murder all the time, even though they were the instigators behind the murder and didn't actually do the killing," said Ashley.

"Yes!" Tim exclaimed. "Exactly! If someone can be put away for life because it was their idea to kill someone, wouldn't that be true of whoever is behind all of these shootings?"

"Not the same thing, though, Timmy Boy," Ashley said. "The question just presented isn't whether whoever is behind all of this could be charged with murder. The question is whether they would be considered a *serial* killer."

Tim grinned at her as they stepped out into the sunlight. There were so many questions that needed to be answered, but he knew wouldn't be till they'd moved forward in the investigation.

"Actually, I don't think that is anything for us to dwell on at all - not at the moment, anyway," he said. "Right now we just need to get to this new town - Kildare - and see what the damage is."

"Let's hope that this time they've left us some clues," Ashley said, feeling much better and more alive than she had been minutes earlier. "Now," she added as she turned to smile at him. "I know what you're about to ask, Moore..."

Despite the horrors that they each knew lay ahead for them, Tim couldn't help but laugh. That was the Ashley that he loved working with - the one who could tease him even when she knew that things were about to get tough.

"I wasn't even thinking about asking who's going to drive to the airport," he said, holding up both hands. He was glad to see Ashley chuckle quietly in response.

"You got it," she said. "I've already got my away-gear with me so I'll follow you to your place and we can go from there."

Tim smiled and nodded before turning to head off to his car. It was easy to temporarily not think about what they were going to be seeing later that day. He knew it wasn't realistic, pretending that horrific images weren't a part of their immediate future, but sometimes a reprieve from serious thoughts was definitely needed. Once they arrived in the town of Kildare, he suspected there would be too much to feel devastated about. It was important to even out that level of horror with something mildly amusing or positive, however and whenever he and Ashley could.

CHAPTER 25

"Here we go again," Ashley said as they exited their rental car and made their way into the police station in the small town of Kildare. On the flight, they'd both read through the file Sarah had provided. The file was based on the number of deaths as had been reported that morning. With so much time having passed since then, Ashley was preparing herself for however high the number might have climbed to.

"With each time this happens, the chances of whoever's behind this making a mistake grows higher," Tim said. "That's a good thing."

"Maybe, but each time this happens, large numbers of people die," Ashley retorted. "*That's* not a good thing."

Tim nodded but didn't respond. While some people in law enforcement might have been focused on not having solved a case - not having cracked the code, so to speak - he knew that the hardest aspect for him and Ashley to accept was that the people responsible were still free and able to keep killing more people. Did Tim care that his reputation as a law enforcement professional might suffer if he and Ashley never caught whoever was behind it? Not at all. If someone else managed to do the solving, he would be very happy. He cared nothing for glory in his job. He just wanted the bad people of the world to be put away so they couldn't keep doing whatever it was that they did to hurt others.

"Agents," a deep voice called out to them as they walked into the police station. "Welcome."

Ashley watched as a middle-aged man held out his

hand to her. Although he was older than her, and it certainly wasn't the right time to think such a thing, she found herself captivated by the darkness of his eyes, the silver shimmer of his salt-and-pepper hair, and the sad smile that he presented.

"I'm Chief of Police here in Kildare - Nick Holden," he said.

"Thank you, Chief," Tim said, noticing Ashley's moment of distraction. "I'm Special Agent Tim Moore, and this is Special Agent Ashley Power."

"You are both very welcome here," Nick replied. "Please come this way, through to my office."

By the time they were seated, facing the police chief, Ashley finally felt her normal self again. It was rare for anyone to capture her attention on a personal level. The idea that the man before her had, both intrigued and disappointed her. She was at the very start of a new case - or the hopeful end of an old one, depending on how she viewed it. There was absolutely nothing about the timing or situation that would allow any form of physical attraction toward someone.

"According to the file we were provided with earlier today, the number of victims then stood at just over a hundred," Ashley said, forcing herself to focus on what was truly important. "I'm sorry to have to ask but…"

She wanted to ask the full question but the words eluded her. Did she really want to know how high the number had climbed since that morning? In both Seaview and Leefton, it had started out bad enough, before each had grown higher and higher. A very definite trend had been set - the death toll in each town was higher than the last. Just how high was the perpetrator intending to take the numbers this time?

"We're currently at 148," the chief responded.

"Oh!" Ashley unintentionally exclaimed.

"You seem surprised," said Nick.

"Yes," Tim responded. "We attended the incidents in

Seaview and Leefton…"

"I am aware of both of those cases," Nick said.

"In both cases, the number began low in the morning but climbed steadily throughout the day, peaking into the high hundreds by the evening," said Ashley.

"And you expect the same will happen here," Nick summarized.

"We did, but if the number hasn't climbed as high, of course that is a good thing," Ashley said.

"Yes, the best thing would have been if there were no deaths at all, of course," Tim said, curious about his partner's sudden bout of being more than a little flustered. "You said you're aware of the Leefton and Seaview cases," he added and saw the mature man nod in reply. "Do you think the details of the killings in those two towns seem the same as what's happened here?"

"We do," said Nick, leaning forward. "All victims that have been found, have one gunshot wound to the head, which appears to have happened during the night. Our medical examiner is still working her way through assessing each of the victims, so our findings might yet change but, at this point, we are treating this as the same type of crime as you investigated in Seaview and Leefton."

"Perhaps on a smaller scale though," Tim said, his mind naturally beginning to wonder why the killer would reverse their previous trend of having more people killed than the time before.

"We hope so," the chief said. "And I understand some of your forensic professionals are currently arriving in town, too, so our findings might change with their advanced level of knowledge also."

"Yes, of course. Do you believe there is any chance that there might be more victims out there somewhere?" Ashley asked.

"It's certainly not impossible, but I've had one of our guys do a street by street grid search to make sure that there isn't anyone that's been left in a public spot - parks and gardens and so on," Nick replied. "That staff member is now visiting homes of people that we know live alone. We don't have a large population here so, by talking to people, we can identify mostly who lives where, and do a welfare check if need be."

"And you know that with the previous two towns where this happened, it was the local residents…"

"Who turned out to be the shooters?" the chief asked. "Yes, we know. I've assigned staff from an external security firm to each of the homes where a victim has been found. They know to not only guard the crime scene, but also make sure that anyone else in the house is kept at home. It isn't an easy job, especially in a town like this where there are some large, well established families that have members scattered across different homes around the town. Of course they want to go and check on their other family members…"

"Yes, of course. That is understandable," said Ashley. "Our forensics team members will be thorough in their scene and victim investigations, but they are also very efficient in their work practices. When we combine all of the information that's gathered, it may be a relatively short amount of time before we know who has done what."

"Just like in Seaview and Leefton," Tim said.

"Although I've read the reports about those mass shootings, I have to admit I'm still a little confused by it all," Nick said. "Have I correctly interpreted what I read? You know who each person is that used a gun in both of those towns?"

"Yes," Ashley replied. "We were able to identify who used their own gun, and who they each shot."

"In both Seaview *and* Leefton?" the chief asked. "And it was the same in each? Every person killed was shot by someone else who lived in the same town? Not a stranger at all?"

"No, in those instances, it was confirmed that all shooters lived in the town, and most knew the person they each killed," said Tim. "We know the who-killed-who. We just don't know the why or the how."

"How they killed their victims?" Nick asked. "They were all shot, right?"

"Yes but, no, what we don't know is how it's possible that so many people could have gone out that night and shot so many *other* people," said Tim. "Even though so many shots were fired that night, there were no reports of anyone having heard them, or of any other kind of disruptions in the towns when the killing was going on."

"Added to that is the mystery of every one of the shooters passing a polygraph test that asked if they were a shooter," said Ashley, finding her anger growing yet again as she thought about the polygraph results from not one but two towns.

"Maybe they weren't the right people...?" asked the Chief.

"No, they were the right people," said Tim. "Where they each said - and seem to believe - they were, we know for a fact that they weren't. *Nobody* was where they said they were on those nights."

"Something wrong with your polygraph test then?" Nick asked.

"There were different tests used, and different testers too," Ashley replied. "Honestly, Chief..."

"Please ... call me Nick."

"Nick," Ashley corrected. "The entire situation has left us stumped when it comes to Seaview and Leefton, but we're hopeful that this time - well, maybe it'll be a case of third time lucky. Maybe, this time, whoever is behind this will have left a clue of some kind."

Ashley watched as the chief took some time to look at Tim, and then settle his eyes back on her for what appeared to be a very lazy appraisal of her outward appearance. Although she fought hard to not let it affect her, she could feel a slight blush appear on her cheeks. To stop it from happening further, she tried to force an image of something horrific into her mind. She had to do whatever she could to not let the mature man facing her affect her in the way that he was. It was unprofessional, to say the least, and professionalism was something that Special Agent Ashley Power was committed to taking great pride in.

"Do you think one person is behind all of these killings?" the chief finally asked, glancing from one agent to the other. "One person could have orchestrated each of the shootings?"

"At this stage, we haven't found any link between the towns, so we have no idea who, but yes, we do think there might be someone pulling strings and somehow forcing the residents of the town to carry out the killings," Tim replied.

"But how would anyone do that?" Nick asked. "I mean, if it was a matter of being forced to kill a complete stranger, that would be one thing, but from what I've read, both of those towns are small, just like here. The chances of someone shooting someone they know…"

"And that did happen," Tim confirmed. "Quite a high number of people in Seaview, in particular, killed people that they knew and, in some cases, appeared to be very close to."

"That's just one aspect that makes it all very difficult to untangle or make any sense of," said Ashley.

After a long period of silence, the chief spoke again.

"It doesn't sound like an easy case to solve, certainly. I assume you'll be wanting to get on with visiting the scenes here now?" he asked.

"Yes, as we said, several teams of forensic staff will be here shortly to begin doing their investigations, and then we'll have an initial idea of whether the system that seems to have been incorporated in the other two towns, has also been used here."

"System?" Nick asked.

"It might be a little complicated to explain right now, but if our suspicions are correct and this *is* the same as Leefton and Seaview, we'll have some definitive answers within a relatively short period of time."

"Can you share with us some addresses of your victims, Nick?" Tim asked.

"Of course," the chief replied before pulling a folder out of his drawer and sliding it across the desk. "This contains full details of the victims we've located. As you indicated, there might be more to come, but this list gives details of victim name, address, and name of anyone that they lived with *or* were known to be involved with."

"Thank you," Ashley said before glancing at Tim and seeing his subtle nod. "We'll be in touch."

CHAPTER 26

Pulling up to the first victim's home, Ashley turned off the car engine and took some time to make sure she was calm and not stressed. Before her, she could see a scene that looked far too similar to many they'd already seen over the past year. Not only was the home they were visiting cordoned off with yellow crime scene tape, but so were several homes in the immediate vicinity.

"It's all too familiar now," Tim said, as if reading her thoughts exactly.

"Yes," Ashley agreed. "If it was a totally separate crime scene, I don't think I'd feel as bad as I do…"

"You can't feel bad, Ash," Tim reassured her. "There are hundreds of people, from several law enforcement communities, who are just as confused by all of this as we are."

"I know but…" Ashley began to argue before turning to face him. "I know you're right. I just wish we could figure this out so that we can stop whoever is behind it all. I mean, what can they honestly gain from delivering all this chaos and pain?"

"That is the question that, I think, once we work out the answer to, we'll be able to figure out who is doing it, and what their full intentions are," said Tim. "For now, we both need to get ourselves together and focus on one crime scene at a time. Even if what's happening here has been done by whoever orchestrated the misery at Seaview and Leefton, right now we need to concentrate just on *here*, and all the people who not only have been caught up in this, but will be hurting and wanting answers."

Ashley took a long moment to breathe deeply as she delivered him a sad smile and nodded.

"You're right. Let's go," she finally said. It was overwhelming when any case went unsolved, but even more so when the perpetrators kept doing what they were doing, and hurting more people. Even so, Ashley knew they still had to hold their heads up high and begin assessing each crime scene for what it was.

On entering that small cottage, the feeling of dread seemed to hang heavily in the air. With the structure being a tiny one-bedroom home, it took little time to find the victim, and to see the damage they'd received. Not far from the body stood a security officer, rigid in his stance.

"Oh," Ashley muttered when she saw the face of the security officer. She was used to getting male attention, but something about the look he gave her almost made her skin crawl. To put the instance out of her mind, she turned to face Tim, catching his look of curiosity. "Never mind."

"Is the person who found...?" Tim began to ask before he saw the security officer nod with his head toward a small sunroom off to the side. "Thanks."

"Hello," Ashley said when they entered the space they'd been directed to.

"I don't understand..." an elderly woman wailed. "My husband ... why can't I be with him? Why am I being kept away from him?"

Ashley glanced at Tim, feeling a depth of despair in her heart for the elderly woman.

"I'm sorry, but that isn't possible right now, Mrs...?" she asked.

It took some time before the woman calmed enough to be able to answer the question.

"Simpson," she finally replied as she began to wipe tears away. "Edith Simpson. My husband is Abe," she added, raising a frail looking finger to point towards the bedroom, and then breaking down into tears again. "I don't understand any of this. Why would anyone do this to him? Everyone loved … Abe."

"We're so sorry for your loss, Mrs Simpson," said Tim. "Can you tell us about last night? Anything you can tell us about your time from yesterday afternoon until this morning…"

"*I* didn't do this!" the elderly woman exclaimed, looking surprisingly animated and strong compared to how she'd seemed moments earlier. "How could you think…"

"We don't think anything, Mrs Simpson," Ashley reassured her. "But it is our job to find out what happened to your husband. Sometimes … sometimes it can be the smallest detail that helps us to find out things like this. Please … if you feel strong enough … can you tell us exactly how you and Abe filled yesterday afternoon and evening? It would help us a great deal in our search for answers about how and why this has happened."

Inside of her, Ashley felt momentarily compelled to inform the woman that many people had been killed in the same manner, not only throughout Kildare but also two other towns previously. Of course she couldn't say the thought out loud. Every individual case needed to be treated as such, at least in the primary investigation of what had happened to each victim.

"It was a normal night for us," Ashley was relieved to hear the elderly woman begin to say. "We had our supper at seven-thirty - just like we always do. After that, we watched a bit of telly, and then we went to bed."

"And what time did you retire for the night, Mrs Simpson?" Tim asked.

"Same time as we always did - nine o'clock," the elderly woman replied. "Always the same, it was, for me and Abe. We hardly ever changed our routine. Hadn't for years."

"And nothing out of the ordinary happened through the night? You didn't hear anything?" Ashley asked.

"No, I didn't, but then I never do," Mrs Simpson said. "Abe snores - oh, how he snores - like a rumbling pig sometimes," she added, her face revealing a blend of amusement and sadness that Ashley had unfortunately seen far too often. "Over our life together, I think I got used to hearing his noisy sleeping habits. Most nights, I get into bed and I'm out like a light. These days I don't tend to hear anything till the morning."

"Sorry to have to ask you this, but do you know of anyone who might have wanted to hurt Abe?" asked Tim.

"Oh, no!" Mrs Simpson replied with passion in her voice. "He's a good man, always helping out in the community. No. People love Abe."

"I'm sure they do," said Ashley, finding it difficult to match the woman's wording of present tense, when the victim was already deceased. "What kind of community work did he do?"

"Abe supported youth who were heading down the wrong path, mostly, but he was always open to helping anyone who asked for help with anything," Mrs Simpson replied.

Tim took some time to consider what she'd just said. Troubled youth might have normally been a direction to at least investigate in any crime. He didn't think they would have had anything to do with the murder of the elderly man who lay in the next room, but made a mental note to look into it regardless.

"Was there anyone who might have not liked him helping the youth?" he asked.

"Not that I know of," Mrs Simpson said. "A lot of the youth here seem to wander around without any direction. It's not their fault, of course. Some of them come from families that don't seem to be interested in providing them with support … or love."

"How did Abe help them?" asked Ashley.

"When he first started to notice the young ones who would wander around far too late for their age, in our opinion, Abe would walk around the streets in the evenings and talk to them," Mrs Simpson replied. "Didn't tell them off or tell them to go home. He believed that sometimes all a young person needs is one person to ask them how they are, and if they're okay, so that was what he started doing. I don't mind admitting I was worried at first. An old man out at night, with who knows who wandering around out there too? Yes, sometimes I was worried, but he still persisted."

"Nothing ever happened to him?" Tim asked.

"No," Mrs Simpson replied with a sad smile. "I don't know if it would have been the same for another person doing what he did, but each night he started coming home and talking about the young ones he'd spoken to, telling me how this one or that one was seeming more friendly and positive than they had on a previous night. Over time, I could see that Abe was finding it rewarding. It still worried me, but no harm came to him. When he told me he wanted to find somewhere for the young people to go in the early evenings, I thought he was crazy, but he talked me into believing it was a good thing. He always had a way with words - a way to change my views on things, with that way he'd look at me," she added, chuckling. "The handsomest man I ever met."

Tim and Ashley exchanged a glance as they waited for the woman to enjoy her memory. They'd both met many people over their years together as a working partnership - many people who'd obviously shared a deep love with a life partner. It was something both agents envied, but which, so far, eluded both of them.

"So the youth center was set up, and Abe went there most nights at the beginning," Mrs Simpson finally continued. "He got some local businesses to donate things - fitness equipment and board games … books … beanbags - anything to provide some kind of interactive activity that the kids could learn and enjoy openly with each other, in a safe environment."

"And it was appreciated and used?" asked Tim.

"Oh, yes!" the elderly woman said. "It was truly a success. He always said it would be, and he was right. After that was up and running, whenever he and I would go out to the grocery store or to the cinema on one of our date nights, always one young person or another would call out to us. 'Hello Mr and Mrs Simpson!' I would hear as we walked around. It made me extra proud to have him by my side as my husband. He was helping those young people, just by giving them a friendly ear and a way to feel safe."

"He stopped going in the evenings?" Ashley asked.

"Yes. After a year of doing that, Abe wanted to hand the reigns of the center over to someone younger, to make sure that after he … after he couldn't go anymore, the youth would still have ongoing support with someone they already knew. Over time, Abe went less and less, and two newer, younger people began to run it in the evenings."

"Were there any problems with the changeover? Anyone angry that Abe wasn't going to be there anymore?" Tim asked.

"Not that I'm aware of," Mrs Simpson replied. "Whenever we would go out, we'd still get the same greeting, and a few of the young ones came up to us to ask us how we were doing, and tell Abe they were missing him. He reassured them that he was still out and about during the day, but just wouldn't be going at night. Nobody said anything negative, that I know of. I'm sure they couldn't miss that we're an elderly couple! Staying out at night wasn't something that he could have done forever. No, I don't think anyone was upset at his decision. They missed him, yes, but upset at him for his decision? No."

After watching a range of emotions cross the woman's face, Tim and Ashley saw her look at them again, finally with the look of curiosity.

"You don't think one of the young ones would have done this to him, do you?" she asked.

"From what you have told us, we don't think so, but we do have to explore all avenues," Ashley replied, uncertain whether the elderly woman knowing other people had been killed in the night would help her, or push her distress even higher.

"May I ask, do you or your husband keep a gun in the house, Mrs Simpson?" Tim asked.

"Oh, no," the elderly woman replied. "No, Abe was very against that. When he found out some of the young ones came from homes with guns, he tried to instill some confidence in the young ones' minds about people - how not everyone was out to hurt them, and so they didn't need guns in this town."

"Did the people he spoke to listen, do you think?" asked Tim.

"I don't know," Mrs Simpson said. "I don't believe anyone in this town could have done … this," she added before beginning to weep again. "You are the professionals, of course, but I think you'll find there must have been someone from out of town here - a stranger. Only a stranger could do… that."

"Yes, of course," said Ashley. "Another one of our team is here now, Mrs Simpson - Tracy. She is going to look after you, and she may ask to check your clothing and hands. If she does, please assist."

"I will do anything I can to help you find whoever took my Abe from me," Mrs Simpson said, her tears beginning again. "Thank you."

Feeling a little tearful herself, Ashley looked at Tim and saw him give his silent and discreet nod. Whatever they'd hoped to find out from the woman, they'd found out, at least until any test of DNA or gunshot residue was complete.

Outside in the fresh air again, Tim turned to face her.

"Are you okay, Ash?" he asked. She wasn't usually as emotional on cases, or even day to day. It both perplexed and worried him.

"Yes," Ashley replied, forcing a smile. "It all seems so unfair, but especially when we hear of a couple like that - married their entire adult lives and obviously in love."

"You can't think like that, and you know it," Tim cautioned her. "Yes, she looked like she was in love with him, but you know things aren't always as they seem, particularly when one partner is dead."

Ashley was surprised by his tone. He was usually the easy going one - the one who told her not to take everything to heart or so seriously.

"That isn't a typical Tim response," she said as they climbed into the car.

"I know, but ... let's just see where the evidence takes us," Tim replied. "We know ... believe ... Abe's death is just one on the list of many for this town, probably orchestrated by the same perpetrator, so..."

"So let's move on to the next crime scene," Ashley said, smiling at him.

CHAPTER 27

Later that night, Ashley and Tim settled into their motel rooms, pulling together all resources they had and laying them out on the long desk in Tim's room. Throughout the afternoon, they'd visited all of the known crime scenes, and talked to everyone who'd been present and/or wanted to talk to them.

"No further bodies found then," Ashley muttered to herself when they were moving pages into a logical order.

"Yes, that is the only good aspect that I can see," Tim responded. "It does prompt the question about why, though. Seaview was in the six hundreds. Leefton was even more than that. Why would the number now be so little?"

"According to the town records about the population recorded here at the date of the last census, there are significantly less people living here than Seaview or Leefton."

"Yeah, that's true," Tim said as he sourced the page detailing the census results. "In fact when you look at these records, and work out the number killed…"

Ashley saw him look at her with an intense stare of contemplation.

"What?" she asked. Still, he continued to look thoughtful. "Tim!"

"Let's do this math, Ash," Tim replied as he put a large sheet of paper up on the wall and grabbed a large marker. "In this town, if we divide the number of those killed by the statistical recorded population of adults -

let's leave kids out of this for now - the percentage killed is ... 21%," he said as he wrote up the details. "In Leefton ... 26%."

"And Seaview?" Ashley asked, knowing he was going to get to his point sooner rather than later.

"Seaview," Tim said as he did a quick calculation based on the census results he held in his hand. When he arrived at the number he sought, he looked up at Ashley, feeling a new level of excitement flowing through him. "Seaview ... 32%."

"*Thirty two percent* of the adult population was killed in Seaview?" Ashley asked, horrified at the realization. "No. It was only a few hundred people..."

"It's a small town," Tim said, nodding.

"And you had a theory at one point about gun ownership," Ashley said, feeling like she was waking up from a long, dull dream.

"Yes, because we know that all of the shooters used their own guns..." Tim said.

"And all of those *killed* seemed to be people who didn't..." said Ashley.

"Not only that, but some of those killed were pretty strongly against guns being allowed at all, not just for themselves, but for everyone in general," Tim said.

"We need to test this theory by..." Ashley started to suggest.

"We need to find out who had a gun registered here in Kildare," Tim agreed as he picked up his laptop and logged into the Bureau interface to find the information he sought. "Search is underway. Shouldn't take long."

Ashley watched as he set the laptop down and began looking over the pages of paper before them.

"Based on previous findings for the other shootings, I think it's safe to consider that all of the shooters, this time around too, will be gun owners in this town," Tim said. "That's been the case twice, so why not this time too."

"True," Ashley agreed. "I wonder, though…" she said before halting her words, her mind active.

"What?" Tim prompted her.

"Well, if this theory is right, do we need to investigate the whole country, and find out any other towns that have…"

"A high percentage of the adult population registered as a gun owner?" Tim asked, finishing her sentence. "If this is the right theory that the people behind this are working to…"

"We could stop the next attack, or at least be ready for it," Ashley said. "But even if we did work out where they're going to do this next, how would we know *when*? As far as we can tell, there's no common ground in the dates of these first three. The shootings haven't happened exactly the same amount of days, weeks or months apart, and none of the dates seem to have any significance."

"That is true," said Tim, thoughtful. "Did any response ever come back to the enquiry you made about whether there had been any instances elsewhere, of people saying they were doing something entirely different when some shootings happened, even though it was proven they were the killer?"

"Tim, pretty much every person who kills someone, says they were somewhere other than where the killing took place!" Ashley responded, taking a moment to enjoy teasing him. "But, yeah, okay, to find out any further places like that, how could we … hmm … I guess it would have to be a town where…"

"The gun ownership to population percentage is high enough to be noticeable," Tim answered.

"Yes," Ashley agreed. "It all sounds a bit farfetched but then so is all of this. I mean, logic…"

"There's no sense in logic in this, I reckon," said Tim as he glanced at the population, gun ownership and killing numbers for each town. I've never heard of anything like this happening, and what could someone get out of it? There's no financial motive - no financial records of any shooters or victims has shown that. We're pretty sure there are no sexual or love connections that would result in this..."

"Not on this grand scale anyway," Ashley added.

"Right," said Tim. "So what?"

"If these findings are right, then what is clear is there's some correlation between the deaths and the number of people who own guns," said Ashley. "If that's the case then that might be the reason for all of it."

"Gun ownership?" Tim asked as he studied her face, his mind active. "The perpetrators have something against guns?"

"Pretty stupid way to deliver that message - by having more people shot," Ashley said before beginning to test that theory inside the silence of her mind. "Stupid … or ingenious?"

Time considered what she'd said. It all seemed too unlikely, but the pieces were beginning to fall into place. He could feel it.

"To be honest, Ash, I don't think *any* of this makes any sense, but I'm not sure there's anything more we can do tonight," he finally said. "Tomorrow will hopefully provide more answers, so what do you say we get some sleep while we can? The remaining test results we're waiting on should be in by morning and we can see how things are looking then. All of this is just an idea," he added as he pointed to the wall. "We really need to see the results of everything before considering it could be a reality."

"Agreed," Ashley said. "Okay, I'll head back to my room now..."

"Make sure you double lock your door and..."

"Text you to let you know I'm safe and sound," Ashley said, grinning at him while cutting short the words she'd heard him say plenty of times. "Yeah, I know."

Tim smiled at her cheekiness. Yes, it was probably an extreme level of overprotection on his part to make sure she was safe each night when they were on away cases, but he'd never apologize for that. She was his work partner and, even though they didn't spend time together outside of work hours, he also considered her a friend. He cared for her deeply, and that was another thing Special Agent Tim Moore would never apologize for.

CHAPTER 28

When Ashley's eyes opened the following morning, she was startled to find a face at the forefront of her mind. For a long time, she allowed it to maintain her focus, ensuring it was lodged deep into not only her subconscious that always seemed to work well in sleep, but also her consciousness.

Picking up her phone, she saw it was another hour till the time she and Tim had arranged to meet up for breakfast and indulge in the first discussion of the day. That didn't deter her. Pushing back the covers from the bed, she raced to the bathroom and turned on the shower.

Throughout her short preparation for the day, she fought to maintain the face in her mind. She'd learned long ago that sleep often provided her with new ideas to test when she was on a case. Usually all she had to do was type up a few words in her phone notepad and that was enough to hold onto whatever detail she wanted to check out. This time it was a face, and she was no artist.

When her preparation was complete, she messaged the Bureau, then messaged Tim. It was early, but she knew him well enough to believe he'd already be up anyway, and probably working his way through the pages of the files they'd received.

A couple of minutes later, after receiving his reply, she knocked on his door.

When Tim opened his door, he delivered a knowing smile. It wasn't rare for his work partner to have woken with something for them to pursue. How her brain happened to process things in her sleeping hours and present to her something new to consider as soon as she woke, he had no idea, but it had proven to be the case so many times before that he never doubted the power of sleep when it came to Ashley Power.

"The security guard," Ashley said, almost breathless in her dedication to maintaining focus. "I've arranged to meet with a sketch artist to get a facial composite done. Come on, let's get going."

Tim was surprised, but said nothing to her, instead grabbing his jacket and backpack to follow her to the car. If she wanted to talk to him, he knew she would. If there was a chance that she could help produce an image of someone who might be of interest, he was going to shut up and support her in remembering as much detail as she could. After the composite was complete, then he'd be asking her some questions.

CHAPTER 29

"Done," Ashley finally said to Tim when she'd gone through the lengthy process of explaining all the details she could remember, and watching as the forensic artist listened to everything she said and worked his magic in producing an image that closely resembled what Ashley could see in her memory. "But you need to look at it too."

"Okay," Tim replied as he allowed her to nudge him to where the forensic artist remained.

As Tim glanced at the image produced, his memory was activated.

"That's the guy you reacted to yesterday at the Simpson home," he said as he glanced at his work partner.

"Yes!" Ashley said, excited. "You do remember him?"

"Yeah, of course," Tim replied.

"Is it an accurate representation?" Ashley asked.

"I can tell it *is* the security guard, so yeah, that's how I remember him," said Tim. "But why do you think he has something to do with this?"

"I can't be sure but, Tim, when I saw him, I first thought that he was just … you know … giving me the eye," Ashley said, prepared to give an eye roll to Tim's usual response to any statement like that when she made it. "But that wasn't it! I remember him from Leefton."

"What?" Tim asked, confused.

"He was a security guard there too," Ashley replied. "I think … maybe the fourth or fifth home we visited, he was there."

"You sure?" Tim asked. "I can't remember seeing him."

"We didn't talk to him that day," said Ashley. "He was one of the guards that was guarding a perimeter that was set up around three homes that were side by side. I don't know why I noticed him, but…"

"And you're *sure* this is the same guy?" asked Tim.

"Tim, you know as well as I do that I could be entirely mistaken, but I don't think I am," Ashley replied. "I am … 99.9% sure that we've seen that security guard before, and it was at Leefton."

"Well we know that the law enforcement there *and here* have used an external security company," Tim said, pondering the possibility.

"They have, and if these were neighboring towns, I'd assume that was a possibility - that the same guards were assigned to the scenes of the two towns - but these towns are nowhere near each other! There are plenty of security firms between here and there, and I'm sure it wasn't even the same firm that was used…"

"On it," Tim said as he pulled out his phone and fired off an information request to his supervisor at the Bureau. "I'll ask Sarah to find out about the security firms used in Seaview and Leefton, and we can ask Nick about who he used here when we see him."

Ashley watched as his fingers worked over the small phone screen. When he looked up at her again, she could see his thoughtfulness. It was understandable. She often got ideas in her head when she woke up in the mornings of an active case, but until they could establish a true lead and find any evidence, that's all they were - ideas.

"Okay, while she's dealing with that … you've sent a copy of the composite sketch to the Bureau to do a search?"

"Yep," Ashley replied. "If he's in the system, I'm hopeful that will provide us with someone to look closer at."

"Good," said Tim. "Okay, I've got a couple of emails to check, but it looks like we're still waiting on quite a few reports to come in so…"

"Breakfast?" Ashley asked, teasing him.

"Oh, how well she knows me," Tim replied, grinning. "Food and coffee. The basic necessities of life."

Feeling the first level of excitement she'd felt throughout the entire case, Ashley happily agreed and followed him. Her thoughts and memory might lead to nothing, but at least she and Tim had some ideas about what was going on, and who might have something to do with it all.

CHAPTER 30

Two hours later, Tim and Ashley sat among a large number of staff from the Bureau plus other law enforcement. All eyes faced the front of the spacious room, studying the chain drawing that had been established.

"This is something I've never seen before," they heard the police chief say. "Special Agent Ashley Power, perhaps you'd like to come up front and share with my staff what, exactly, we're seeing."

Ashley glanced at Tim. Why she'd been summoned alone to address the group, she could only guess, but she knew Tim would follow her lead for the two of them to go to the front of the room.

"Thanks, Chief," she said when they turned and faced the crowd. "What this represents is the flow of shooters, with who they've shot. For those of you who live here, I have no doubt that you might not agree that some of these people have done what our forensics testing has found, but, unfortunately, there's little doubt."

"You're saying that those people whose names have been written up in red, are all of the victims?" one police officer called out.

"Yes, these are the people who have been killed," Ashley confirmed. "The ones in the black are their killers."

"But I *know* John Brown," one officer said, disbelief obvious in their voice. "He'd never…"

"One thing we've learned from the previous cases of Seaview and Leefton, is that hardly anybody who pulled the trigger of their gun, seems to be a person who would be expected to do that," Tim said. "That is just one piece of this very large and very complex puzzle surrounding these shootings."

"But I don't understand. Why would all - or *any* - of these people do that?" an officer asked.

"That is something we have to find out," said Ashley. "As of this morning, we do have an interest in one person, and this is currently being delved into by staff at the Bureau. We're hopeful we'll have a lead from that within a few hours. In the meantime, this is a composite sketch of the person in question. Do any of you know him, or remember seeing him anywhere?"

Seeing all the people in the room shake their heads surprised Tim. Some of the people sitting before them had been at the Simpson scene.

"Nobody has seen him at any of the crime scenes?" Tim pressed. Again, there was only silence and blank looks.

"Who here was at the Simpson house?" Ashley asked and saw three people put up their hands.

"Yes!"

"Okay, can you guys please look at this image again," Ashley instructed, but still saw no look of comprehension on their faces. "You really didn't see this person there? He was in a security guard uniform."

"No, Ma'am," one of the officers called out. "Unless he changed how old he was, and changed his hair color. The security guard I saw there was much older and had white hair."

"What about you two?" Tim asked, pointing to the other two officers who'd said they'd been at the Simpson home.

"Same," one officer called out in reply.

"Yep, the guy I saw at that home was older, too, with white hair," the other officer called out at the same time.

"Right," Ashley said, silently filing away in her mind

the information she'd received till she and Tim could further talk about it away from the crowd.

"What we did find in Leefton and Seaview, is that everyone who had a gun registered - and only one who didn't - used their gun on those nights to shoot someone who didn't own a gun," Tim added. "For whatever reason, it looks like people owning a gun has possibly been a driving force behind who was chosen to do the killing. How or why, we still don't know, but that's how things are looking at this stage."

"The other part of this puzzle is that even though we know that these people pulled the triggers, they *think* they were somewhere else - in the case of Kildare, all of the shooters we've had the opportunity to talk to so far, think they were in your town square, having a friendly get together."

"I was on night shift that night, and I didn't see anyone in the town square," one of the officers said. "So they're lying. Is that what you're saying?"

"Possibly yes … but possibly no," Tim said. "We haven't started any polygraph testing yet, but we do know that in the previous two towns where this happened, all shooters, when asked about their whereabouts on those nights, believed they were somewhere they weren't…"

"And passed the polygraph with no problem," Ashley added.

"Right," said Tim.

"Some people can pass polygraph tests, even when they're lying," called out an officer.

"You're absolutely right. Some can," said Ashley. "The problem we have with that argument, when it comes to Leefton and Seaview, is that *all* of the shooters passed the polygraph. And before anyone suggests the test was flawed, there were multiple polygraph machines used, and multiple polygraph examiners. No matter what machine was used, or who used it, the shooters all passed."

"But how can that be?"

"We believe the reason they all passed is because, for whatever reason - at this stage we have no idea - but for whatever reason, all of the shooters we've talked to, do actually believe they were at the location they said they were, doing what they claimed to be doing," Ashley replied. "As far as we can tell, not one of our shooters can remember shooting anyone."

"And there's no possibility that *that* is the error?" someone called out. "That all of the people were doing what they've said they were, and it's the testing of evidence - ballistics and what not - that could be wrong?"

"Not possible," said Tim. "We have seen hours of CCTV footage, looking for any of the shooters in the places they think they were, and there was never any sign of any of them."

"Could someone be teaching people to defy the polygraph?" a voice asked.

"That is certainly a possibility," Ashley conceded. "How they could find so many people to be able to do it, however, is a mystery, especially since everyone who has fired a gun, owned a gun. When you think about the odds of finding someone who's a gun owner *and has* the ability to beat a polygraph, it starts to look even less likely to be possible."

"Just like everything about this case," Tim said quietly. "As with all cases, though, we could be wrong about this, just as we could be wrong about lots of things. What we absolutely are sure about is that someone must be pulling strings for this to all happen. The odds of so many residents in a town, waking up in the middle of the same night and going to shoot someone, then going home to bed and forgetting it happened, are too slim. With each additional town that this happens in, it seems more likely that these are targeted attacks - like we've said, possibly to do with gun ownership, given that all shooters had guns registered to them and all victims didn't. *How* someone could be coordinating it all, who knows. We just have to keep an open mind. For now, take a bit of time to look at, study, and become familiar with this diagram. You may see on it some names that you can't believe would hurt anyone. Be accepting of that! This is the same situation as has been the case in the other two towns!"

A long period of silence ensued as people studied the chain diagram. Looking out at their faces, Ashley could see similar expressions to what she'd observed on the local police force in Leefton, and Seaview before that. The people on the diagram were all people who might be at least familiar to the law enforcement officers of that town. Ashley couldn't imagine how hard it would be to see that they knew not only some of the victims, but also some of the killers. Fortunately, in all three towns, law enforcement seemed to be the exception to the 'gun owner equals shooter' rule. Why was that? It was another link of the mystery puzzle.

"Is that diagram supposed to run together as a continuous loop then?" one police officer called out, breaking the lapse in conversation.

"Yes, it is a continuous representation of who shot who," Tim replied. "It shows that everyone who pulled a trigger that night, is an owner of a gun - the shooters. All the people over here are our victims. None of them owned a gun."

"I can see that most of it seems to flow, but why is there a gap *there*?" they heard the officer ask. "It's like everything fits … except that one spot. Like … you've got an extra person who owns a gun up there…"

Hearing the observation voiced, Ashley and Tim both turned to look at the diagram. So many names were on the board that they hadn't noticed at first, but when they looked closely, they stepped closer to the diagram.

"Here?" Ashley asked.

"Yes," the officer replied. "What does that mean?"

Ashley looked at Tim. It was easy to see he'd just come to the same realization she had.

"It means there's one person in this town who has a gun registered to their name..." Ashley said.

"But didn't use it," Tim surmised. Glancing up at the board again, he followed the line of the chain until he came to the gap. "Kane Garmin," he read. "Does anyone here know someone called Kane Garmin?" he then called out.

"Yes, I know Kane," an officer said. "I haven't seen him in a long time, but we were in the same class in high school."

"You know where he lives?" Tim asked and saw the officer nod.

"I know where his family home was," he said. "I can't say if he lives there now, but I know his parents passed a while back so he might have moved back in."

"Great. You're coming with us. We need to speak to him."

As Ashley and Tim both felt intrigued by a new development in the case - and, quite simply, something feeling *different* - they began to extract themselves from the front of the crowd.

"Is there anything I can help with?" Ashley heard the chief, Nick, ask as he approached her. It wasn't lost on her that he'd stepped a bit closer to her than he needed to.

Looking up into his eyes, she was again struck by just how attractive he was - a 'silver fox', as she'd heard people say about someone or other. She'd always regarded it as a silly phrase, but couldn't deny just how easy it appeared to be for the Kildare police chief to have a physical effect on her.

"I don't think so at this stage, thanks, Chief," she said.

"Nick," he corrected her with a wry grin on his face.

It was such a surprising - and somewhat unprofessional - thing to happen that Ashley was instantly broken from her momentary lapse in focus on the job at hand.

"We'll take your officer along with us, if that's okay with you, and go and speak to our missing gun owner," she said as she saw Tim take a step closer. She couldn't help but smile at him, knowing full well that, when it came to her, he had a very protective side. Any sign of anyone giving any kind of potentially unwanted attention to Ashley, and Tim was always there, right by her side. Some women would have found that insulting. She found it comforting.

"Yep. And these guys can be released then?" Nick asked, glancing around the room.

"Yes, thank you for bringing them all in for this," Ashley replied. "I know it was brief, and I wish we had more to give them, to help them with everything they're dealing with. I expect some of them have friends or family members who've either been killed, or…"

She stopped speaking, out of respect, but Nick didn't hesitate to finish what he suspected she'd been about to say.

"Or were one of the shooters," he said.

"Yes," Ashley said.

For a long moment, she caught the chief focusing on her lips. Even though she suspected she might have enjoyed his attention in another setting, at another time, in that moment she just found it unnerving. She was relieved when the officer who knew the person of interest stepped forward.

"I'll go with these guys, Chief?" he asked Nick, who nodded in reply. "My car or yours?" he then asked the agents.

"Probably best if you lead in your car and let them follow you," Nick replied before Ashley or Tim could speak. "He's on duty. He needs to be able to leave you if something happens," he added, addressing the agents.

"That works for us," Tim said, finding himself surprisingly eager to get Ashley away from the police chief.

"Okay," the officer said as he grinned. "I'll wait for you out front."

CHAPTER 31

On the drive to Kane Garmin's home, Ashley's mind was active. They thought they'd found a reason why certain people in a town were shot, and other people in a town were shooters. In Seaview and Leefton, the list of people with guns registered had entirely matched the list of people who'd fired their guns. Now something was different, casting doubt on whether their growing suspicions might be right.

"You're thoughtful," Tim asked her after watching her face for several minutes. "I hope it isn't due to the chief…" he tentatively suggested, pausing to see if that was going to be a subject he could tease her about or not. Seeing her turn and look at him with a distinctive Ashley-frown, he chuckled. "Nope, not due to that, I can see."

"Hardly, Timothy!" Ashley replied, not minding his teasing at all since she'd gotten so used to it over the years they'd been working together. "No, it's *this* - this difference in what we'd been believing till this point."

"I agree," said Tim. "It's disheartening if we've had it wrong up till now, but let's see what meeting this person brings us."

"If he's there," said Ashley. "Maybe that's why he wasn't involved - he isn't in town. If he went to school with that officer, he's not a young man. His life could have taken him anywhere in the time since that guy last saw him."

"That's true," Tim agreed. "We'll know in a few minutes, it seems. Looks like the officer's pulling over in front of that place."

Both agents watched as the police car slowed and stopped, and the officer got out of his vehicle and motioned for them to also stop.

"This is it?" Ashley asked, just to be sure.

"Yep, this is where he used to live," the officer said. "Like I said, I haven't seen him in a long time, and I'm only guessing he might have moved back into his family home, but I'll knock on the door for you if you like."

"Yes, please," Ashley said, knowing there was no reason to have a police officer to escort them, but wondering if a familiar face might put the man in question more at ease if he was at home.

It took only a short time after the officer knocked before the door opened and a man around the same age stood in the doorway.

"Tony?" the man asked, his eyes glancing over the uniform facing him and then towards where Ashley and Tim stood. "It's been a long time. What's up?"

"Hey, Kane," the officer said as he held out his hand. "These agents from the Bureau of Investigation are keen to talk to you. Is it okay if they come in?"

"Yeah, sure, but what's this about?" Kane asked, surprised.

At that moment, the officer reacted to something that came through his radio.

"I have to leave, sorry," he said, turning to face Ashley and Tim. "You'll be okay here?"

"Yes, thank you," Ashley said before she watched him begin walking swiftly toward his police car.

"How can I help you?" she heard the voice ask from the doorway.

"Mr Garmin?" asked Tim. "I'm Special Agent Moore and this is Special Agent Power. We'd like to talk to you about your whereabouts over the past three days, if we may."

On the face before them, Ashley and Tim could see

surprise, but that didn't stop the man from opening his front door wider.

"Sure. Please come in and tell me what this is all about," Kane replied, confused.

Once seated, he waited for their questions to come.

"Two nights ago, there were a number of shootings in the area," Tim began.

"Yes, I heard about that on the news," Kane said. "But … what has that got to do with me?"

"Can you tell us where you were two nights ago?" asked Tim.

For a long while, Kane felt conflict. He knew he'd gone out to a dance party. Did he want to tell law enforcement *that*? Would they even believe him? He was almost fifty years old, and then there were the conditions listed on that invitation. What *would* be the consequences if he told someone about the dance party?

After consideration, he sighed. He had no family left. If whoever organized the dance party was going to get nasty because someone told someone about it, he guessed he would be the only one who would suffer for it.

"I was … dancing," he finally said.

"Dancing?" Tim asked. "Can you please elaborate?"

"I can," Kane said. "I was invited to a dance party, and I went along."

"Do you mean a dance party … in a local bar?" Ashley asked, quite prepared for a bizarre story to be told, and the story to later be proven to be untrue.

"No, not at all," Kane replied. "It was … wait … I still have one of the invitations here. It has a strict instruction to take it on the night, which I did. That one - the one I received - they took off me and destroyed before we got inside, but when I saw this on the ground after I passed the security guys, I grabbed it. Thought it might be a cool keepsake since I'd never seen so many conditions on any document in my *life*."

When he returned and handed the invitation to Ashley, she glanced over it and then passed it on to Tim, taking care to hold it carefully by the edges.

"And, can anyone confirm you were there?" she asked.

"I'm guessing that probably ... oh ... well over a hundred people were there, I'd say, but that's only a guess," Kane replied. "Look, I'm confused. You said you wanted to talk about the people who were killed, but I still don't know what any of that has to do with me. Do you think I'm a relative, or..."

"Do you own a gun, Mr Garmin?" Tim asked.

"I do," Kane confirmed.

"Is it here in your home?" Tim continued and saw the man nod in reply. "May we see it please?"

Kane felt nervousness flow over him. He knew he hadn't done anything wrong, but it was always the way when he was questioned - he always felt like he probably looked guilty. It had always been the way, particularly during his military years, having to give reports and explain his actions after major exercises.

In spite of his uncertainty, he retrieved his revolver and showed it to the agents, holding it at a distance so as to not let them touch it. That was something he'd never do, as he'd been rigidly taught during his time in the army. His weapon. His responsibility.

"Now can you tell me what this is about?" he asked as he sat down, keeping the revolver inside its case and tight in his hands.

"Can you..." Ashley started to ask before she could decide which question to ask first. "Is there anyone in town that you know personally, who also went to this dance party, Mr Garmin?"

"Yes, of course," Kane said before he named four people he'd seen there, who he knew from growing up in the small town.

As the four names were said out loud, Ashley saw

Tim's face look as surprised as she was sure her own would look.

"You're sure all four of those people were there?" she asked and saw Kane nod. "Did you … meet anyone new there? Anyone at all that you can name?"

Kane took some time as he wondered about mentioning Nancy. They'd spent a lovely time together, both at the dance and for a short time after. He was saddened that he hadn't heard from her since then, and she hadn't answered any of his calls or texts, but he accepted it. She was a beautiful woman, and even though she'd indicated she was single, Kane had accepted that might not have been the truth. Since his efforts to reach out to her had gone unanswered, he suspected he never would hear from her again, and that was okay. One thing he'd always known he'd never do was push himself onto a woman.

"There was someone that I met," he finally began to say. He didn't really want to mention her, but it was law enforcement and, somehow, something to do with him must have had something to do with the mass shootings in the town. Otherwise, why would the agents in front of him even be there? "A woman."

"Her name?" Tim asked.

"Nancy," Kane replied. "I really can't tell you anything more than that. We exchanged first names and that was about it. I didn't ask her for details."

"And you met Nancy … at the dance?" asked Ashley.

"Yes, but there were lots of people there," Kane said. "As you'll see on that invitation, it says that the invitation itself is supposed to be destroyed, and whoever gets one is not supposed to tell anyone about it, so I can't say that if you talk to her, she'd confirm she was there or not."

"Can you describe Nancy? What she looks like?" Ashley asked.

"She's … I dunno … maybe 5ft 9, medium build,

blonde hair that's about the same length as yours," Kane replied. "I'm not good with ages - especially women - but I thought she might be in her 40s; maybe older but I'm not sure."

As Ashley listened, she felt a level of dread fall over her. She knew there was one Nancy on the list of shooters, and she fitted the description Ashley had just heard, almost perfectly.

"And … forgive me for having to ask, but did you … spend the night with Nancy?" Ashley asked. She hated delving into people's personal lives, but it was always necessary for her job.

"What…?" Kane began to ask, then accepted he'd been asked a question and should answer. "The whole night? No, but we did … we were intimate. After a couple of hours of dancing, we left together and came back here. We were probably here for … I'm not sure, to be honest. Maybe an hour? Maybe two? I invited her to stay but after a while it was clear to me that she wanted to get out of here, and I didn't try and stop her. Sometimes that's the way things go. I'm guessing it was probably around 1am when she left here. I didn't look at the clock so that's only a guess. She said she had something she had to do, which seemed a bit odd at that time of the night so I think it was probably an excuse and she wasn't enjoying my company as much as I was enjoying hers, but I mean, I don't *know* this woman, so who was I to judge."

"She didn't seem odd to you, then, I take it," Tim suggested.

"Until the moment that she seemed to become almost desperate to leave, she seemed lovely," said Kane. "Very easy going and happy. To be honest, I thought she seemed a bit *too* happy when we were dancing - like not just happy but … almost as if she was high. I remember thinking that she couldn't be since the security of the event was so tight. Phones, alcohol and drugs were being found and taken off people at several different checkpoints on the way into the venue, and from the moment she and I met inside, she was in my arms almost non-stop. Even if she'd had a pill hidden on her somewhere, I'd be surprised if I missed her slipping it into her mouth, although I suppose she could have taken something before she went in. I just accepted that she was having a good time ... as was I, and everyone else around us looked just as happy as well, so it was just a ... feel-good night."

Tim pondered what they'd just been told. He knew from toxicology tests completed that none of the shooters had been found to have any type of drug or other stimulant in their system when they were tested, and the lab confirmed that it was unlikely any of them had drugs in their system that would have been gone by the time they were tested. And yet, the way Kane was describing one of the shooters, before she went off and killed someone...

"Can you tell us a bit about yourself, Mr Garmin?" he asked, curious.

"Not much to tell really," Kane replied, his mind having once again drifted to wondering if Nancy was okay. Was she just not wanting to talk to him after their time together, or was she *unable* to talk to him? "I was in the military from when I was eighteen, until just over a year ago. Now I don't do much - except run, that is. I do enjoy that. I just appreciate the quiet life."

"You retired from the military?" Tim asked.

"Yes, I did three tours in war-torn areas," Kane replied. "That was enough for me. By the time I came back from the third tour, I knew I'd had enough of that life. I was offered a position here at home, but I wanted to try and forget the atrocities that I witnessed. One thing I had to learn in that part of my life was the art of compartmentalizing - closing off my brain to certain things, and making sure I can't be as easily manipulated as some people are. I think it affected me more than I realized when I was still in service, but who knows - maybe one day someone will try and persuade me of something and they'll actually succeed! For now, though, I just want to keep trying to move on from the wars I've witnessed, and have a peaceful life, free of those memories."

"Do you think you can?" Ashley asked, intrigued. She'd met and interviewed a lot of ex-military people over her years as an agent. From those interviews, she always came away wondering how people could move forward from what they saw in war scenes. It was hard enough when she had to see human destruction in her job, and that wasn't anywhere near on the scale of war.

"I try, and I remain hopeful but, as yet, it hasn't happened," said Kane. "Maybe that's why when I got that invitation, it made me happy. Reading it, I thought, why not? I'm just an old guy who hasn't really had much reason to smile for quite a while. To be honest, I did consider that it might be some kind of joke or something, but once I was there, it all seemed pretty legit. There was nothing about it that made me think it was run by amateurs."

"Do you know who *was* running it?" asked Tim.

"I don't know *who*, but there was a DJ on a small stage in the center of the venue," Kane replied. "Looked like it was a one-man show. Other than him and the security personnel who searched everyone on the way in, there wasn't anyone else working, that I saw."

"And you said this wasn't held at a bar in town?" Ashley asked.

"No, it was in an old building just out of town," Kane replied. "Looked like an abandoned site. I grew up here and I'd never noticed it at all so I don't know what it was originally used for."

"Do you remember exactly where it was?"

"I do, but if you want to take that, it has the

coordinates on it at least for where we met," Kane said as he pointed to the invitation. "It took a bit for us to walk to the building itself, which I do remember was a really old place, like a building so dilapidated that it really should have been demolished decades ago. I'm guessing that's why the organizers wanted to make sure the invitations were disposed of - to hide any evidence that the dance happened, although why they'd want that to be the case, I have no idea. It was just a fun night. Nothing bad happened there, as far as I could see, and I think I'm pretty vigilant and observant."

"Okay. And is there anything else you can tell us about the DJ?" asked Ashley. "Did he introduce himself, or say anything to the crowd at all?"

"No, I saw him get on the stage and begin playing, but shortly after that I met Nancy. I guess I don't even know if that's her real name now," he said, scoffing. "Ah, the joys of being a single man. Anyway, no, once I met her, she was pretty much all that I was focused on. Her and that darned look of ecstasy on her face. I don't think I'll ever forget that. But to answer your question, no I don't remember him even introducing himself. He got up and started playing, and then, at some point later, he stopped playing and disappeared from the stage. Not long after that, security ushered us all out of there and demanded we go home and not tell anyone about the event."

"Can you describe what he looked like? The DJ?" Tim asked.

"I'm pretty sure he was wearing a cap that sat low over his eyes, so it wasn't easy to see his face," Kane replied. "I did notice he was lean and fairly tall but, to be honest, I only noticed him in the few minutes from when he got on the stage until when the first song started. After that, I … yeah, sorry but I was distracted."

"What about what he was wearing?"

"No, sorry, I really didn't take any notice," Kane said.

"Usually my mind is pretty sharp and I take in details easily but, I don't know, since I've been back, it's been kind of nice to try and not scrutinize everything quite so much. Sorry, I wish I could provide you with more detail."

"That's okay," Ashley said as she pulled out a range of images she'd brought with her. "Would you be able to look through these and see if you recognize anyone?"

Sitting back, she watched as Kane accepted the selection of police sketch images and looked through them.

"I really can't say any of them look familiar, sorry," Kane finally said after shuffling through the images a couple of times and then passing them back.

"No problem. Thanks for that," said Ashley. She knew it was a long shot that he might have been able to identify a familiar face from the selection - particularly the sketch of the security guard she remembered - but it was worth a try.

"And nothing about his voice stuck out to you?" Tim asked. "The sound of it, or the way he spoke? Maybe he had an accent?"

"No, not that I noticed," Kane replied. "Yeah, I think that even if I was distracted, hearing something different about his speech *would* have stood out to me, so I don't think he had an accent or any out of the ordinary speaking pattern. If he did say anything - and I'm not sure that he did, to be completely honest - he must have sounded just like an average sounding guy from around here."

"Alright, well, thank you," Tim said after a knowing look and nod from Ashley. "We'll leave you now, but if we need your assistance again, we can call on you?"

"Yes, of course," said Kane as they walked toward the door. "But like I said, it was a dance and it was fun. I can't see how it could, in any way, have anything to do with whatever happened in town the other night."

"It does seem a long shot, but thanks for your time anyway, Mr Garmin," said Ashley. "We'll be in touch."

Once in the car, she turned to face Tim.

"A dance party?" she asked, her face revealing a blend of amusement and curiosity. "It couldn't be…"

"Related to the shootings?" asked Tim and saw her nod. "It seems farfetched, but then so does everything about this whole case. One thing we do know is that all of those names that Kane mentioned just then, have proven to be shooters in this."

"Yeah, but he didn't mention the DJ saying anything at all, let alone telling people to go and shoot someone," Ashley retorted. "If he didn't speak, there's no way he could have given instructions to them. Is it possible that all of these people were guided by someone in the crowd?"

"Maybe," Tim replied. "I think the first thing we need to do is find this dance location. If we can, and we can get scene investigators there, maybe they can find something to begin tying this all together."

"Agreed," said Ashley before starting the engine. It was a weird journey they were on, but at least she finally felt like things were starting to fall into place.

CHAPTER 32

Once at the coordinates provided on the invitation that had been housed carefully inside a clear evidence bag, Ashley and Tim stood and looked in all directions. Kane had indicated it was a hefty walk from the meeting point to the event venue. Both agents had thought they'd still be able to see a building. Both were disheartened by what they saw.

"There's nothing that I can see, at all," Ashley said after they'd both looked around in all directions. "I mean, how far could the organizers of the event expect people to walk?"

"Ash, it was a dance party," Tim teased her. "If they were able to dance, they were probably able to walk!"

Ashley took a breather to deliver him a sarcastic eye roll. In her opinion, some things that came out of her work partner's mouth didn't need to be responded to in any other way.

"Besides, Kane did say that it seemed like a bit of a hike to get from the meeting point to the building they ended up going into. But let me have a quick look online," Tim continued after he'd received the response he always liked to witness. "If I can find an old map of the area..."

Ashley remained quiet as she waited for any result to be reported. Everything she'd learned from Kane Garmin played over and over in her mind. There was every chance that everything he'd said could prove to be pure fiction, and if that was the case, was there a chance that he had something to do with the crime? He was the one person out of the whole town who hadn't shot someone even though he had a gun not only registered to his name, but also in his possession. It wasn't impossible that he wasn't just someone who hadn't followed instructions provided, if that was how things had gone, but instead he was the person who'd given them.

"Got it," she heard Tim say, breaking her out of her thoughts and doubts. "In this direction, there was an old wool processing factory that stood over a hundred years ago."

"I still can't see anything over there though," Ashley muttered.

"Exactly, Special Agent Power!" Tim said, grinning at her. "Does that not sound like the absolute *perfect* location for a secret dance party?"

As annoying as he could be on the odd occasion, Ashley knew his efforts to make her smile and to keep her from falling into disheartenment during cases. Knowing that, she kept silent as she nodded, smiled, and forged ahead. If nothing else, the sunshine made it a good day for a cross-country walk.

CHAPTER 33

"Oh, wow," Tim said in surprise as they approached a dilapidated building. Getting closer to it, they realized just how well hidden it was from where they'd been. Over the many years it had obviously been standing, trees and vines had grown up and around it, providing it with a level of privacy that made it impossible to view from anywhere around it.

"You think *this* is where this dance was held?" Ashley asked, horrified. "I'm pretty sure any health and safety officer would have a field day trying to stop *anything* from being held here!"

"Yep," Tim agreed. "And I'm thinking that if you wanted something to be kept secret, this is just the kind of place you would want to use - *and* keep health and safety from knowing about."

Tentatively walking around the outside, they were glad to find a door that stood ajar.

"You don't have any fears about haunted houses, do you?" Tim teased her again as they took a step inside.

"Haunted houses? Yes," Ashley replied. "Old factories? Don't be silly, Timothy Moore."

Tim smiled. Any time his work partner sounded like she was in a more lighthearted state of mind, was glorious to him.

"No stage," he said when they'd moved to near the center of the large, open space.

"No, but definitely an indication that something the shape of one was here," Ashley called out when she noticed an outline in the dirt floor. "Lots of fairly fresh-looking footprints too."

"Yeah, I think we may have found the location of what Kane was telling us about," said Tim. "That at least makes his story credible."

"Did you have any doubt?" Ashley asked despite her own uncertainties about what Kane Garmin had told them.

"There's always room for doubt, Ash," Tim said. "That's what drives us on in our jobs, after all - proving something *beyond* reasonable doubt!"

"True. Well, let's get some of the crime scene techs here…" Ashley began to say as she pulled out her phone. "Cancel that. No cell phone reception here."

"I guess that's yet another reason this place would be ideal for someone wanting to make sure people couldn't call their friends and invite them over while the event was happening," said Tim.

"But you managed to open your maps app…"

"That was back near the car though," Tim said. "Must be a line somewhere between here and there, where the closest cell tower loses its range. That's pretty interesting. I wonder if the organizer of this dance party went that far - to calculate a building that would be out of cell tower range."

"Whoever it is does seem to do a lot of homework, if our theory about gun ownership is right, and that amount of research is in line with someone who's spent a large chunk of their life in the military," Ashley said. "This really could all be a ruse by Kane Garmin, you know. I'm certainly not ready to discount him as a suspect."

"Yeah, his story is weird, granted," Tim agreed. "But let's see where this current path of enquiry takes us. We've still got some of the known shooters to talk to. It'll be interesting to see what each of them says about their whereabouts - if they all share the same story that others have told. I also want to see if any of them mention this dance party."

"Yes, I'm particularly interested in speaking to the woman that Kane said he was with that night - Nancy," said Ashley. "Will she tell us the same story as what he's said? That she was with him?"

"Or will she tell us - and then seem to believe - that she was doing something entirely different, like being in the town square?" Tim suggested. "All of the shooters have already given that story. I'm not sure Nancy will tell a different one if we speak to her now."

"Only one way to find out, Partner. Come on," Ashley said, making a beeline for the door. "We need the techs to get here to see if they can find us some answers, and I need to get away from this building to be able to call them."

"Sure thing, Boss," Tim teased her as he fell in step beside her. "I gotta say. I'm starting to like this case more now."

Ashley wasn't sure she could agree, but couldn't deny she finally felt more invigorated by their current finding than she had throughout the entire Seaview / Leefton / Kildare case to date. Were they on the right path to finding out anything at all? She had no idea, but in her gut she was getting more and more hopeful with each new person she talked to.

CHAPTER 34

"I'll make sure any DNA or other scene findings testing is pushed through as a priority," Bureau of Investigation supervisor, Sarah Johnson, said through the speaker of Tim's phone later that afternoon. "I have to say, though, that this all sounds like something out of a fiction novel."

Tim smiled at Ashley as they both listened to their supervisor's words.

"Yeah, we know, Sarah," Ashley replied. "We have no idea where this'll lead, but we haven't ruled out the possibility that Kane Garmin has something to do with all of this."

"Good. The findings from our investigation into him are that he has an impeccable record from his time in the military, but we know not everyone who comes home with a record like that, comes home with a healthy mind," Sarah said. "In saying that, everything that you said he told you, at least as far as his army days go, does seem to be true. That doesn't mean he's still that good guy, of course."

"No, it doesn't," said Tim. "Don't worry, we're keeping an open mind where he's concerned."

"Well, just don't let him slip through your fingers," said Sarah. "His time in the military will have helped him hone skills in acting with stealth. Turn your back on someone like that, and he could be gone in an instant, never to be found again."

"Yes, Boss," Ashley and Tim both replied at the same time, making them chuckle.

"Alright, enough said for now," Sarah said. "When the results come back for the test samples taken from the event scene, I'll send them through to you."

"Thanks, Sarah," said Ashley. "Can you also follow up to see if anything has been found from the sketch of the security guard? Nothing's come through to us yet, but I don't know if that means there's nothing to learn about the guy, or the search hasn't been done yet."

"Oh, no, hang on," Sarah said, her voice fading away for a moment. "No, nothing came back from that. If he's got anything to do with all of this, and the sketch is accurate enough, he isn't in the system anywhere."

"Hmm," Ashley said, disheartened. "Okay, thanks for that, Sarah."

After hanging up the call, Tim turned to face Ashley.

"Where to now?" he asked.

"Well, we still need to chat to a few more of the shooters," Ashley replied.

"Yeah, I think this Nancy could be real interesting to talk to," Tim agreed. "I am curious to see if she can confirm Kane's story about this dance party."

"We'll have more of an idea about that once the scene forensics test results come in, too," said Ashley. "In the meantime, while we wait for those..."

"Lunch?" Tim asked as his tummy loudly expressed its thoughts on eating.

"Wow, yeah, we need to get you fed, and stat!" Ashley said, chuckling.

CHAPTER 35

"I feel like we've come up with some theories about what *might* have been happening, and how people *could* have been selected as who's going to shoot and who's going to be shot, but..." Tim began to say as he and Ashley sat, waiting for their meals to arrive.

"It all feels all over the place?" Ashley asked.

"Yes!" Tim exclaimed. "So much time has passed since that first day in Seaview, but it still doesn't really feel like we've got a sound handle on what this is all about."

Ashley took some time to study his face, and the frustration she could see on it. He was usually the more easy-going of the two of them. She had to admit, it was difficult for her to see him not confident in their work.

"Usually it's me who feels it the hardest when we haven't achieved momentum in a case," she said. "You're okay, right?"

Hearing the genuine concern in her voice, Tim grinned. A moment earlier, he had been feeling the heaviness of not having solved the case. It was refreshing to have someone divert his mind, even if it was only for a misdirected question about his state of mind.

"And that's usually *my* role - asking how *you* are," he said, teasing her. "But yeah, of course I'm good. I just want to get this thing done and dusted. As long as we haven't solved this…"

"There's always a chance that it might happen again," Ashley said.

In response to her finishing his sentence, she saw the smile fade on Tim's face. There was still a remnant of it - the piece that he was able to plaster on his face even though he didn't necessarily feel happy - but she could see everything about the investigation was affecting him.

"We're going to get whoever's behind this, Tim," she said. "I really do believe we're heading in the right direction. Once we have results from all of the tests done…"

Seeing his facial expression change, Ashley stopped speaking.

"What?"

Tim took his time reading the email that he'd opened after hearing the distinctive notification sound. It was a long while before he finally looked up at Ashley and delivered a smile she knew could melt hearts.

"*What?!*" she demanded, knowing he was toying with her by making her wait for some important news.

"The tests from the building we thought might be the one Kane Garmin was talking about," said Tim, his mind darting over lots of considerations. "DNA secured from random pieces of hair mainly … seventy six in all that actually had some traceable DNA attached … they're *all* matches to our shooters."

"All?" Ashley asked, surprised. "The scene investigators who went into that dilapidated old building found hairs with enough DNA on them to show they were from seventy six people? Seven six *shooters*?"

"Yes," Tim replied, understanding the surprise he could see on his work partner's face.

"But that means…"

"Yes," Tim said, anticipating what Ashley had been going to say. "Our shooters - the majority, at least - all went to that building recently."

"To that dance party…"

"Well, that's a bit harder to prove since only one person in this town seems to remember - or know -

anything about that," Tim replied. "But knowing that it's looking more and more likely that Kane was telling us the truth, I want to go and talk to *all* of the shooters again."

"Maybe us prompting them, talking specifically about the dance party, will nudge their memories, even if they've actually forgotten they were there," said Ashley. "Come on," she added, gulping back the last of her cup of coffee and standing up. "The first person I want to see is Nancy. Kane said she's the one he was dancing with. I really want to see what she remembers … if anything … about that whole night."

Tim didn't object. As weird as the entire case was, and as much as it all sounded like a fictional story, it was their job to investigate all possibilities. Usually, the investigations they worked on were all pretty standard - kidnappings or the occasional murder - and all generally turned out to be someone with some grudge or reason for taking or hurting someone else. With everything about the current case being so unlikely to happen, he was aware that if they did ever solve the case, they still might not find the absolute answer they'd like to - the *why*.

CHAPTER 36

After traveling to the military base where all shooters had been housed since their role had been determined in the Kildare shootings, Ashley and Tim waited patiently to see the woman they hoped would hold some answers. On the way, they'd called in to see Kane Garmin again to get a photo of him. On their return visit, he'd been as straightforward and relaxed as he had been when they'd first seen him. Even so, Ashley still kept her thoughts about him in check. That was necessary on every case, but especially one where evidence so strongly contradicted the results of polygraph testing on such a strong level.

"Hello," they heard a woman say as she moved around from behind where Tim and Ashley sat. It was easy to see confusion on her face. "Do ... do I know you?"

Ashley watched the woman sit down and face them over the stark table. As was the case with all shooters Ashley had spoken to, it was difficult to look at them without judgment, but Ashley did find she couldn't help but also feel a little sorry for them. It made no sense, but it was what it was.

"Hello Nancy," Tim began. "We haven't spoken to you before, but I'm Special Agent Moore and this is Special Agent Power, from the Bureau of Investigation."

"I didn't do what they say I did," Nancy said before resting her head in her hands. "Why am I here? I could never hurt *anyone*."

"Nancy, can you take us through what you *did* do that

night?" Ashley asked. "I know you've gone through this with different people, but if you can recount your movements one more time for us, we'd really appreciate it."

When the woman looked up, Ashley and Tim both studied her face. Yes, she had tears flowing down her face, but were they real? With some people, it was easy to see the façade of fake tears by seeing the simultaneous hardness of the person's eyes. It was difficult to make out what was real with anyone on the current case.

"As I already told the other guys, I was out with friends in the town square," Nancy replied. "We weren't doing anything illegal or anything! Just talking! I … I don't understand how doing that has led to me being here."

"And you say that everyone else who you've seen in here, from that night…"

"Yes! They were there too!" Nancy exclaimed. "None of us know what is going on, or how we've come to be here. This is just some … misunderstanding … or a nightmare that I'm not waking up from."

"Can you tell us why you were all there that night?" Ashley asked. Ever since the first event in Seaview, although their job was to find out who was behind the shootings, and make sure they couldn't do it again, she couldn't deny being intensely captivated by the alibis that the shooters all spun, even after evidence was found that proved their guilt. "Was that a normal thing to do - to assemble in the town square late in the night?"

She watched as confusion settled deeper on the face of the woman in front of them, as if that was one question that hadn't been asked of her before.

"I don't understand," Nancy finally said, her frown deep.

"You don't understand?" Tim asked. "Had you met with all of those people in the town square that late at night before?" he nudged and saw the confusion deepen further still.

"No, I don't ... think ... so," Nancy replied.

"So why did you meet that night?" Ashley asked.

"I..." Nancy started to say. "I ... I don't know. I know that sounds ... *flimsy* ... but I really don't know. It just ... seemed..."

Tim and Ashley watched as the words drifted off and left silence again. Both could see the woman's face indicated she did not know what had happened, or why she'd done what she'd done.

"Nancy, I have some pictures here," Ashley said as she pulled out a handful of photos and laid them out on the table. "Would you be able to look through these and tell me if you know any of these people? Or have even met them?"

Once again, Tim and Ashley watched the woman. Not only did her words sound vague, but the way she moved, with movements slow rather than regular, prompted the two agents to share a glance at each other.

"No," they finally heard the woman say. "No, I don't know any of those people. Should I?"

"We just wanted to check," said Ashley. "And you're sure? Could you look again?"

"Hmm," Nancy mumbled but then did as she'd been asked to do. "I don't know any of them, but..." she said as she lifted a finger and touched Kane's photo. "No, I am sure I have never met him, but he does look familiar somehow."

"Think, Nancy," said Tim, knowing there was always a fine line between nudging someone's memory, and pushing them too far. "Does a name come to mind when you look at his photo? A name, or a place where you might have met him?"

"I..." Nancy started to reply before shaking her head, as if in disbelief. "No, I don't think so."

"Did you have a thought then?" Tim pressed. "Anything you can tell us is welcome, no matter how likely or unlikely to be important it may seem."

"Oh, no, it's just … dancing?" Nancy replied. "It's silly but I keep thinking of dancing when I look at this photo."

"Okay, and why do you say that's silly?" Ashley asked.

"Well, because I haven't … I haven't danced for years - decades, even, if I think about it," Nancy replied. "I loved it when I was in my twenties but since those days - since the days of going out to nightclubs and all - I've never set foot into anywhere where I'd dance."

"But you think you may have had some kind of connection with this man?" Tim asked.

"Yes … and no," said Nancy. "Oh, I can't explain, sorry. I'm sure I've never met him before, but there's just something about this photo…" she said before scoffing, with a small smile on her face. "It's probably just because he's so handsome, to be honest. Yes, I'm sure that's it. He's a handsome man who probably reminds me of a film star or something."

As Tim watched her speak, he studied the way her face moved, and the tone of her voice. He felt dismayed that, just like all shooters of all three incidents so far, the woman in front of him was incredibly convincing about what she was saying. Was it an act? Were they *all* acting? Were they all that *good* at acting?

"I'd like to show you something else, Nancy," Tim said as he pulled out the clear plastic evidence bag housing the invitation and showed it to her.

"Oh," Nancy said as she received it into her hands. "Why … why does *that* look familiar to me?"

Tim saw Ashley give him a look that he knew was one of hope. In a fleeting moment, he found himself hoping as well - hoping that something was going to click into place sometime soon.

"You have seen this before?" he asked.

"I … this is insane," Nancy said. "I must be insane, or

at least *going* insane."

"Why do you say that?" Ashley asked.

"Because … because when I look at this, I feel the same thing that I felt when I looked at that particular photo - like I have seen it before, but I'm equally sure I haven't," Nancy replied. "I … I probably should see a doctor. I really do think I must be getting dementia."

"Have you heard anyone else speaking about a dance party, or a dance night, that they attended?" Ashley asked, her mind working quickly.

The look she received from Nancy then was one to give both agents some hope.

"How did you know that?" the woman asked.

"Know what, exactly?" asked Tim.

"Know that a couple of the people who've also been tossed into this place, have mentioned something about a 'dance party'," said Nancy.

"Who has talked about that?" Tim pushed.

"Oh, um … let me see," Nancy began. Within a couple of minutes, she'd listed off four people. "I'm sure they said something along those lines. Maybe not exactly 'dance party', but some kind of event where there was dancing…"

Seeing her drift off in her speech, both agents watched and waited.

"Was *I* there?" she finally asked. "I feel like maybe I was, but I can't understand why," she added before she picked up the invitation again. "There was a DJ? And…" she continued before placing down the invitation, then reaching out with one free hand to pick up the photo of Kane Garmin, and the other hand to pick up a sketch she'd seen among the printed images.

As Ashley watched Nancy pick up the sketch of the security guard she'd seen at one of the crime scenes, she felt her heart pound.

"No, sorry, I can't remember," Nancy said after looking at the images for a long time, moving her eyes back and forth from one to the other. "There's something about these two people that seems so familiar to me, but I know I've never seen or met them before. Sorry. I just don't understand what's happening to me."

Watching the woman begin to look distressed, Tim exchanged a silent nod with Ashley.

"That's okay, Nancy," he said. "We will leave you now, but thank you. You've helped a lot."

"Have I?" Nancy asked, scoffing as the guard approached. "Personally, I think I'm losing my mind."

CHAPTER 37

An hour later, Ashley and Tim made their way to the car. They'd taken the opportunity to speak to the other people that Nancy had said she'd heard talking about some kind of dance night. As odd as it all was, when the agents listened to each story, they felt as though something had definitely happened to the people who were being held for the shootings.

"I just don't understand," Ashley said when they climbed inside. "The majority don't remember dancing at all, even though we know they were all there, and the few that do have some kind of memory of it, don't *believe* their own recall of it."

"Yes, the few that said they must have dreamt it all were particular hard to listen to," Tim agreed. "They seem to think they all had a shared dream, which is pretty crazy."

"Crazier than hundreds of people attending a dance party and then leaving to grab their gun and go shoot someone?" Ashley suggested. "If you ask me, you and I might be the crazy ones, for starting to believe any of this could be true!"

"Well, one thing is for certain," Tim said as he fastened his seatbelt. "Somewhere out there could be a DJ who is running these secret dance parties, and he just might be the key to everything."

"And your thoughts about Nancy picking out that sketch?" Ashley asked.

"The one of the security guard you noticed?" asked Tim.

"Yes."

"I think that, even though she said she didn't recognize Kane or the guy in that sketch, she *did* pick up those two images and study them for quite some time," Tim replied. "Even if she can't actually remember the facts about what happened that night, maybe it is all in her subconscious. That's worth keeping in mind."

"Right, but how do we go forward from here?" Ashley asked.

"I wonder…" Tim began, pondering options.

"Yes, Timmy Boy?" Ashley asked, hopeful. "What do you wonder?"

"I wonder if we should go back," he said, turning to smile at her. "If some of these shooters seem to have some kind of residual memory of that night, I am wondering if any from the other two towns might have since remembered something as well."

"You want to go back … to Seaview and Leefton?" Ashley asked, surprised.

"I do wonder if it might be a good idea," said Tim. "It might not turn out to be anything, and it could end up being a complete waste of time, but what if … what if somehow these people's minds were manipulated so that their memory wasn't correct…"

"Like making them think they were somewhere they weren't," Ashley suggested. "Which *is* what we do think has happened."

"Yes, let's say they were all … *conditioned* to believe something other than reality, but after some time passes…"

"Their true memory starts to come back?" asked Ashley. "The only problem with that theory is that we talked to the people of Leefton and Seaview for even longer after those events than we've been talking to people here, and nobody offered any kind of memory story there, even that long after the event took place."

"Yeah, that's true," said Tim. "Hmm."

"But I agree it's worth looking into," Ashley said. "We now have an idea about what might have happened, and we can show the sketch of that guard..."

"Who we're thinking could be the DJ, or the person behind it all, right?"

"Absolutely," said Ashley. "We can show that sketch, and we can show the invitation. And you're right. The only way to know if anyone's memory might be stimulated by them is by going out to each of those towns and talking to everyone again."

"Yes, and the other thing that keeps playing on my mind is how does the person running all this know who has a gun registered to them, and who doesn't?" Tim pondered out loud.

"The gun ownership registers are available for the public to view," Ashley replied. "Anyone could see them."

"Yes, but they have to access them somehow - either online or in a public records office," Tim said. "I want to see..." he added as he pulled out his phone and typed into it for a few minutes. "I've asked the guys at head office to find out if there's any way to find out who might have been completing any kind of search for gun-ownership populations."

"Good idea," said Ashley. "If they can figure that out, maybe they can also zero in on who might have done a search that showed Leefton, Seaview and Kildare as high percentage results."

"Yes. Okay, I've put through the request so we can leave the tech professionals to figuring all that out," said Tim. "For now, should I ask Sarah to get us back to Seaview?"

"Do it," Ashley agreed as she started the car. "Hopefully Sarah will agree and can get us on a plane out of here pretty soon."

"You look like you're excited," Tim said, chuckling at her. "You know we could be right off the mark, because if anyone in Seaview or Leefton *has* since remembered something more, I do think they would have made that known, and we would have heard about it by now. Even though I do want to go and speak to those shooters again, I do expect the chance to be slim that we're going to learn anything new."

"Of course, but it at least feels like we're gaining some momentum, even if all of this does go nowhere."

Tim knew it was silly to be too confident about their current path of investigation, but he did love to see Ashley become excited and animated once again.

CHAPTER 38

Perched on a wooden fence high up on a hill overlooking what looked like a desert landscape, Jaz McMenamin used the beauty before him to try and clear his mind. On his last two jobs, he'd carried out his latest obsession - seeing if he could meet the law enforcement agents who'd worked on each of the sites he'd caused chaos in.

Where the idea had come from, he wasn't sure, but ever since seeing the two Bureau of Investigation agents on a news report he'd casually spotted in a coffee shop while on his travels, he'd wanted to meet them. And he had, even though it was under the guise of being one of the security guards.

How had it felt to stand right beside the very people who could put a stop to the ideas that continued to plague his mind? Had he felt empowered, knowing they had no idea they were in the presence of the one person who was causing so much destruction? No. Not empowered. Perhaps if it had been his intention to cause destruction - to want to cause pain just for the hell of it - he might have gotten more joy out of it, but that wasn't what he wanted. What he wanted to happen, still hadn't. For him, that was the most frustrating aspect. Why could they not see? Why could they just not get it?

Feeling his anxiety start to rise again - and his blood begin to feel like it was starting to boil as it pumped through his veins - he closed his eyes and focused on his deep breathing. When he'd started to embark on his current life journey, it had all seemed so easy, with so much potential to help change the way things had become in the world. When he'd stood in that last scene, it had been a thrill to see the law enforcement agents in person, but it had also driven home to him that near where he'd stood as he'd waited for the agents to arrive, had been a dead body.

Whenever he actually thought about death, his mind always returned to the day he'd learned that Christie had been killed, and had died for no reason at all. In that case, nobody had worked out why the shooter had done what he'd done. He'd left a suicide note that made it clear he'd intended to kill and then be killed himself. To this day, nobody knew why he'd done that, and that was one of the greatest frustrations of all. Why did that shooter kill those people, and why were people now being killed on such a large degree in the towns that Jaz had left so much damage? He didn't want to put himself in the same light as the psycho who'd killed Christie and all of those other students, but he could see that he was beginning to be.

More and more people were dying with each new town that suited his study results. He'd studied news of the whole country, in the hope of seeing someone say they want to make changes because of the events that were taking place, but nobody ever did. They talked about the shooters. They talked about the victims. They even talked about the people who were trying to figure out what was happening and who could be behind it all. They never talked about what could be done to stop it.

Opening his eyes again, he pondered the point of continuing his mission. If nobody wanted to sit up and take notice, was it even worth it? If nothing good came out of it, was he wise to keep going? Where he currently was - free and easy with the world at his fingertips and nothing to worry about - was a place where many people would love to be. Yes, he'd lost Christie, but he still had his health and he still had many years ahead to look forward to in his life. What would Christie think if she was up in heaven, looking down on him? Would she admire him for standing up and fighting for what he believed in? Or would she be shaking her head in that way that she used to do whenever Jaz did something stupid that Christie couldn't make any sense of?

He'd wondered about that many times - what Christie would think. In his heart, he knew she wouldn't want him to do what he was doing, even if it was for a good reason. Hurting people was hurting people. Even if his plan worked, there would always be murderers in the world. To eliminate them all was something that could never be done. Even if all of his hard work paid off and gun laws were changed - even if guns were never seen again - people would still be killed. It was a sad fact about humanity. Since the beginning of time, everybody could have always lived in peace with everybody. Human nature made far too many people think that would be no way to live, and peace wasn't all it was cracked up to be.

Taking one more long moment to study the landscape around him and breathe in the fresh air, he thought about his upcoming plans. He'd already done his research and knew the next town on the list. Should he go ahead with it? Would one more town make a difference, finally? Or would more people die and still nothing come from it? He'd monitored enough news online to know that no matter what people thought of the mass shootings, nobody ever grabbed it as a reason to stop things from being the way they were. Once again, it crossed his mind as his biggest frustration - why couldn't they just *see*?

Thinking about the choices that lay ahead for him - to repeat what he'd been doing already, or to leave it be and move on as if nothing had ever happened - he didn't know what the right decision would be. What he did know was that if his heart wasn't in it - if he wasn't excited to get on with the next level of destruction - then it might not be the right time to do it.

With the level of dissatisfaction he felt at that moment, he knew it was the right time for him to step back and do nothing. He wouldn't put his plan away forever but, for that day, he would.

Resolved, he jumped back into his RV. He wouldn't do anything to hurt any more people for the moment. Instead, he would drive until he found a nice quiet camp spot, and take some time to enjoy peaceful thoughts, in a peaceful environment. Sometimes he needed that, just to make sure that he didn't rush into anything and make a mistake.

Yes. Somewhere peaceful. Perhaps somewhere amongst forest, with a small river and friendly people in the surrounding area. Even though he still wanted to get on and do what he believed he was meant to do, the idea of peace won out - at least for that moment. He knew where he was going to go next, and how he would approach that. There was always a time for everything, and today wasn't the day to go where he was planning to play his next move.

Not today.

Definitely not today.

But maybe tomorrow.

CHAPTER 39

"Sarah?" Tim asked into his phone after he saw the incoming call. "What's up?"

"Are you guys already at the airport?" Sarah Johnson, Tim and Ashley's Bureau supervisor asked.

"Yeah, we're just about to board the first flight on our way to Seaview," Tim replied. "Has something happened?" he asked, dreading what he might be about to hear.

"Relax, Moore. It's nothing bad," Sarah said. "I have news about an identity."

"Yes?"

"A partial fingerprint on that invitation has come back with a match to someone that police interviewed a long while back," said Sarah. "I won't hold you up now if you're just about to head off..."

"We have a few minutes till we'll be on the plane," Tim said. "Tell me what you've got for us."

"Years ago, there was a mass shooting at a college," said Sarah.

"There have been quite a few college shootings, Boss..."

"Indeed there have," Sarah said. "This one, I'll email you details of. Anyway, this guy wasn't a suspect at all - the shooter turned the gun on himself and that was the end of the case - but this guy was someone that police interviewed and, at that time, the police department took fingerprints of everyone they spoke to in an official capacity."

"Okay," said Tim. "So you have an identity, you

said?"

"Yes, I'll send you everything I have about this person, and about that shooting incident," said Sarah.

"But we ran that sketch through the system and it came back with no matches…"

"Correct," Sarah said. "It didn't find a match in our system because this person has never been charged with anything. His fingerprints were, however, kept on file after that incident, and our experts are sure there's no doubt that it's the same guy. I'll send through his file photo as well as the other details. Get Ashley to look at it and confirm if it looks like the guy she thought was a fake security guard in Kildare. It would be beneficial to find out, for sure, who that was, and what his role was in playing a security guard out there."

"True. Okay, we'll have a read and look through," said Tim. "Do we have any physical address for this guy?"

"No, not at this stage," Sarah replied. "We know where he was living at the time of the shooting that killed his girlfriend, but there's no record of any address for him now. There's also no trace of him on any social media."

"Okay," said Tim. "We're being called to board now, but we'll give you a call when we're on the other side."

"You really think you might find something new in Seaview?" asked Sarah. "After all this time?"

"We're wondering if there might be a period after this … brainwashing, or whatever it is … when the memory might slowly return to reality," Tim replied. "Maybe it'll come to nothing, but I think it's worth looking into, and if the photo you send through turns out to be the guy Ash saw, we'll now have one more thing to show the shooters."

"Alright, go and get on that plane and I'll hear from you when you have something to report," Sarah said before disconnecting the call.

"What was that all about?" Ashley asked. Usually Tim was good about putting calls onto speaker. It was understandable that, for that particular call, he wasn't going to share information with the hoards of other people around them at the airport gate.

"We might have another lead," Tim said quietly as they were welcomed to walk through the air bridge. "When we get to our seats, I'll quickly download some files Sarah's sending through now, and we can work through them before we land."

"Sounds positive," Ashley said, hopeful there might be something new for them to look into, at the very least.

"Let's hope so," Tim said, turning to grin at her as they made their way into the cramped airplane aisle. "Looks like we're right at the back, Partner."

Ashley rolled her eyes at him.

"Of course we are, Moore," she said. "Of course we are."

CHAPTER 40

"Is this the guy you saw at the Simpson home in Kildare?" Tim asked once he'd downloaded his emails and opened up the files.

Ashley took some time to study the photo being presented to her. Was it the same guy she'd noticed, who might not have been a true security guard?

"It does look a little like him," Ashley said as she took her time to make the assessment. "He's a bit younger there but the eyes look the same. You saw him too, though. What do you think?"

"I can honestly say that I didn't notice him like you did," Tim said, smiling. "But seriously, you'd have a better idea than me. You indicated at the time that you thought he was a bit…"

"Creepy," Ashley said. "I thought he was looking at me because he liked the look of me but now, of course, I'm wondering if he was looking not just at me, but both of us."

"Like a serial killer who likes to play a bit of a game with law enforcement?" Tim said. "As yet, we don't know if this guy has anything to do with any of this."

"They identified the partial fingerprint on the invitation as his," said Ashley.

"Yeah, but where did we get the invitation from?"

"Kane Garmin," Ashley admitted. "I see your point. Despite how helpful Kane has been, is there still a chance he's behind it all…"

"And if so, has he set this guy up to take the fall for everything?" Tim suggested. "It's only a partial fingerprint, so maybe this guy didn't actually handle the invitation much after all. For all we know, he could be the printer of the invitations, or the deliverer. We can't yet be certain that Kane isn't behind everything."

"But ... when we showed the sketch to him, he didn't seem to know who the guy was," Ashley said. "Of course, I guess he wouldn't if he is setting someone up. He'd want us to believe they don't know each other and have never met."

"Which might be the case, although if it is, then how did this guy's fingerprint get on the invitation?"

"Okay, so, this guy - what's his name?"

"Jaz McMenamin," Tim replied.

"Jaz? Hmm," said Ashley. "If he is the one behind all of this - or at least *one* person who's behind all of this - why would he risk handling the invitations without wearing gloves? Even someone who's never been a criminal would know that fingerprints or touch DNA can be collected from surfaces, for use in crime solving."

"True," Tim agreed. "Maybe he did wear gloves for handling the invitations, but then absent mindedly touched one by mistake."

"And that one invitation just happens to be the one that gets given to us?" Ashley asked. "Come on, Timothy, you know the odds of that happening are slim to none. No, it seems a little *too* unlikely that only one invitation was handled so flippantly. Either this guy is our guy, or he is being set up."

"Well, we only have one invitation, Ash," Tim said, chuckling. "For all we know, this guy's fingerprints were over the whole lot of them that were printed," he added before growing serious. "You're still leaning towards Kane Garmin having something to do with this, huh?"

"I think ... I think this guy - this Jaz McMenamin - might have something to do with this," said Ashley. "If he doesn't, why was he dressed up as a security guard at one of the scenes, when we've established by others who were at that house that he wasn't there when they were?"

"Plus the security company has confirmed they don't have him on file as an employee," Tim added. "They think he might have swiped one of their uniforms from their HQ."

"Right, which we now know is the same thing that happened in the security firm assigned to guard scenes at Leefton too," said Ashley. "Says a lot about my ego, doesn't it, that I'd assume a guy is looking at me in that way, instead of realizing that he was a guy I'd possibly seen before at a crime scene previously."

"You really think he was at a Leefton property as well?" Tim asked. "You haven't sounded so positive about that before."

"To be honest, Tim, I'm not sure, but I noticed him for some reason," said Ashley. "I do wonder if it was because I'd subconsciously seen him at an earlier site. I can't actually remember that, but you know what it's like when we get to a scene. We're so focused on the victim, or the building, or the other law enforcement personnel. The people assigned to just stand guard and make sure nobody else comes in, we hardly speak to."

"True," Tim said. "Well, either way, this guy - this Jaz McMenamin - is someone that the tech team are keeping an eye out for on CCTV and, reading through this, there are some aspects that are interesting."

"Like what?" Ashley asked.

"Says here that he was the boyfriend of someone who was shot in a college shooting," Tim replied.

"That … would certainly present a motive to *not* shoot people, if he's felt what it's like to lose someone at the hands of a gunman," Ashley said. "If anything, surely he would be a person *against* shooting, not *for* it."

"Yeah, I agree. It doesn't make sense," said Tim. "But the police report says he was pretty angry - understandably."

"As any of us would be," said Ashley. "Every time

I've heard on the news about a mass shooting - especially one directed at young people who've hardly started their lives yet - I find myself trying to imagine how the families are feeling. And there never seems any sound explanation for it. It's like someone just has this whim..."

"But there must be a reason," said Tim. "Even if it makes no sense to anyone else, inside of those shooters' minds must be some logical reason why shooting multiple people - strangers that they've never met - makes sense."

"To make a statement, I suppose," Ashley said.

"And if that's how it sometimes goes, what if our guy - the person behind the shootings in Leefton, Seaview and Kildare - also wants to do that?" Tim pondered.

"If that's the case then he must be as crazy as all those other people who've killed masses of people for no good reason," Ashley replied.

To that, Tim didn't say anything. Sitting back in his seat, he let his mind begin to formulate theories. Why would someone shoot so many people? Why did anyone ever shoot anyone? None of it made sense to him, but then, he knew it didn't have to.

CHAPTER 41

At the end of what seemed like a very long day, Tim and Ashley walked away from where the Seaview shooters had been housed since the event had happened. Both agents had been hopeful when they'd arrived, enthused by the possibility that some of the shooters might have at least started to remember a dance party, once they were shown the invitation and asked specifically about the night, or they might have been able to recognize the face of the man who'd become a suspect.

"Do we even bother going to Leefton?" Ashley asked, feeling disheartened.

"Come, now, Special Agent Power," Tim said, grinning at her. "Of course we're going to Leefton! We knew it was a long shot that anyone would have remembered what they were really doing that night."

"But why isn't it a problem for Kane Garmin?" Ashley pondered.

"I was thinking about that on the flight here," Tim replied.

"And?"

"Well, Kane did say that part of his military training entailed being trained to resist any form of mind manipulation," said Tim. "I'm wondering if his remembering what happened that night, when no-one else does, could just be because his mind is more resistant to whatever was done to everyone else."

"It's a possibility, I guess, but I also think that's something we'll never really know," said Ashley. "But knowing now that none of our Seaview shooters have remembered anything more, even after all this time, do you think it's still worth going to Leefton to talk to the shooters there?"

"Yes!" Tim said. "It's getting pretty late now so let's go and check into the motel that Sarah's sent me details about, and tomorrow we can get up early and get back to the airport, ready for another day of this."

"Okay," Ashley agreed. "Come on then."

Back in her motel room, she and Tim took some time to go over the day's conversations, comparing notes about their thoughts.

"I think it's the number of shooters in Seaview and Leefton that still gets to me," Ashley admitted. "Any deaths are horrid, but the number of people that were found to have shot someone - and even now, none of them seem to understand why they're not allowed to go free."

"Yes, in some ways it does seem unfair, but there have been a few cases in history where someone seems to honestly have no idea they've committed a crime," said Tim.

"And if someone has no recollection of hurting someone - or worse, killing them - how can they be charged for it?" Ashley pondered. "I mean, most criminals will claim they didn't do what they did, or that they don't remember doing something, but what about when it's been proven that they truly don't remember it?"

"Okay, but what about if someone can't remember because they were under the influence of alcohol or drugs at the time?" Tim challenged her. "Do you think that, in those cases, the person shouldn't be charged, even though evidence proves they did it?"

"No, of course they should be charged," Ashley replied.

"But what's the difference? Those people - those who have blackouts after extreme drinking or drug taking - also might not actually remember having done the crime."

"But in this case, these people have all passed a polygraph test," said Ashley. "Evidence seems to say that while they did do what they did, they truly don't know that they did it."

"So what?" Tim asked. "Like I said, some people get drunk enough to never know that they did something too. Those people might also be able to pass a polygraph since they truly don't remember what they did."

"Hmm, yeah, I know you're right," Ashley said, smiling at him. "And, of course, that's why none of the shooters have been freed. As far as the law sees it, they *are* all murderers."

"I hear a 'but' coming," Tim said, chuckling. He knew his partner well, and he did love the way that their minds sometimes saw things so differently. It helped not only in the investigation process, but also in opening up his mind to the many different ways something could be perceived.

"But … what if this happened to you or me?" Ashley suggested. In truth, she was playing with Tim, knowing it felt good to twist things around in their conversations and opinions now and then. "What if you were … let's use the word *brainwashed* ... into doing something terrible - or maybe hypnotized. Actually, yes, let's go with that. You go on a night out to see a live show of a hypnotist. Once there, the idea to do something is subconsciously put into your mind, and you go and carry it out, but you have no idea that you did it. And let's say that what the hypnotist got you do wasn't something silly like walking around on stage, quacking and looking like a duck, but was actually something criminal. Would you really think it's fair that you're then charged with that crime?"

"Ashley Power, I do think you're purposely trying to get a reaction from me," Tim said, grinning as he completely avoided the question. "Look, you, you know as well as I do that it's our job to figure out who has committed a crime, but it isn't up to you or me to decide what happens to those people after that. So stop trying to start an argument with me - especially one that is pointless."

Ashley chuckled as she shook her head. While Tim fairly frequently enjoyed teasing her about anything he could, it was always nice to now and then get a bit of a bite out of him in return.

"Yeah, you know me too well," she said. "But…"

At that moment, both heard Tim's phone give an audible notification.

"It's Sarah," Tim said before answering the incoming call.

"I have some further results for you," Ashley and Tim both heard their boss report over the phone's loud speaker. "And they might make a difference to your entire case."

"Yep," Tim said succinctly, waiting in anticipation.

"You put through a request a while back, asking the tech team if there was any way for them to figure out if someone had used a digital means to access the national gun registry database," Sarah reported.

"And they've found something, Sarah?" Ashley asked, feeling her heart beat just that little bit faster.

"They have indeed," both agents heard Sarah say. "What they've reported is that someone accessed the database eighteen months ago, and conducted the exact search to produce the data you guys have said could be the reasoning behind all of this."

"Someone searched … for which towns had the highest percentage of gun ownership population?" asked Tim.

"Right," Sarah confirmed.

"Were they able to find out who did the search?"

"Not the who, but they were able to find an IP address that's linked to the computer used to do the search," said Sarah.

"Then they have an address?" Ashley asked.

"Not an address of a physical location," Sarah replied. "What they believe, based on what they've been able to find out, is that the IP address is linked to a mobile hotspot setup, so…"

"So it's always moving?" Tim asked.

"Yes, it seems so," said Sarah.

"But the mobile is registered to…?" Ashley asked.

"Unfortunately, nobody," Sarah replied. "It's not on a plan, so there's no account details and whoever purchased the phone immediately paid a lot of cash to get months in advance worth of data, *but* there is some hope in this search. Firstly, because the tech team were able to see that the search had been done, they've also been able to see the results of the search."

"So they could see that Seaview has the biggest gun ownership ratio, then Leefton, then Kildare…"

"Yes," Sarah confirmed.

"But we already knew that, Sarah," said Ashley. "Is there something new to report?"

"Yes. The tech team have pointed out that they can also see the fourth town on the list," Sarah said. "Welburn has the next highest gun ownership population percentage, so the guys have done an extended search to see if any more recent searches have been done about Welburn."

"Surely, lots of people would have searched…"

"Not many at all, actually, but what you need to know is that whoever is associated with that IP address, has today logged into the network from within range of one of the cell towers just outside Welburn," Sarah said.

Tim and Ashley looked at one another in surprise. They always put full faith in the tech team at the Bureau, who appeared to have skills that were godly in the eyes of the agents.

"Sarah, just to make sure I'm accurately interpreting

what you're saying," Ashley finally said. "Are you telling us that whoever did an original search to find out gun ownership population percentages, and subsequently found out that Seaview, Leefton and Kildare are the top three on that search list, is right now within close vicinity to the fourth town on the list?"

"That's exactly what I'm saying," Sarah said. "Hence, I've cancelled your travel plans to go to Leefton. If you two do feel you need to get back there at a later time, I'll rebook your travel and accommodation but, for the moment, I've booked what I'm deeming as more urgent travel, for both of you to get to Welburn."

"Tonight?" Tim asked.

"I wasn't able to get you on any flight tonight so you need to be at the airport by six tomorrow morning to catch the flight," said Sarah. "I'm emailing you tickets now," she added, just as a further audible alert sounded.

"Got them," Tim confirmed as he opened his email app on the laptop in front of him.

"Are you informing local law enforcement in Welburn as well?" Ashley asked, suddenly feeling alarmed at the thought of arriving in the town too late. "We can't do anything about this tonight? What if this person is heading there to do the same thing right now? Tonight?"

"The tech guys are watching the movements of the phone that's been used to access the Internet for the search," said Sarah. "Don't panic. I've got other staff heading to Welburn now, and the local Sheriff's office there is on guard as well."

"And they have the photo of the guy associated with the partial fingerprint on that invitation?" Ashley asked.

"Yes. I've sent it to them and asked them to make sure all of their officers are made aware of what the guy looks like," Sarah said. "The sheriff also said that since his town has only two roads that someone can take to get into it, he's ready to set up some road check points."

"I don't know about that, Boss. That could really spook our guy if he does try and enter the town," said Tim. "Do you think that's a good idea?"

"No matter what this person does - or where he goes - our tech guys are watching his movements," said Sarah.

"They're watching the movements of his *phone*," Tim argued. "If he gets nervous and thinks law enforcement being set up on the roads going into Welburn has something to do with him, he could ditch that phone, and then we'd never be able to find him. We don't want that happening."

"The sheriff had that same thought, too, which is why he said he'd find a way to monitor who's coming into his town," said Sarah. "He was convincing in saying his team will find the guy if he's around."

"Okay," Tim and Ashley both said at the same time.

"Is there anything else we need to know right now?" Ashley asked.

"Only that I have staff on shifts, monitoring the limited number of CCTV cameras in Welburn," said Sarah. "There aren't any around the outside of the town, but the team are watching all the town cameras, and they've sought permission to monitor some areas via home security cameras."

"Home owners have said Tech can access their personal security cameras?" Ashley asked, surprised. "Really?"

"They haven't been told that a murder suspect might be coming to their town, if that's what you're worried about," Sarah said, immediately putting Ashley more at ease. "And the permission extends only to the exterior views of the homes - the roads and streets in the area."

"Okay," Ashley replied. Sarah hadn't expanded on what the tech guys *had* told the people who'd given permission to view neighborhoods through their home cameras, but Ashley was happy to trust Sarah knew what she was reporting.

"Alright, we'll get organized here and be at the airport first thing in the morning, Boss," said Tim. "If you hear anything from the sheriff's department in Welburn, you'll let us know?"

"When I hear something, *you'll* hear something," Sarah said. "I won't hold you up any longer, and I know it might be tempting to not get much sleep tonight, but both of you *try!*"

"Yes, Boss," both agents replied.

After the call disconnected, Tim took a long moment to process what they'd been told. Glancing at Ashley, he could see that her mind was active as well.

"This could be what we've been waiting for," Tim said quietly. "We've been wondering how we might be able to get ahead of this person or group of people. This could be it."

"I want to believe it…" Ashley started to say.

"What are you thinking?" asked Tim.

"Just that it would make things a bit too easy, wouldn't it," Ashley replied. "If this is the right guy - the person behind all of this - he must know that law enforcement everywhere is keeping their eyes and ears open, and somehow trying to be prepared for what might come next."

"The fact that he's managed to avoid being questioned about anything to do with this, makes me think he could be right where we want him - with an out of control belief that he'll never get caught. That law enforcement don't even have him on their radar."

"Maybe," Ashley said, not convinced. "I know we do need to sleep tonight, but…"

"Worried we'll be too late to stop it all happening again, this time in Welburn?" Tim asked and saw her nod. "I know. Of course there's a good chance that this is the night that he's chosen to strike the fourth town. If that's the case, we might not be able to stop him from doing whatever damage he's aiming to do this time."

"You say that so easily," Ashley said. "But so many people have died already."

Reading her expression of almost defeat, Tim stood and walked to her, holding his arms open. He was glad when she accepted the offer and walked into them.

"We're going to get this guy," Tim reassured her.

"Maybe, but we aren't even sure if this guy *is* who's behind all of this," Ashley replied as she pulled away. "We could be on an entirely wrong track."

"And if we are, there's no point in worrying about the people of Welburn tonight," said Tim. "If we're on the wrong track then we have no idea who is behind this, when they'll strike again, or where they are right at this moment."

"Thanks, Partner," Ashley said, rolling her eyes at him. "Way to go to make me feel better."

Tim grinned at her before beginning to pack up his laptop and notes.

"Don't dwell on it tonight," he said. "I'm going to leave you now, so you can get some rest."

"You're going to rest too, I hope," Ashley said.

"I am," said Tim as he made his way to the motel door. "But as you and I both know, Special Agent Ashley Power, you are often rather brilliant when you sleep."

Ashley scoffed but smiled regardless. She usually maintained a fair amount of confidence in her abilities as an agent. For the current case, her confidence had been tested to the limit. She hoped that would change - and preferably before the death toll went any higher.

"Sleep well, Ash. See you in the morning," she heard Tim say as he headed out the door, and then was gone.

Alone in the motel room, Ashley activated all door locks and stood still for a long time, leaning her back against the door. She wasn't sure she'd be able to sleep during the night - not knowing that someone they suspected to be behind everything, might be so close to the town that might be next on his list of targets.

Sighing to herself, she finally moved away to prepare for a long bath and, hopefully, sleep that would enable her to feel far more confident when the sun rose again.

CHAPTER 42

On the outskirts of Welburn, a white RV perched high up on a hill, parked at a roadside stop. The stop itself seemed to be situated purely to allow motorists to stop and take a moment to enjoy the view out over the valley below. As Jaz glanced over the entire vista before him, he could see that something might be going on in the small town.

No cars that he could see were marked cop cars, but there was something about the way the vehicles moved and interacted with one another that made him question why anything would be going on in Welburn. Was there going to be a concert there, or some kind of sporting event? Before he'd embarked upon his journey, he'd checked the weekly events page for the town, and nothing had shown up. For him, that had been good news. If there was nothing else on, the people who were going to receive invitations would almost certainly be tempted to go to his event. No matter who they were, egos always won out when it came to people getting those very special invites. It was humanity's way to give in to anything that made someone feel more important than the next guy.

Not in any hurry to move, he pulled out his phone and did what any good tourist would do - take photos of the beautiful views. When he took a moment to look at the images he'd captured, he zoomed in on the cars that had just happened to be in the photos as well. Were they law enforcement in plain clothes disguise? Wherever he'd gone, he hadn't worried about running into anyone like that. He had a system that worked. There was never anything to worry about.

Except, as he remained where he was and watched the activity below, he did feel an inkling of concern. The odds of anyone anticipating him coming to the small town and then doing what he always did, was pretty much zero. Why then, did his heart feel like it was racing a little more than usual?

Smiling to himself, he shook his head. Nothing was going on, and nobody knew anything about him. He was having a mild case of nerves, that was all. And besides, if someone did suspect him of something, it was in his full control to change their mind - literally.

Walking back into the body of the RV, he glanced around. Before he'd left the previous town, he'd gone to the supermarket and done a full stock up of everything he'd need for the coming month. The RV had been through some checks, and everything was fine there. Jaz had been through the routine many times, making sure that once he arrived where he needed to be, he could sit still and hide away for as long as he needed to, sleeping and keeping out of sight of the general population during the daylight hours, then coming out only on the one night that he'd use to deliver the invitations.

For a moment, he wondered if he *had* covered everything. He was stocked up so could easily isolate himself. With the gloriousness of the maps app on his laptop, he'd already studied the town and where he'd be holding his next dance party. The gear was all ready to set up at the venue when he'd decided which night was going to be the right night. All he had to do was get in position, sit tight until he felt the right time had come, then put into effect everything for the dance party and get the invitations out. It might have all seemed impossible for someone else to comprehend. For Jaz, it had all been done so many times that it now worked like clockwork.

Nothing at all for him to be nervous about.
But he was.

CHAPTER 43

"Ready to go and get this guy?" Tim asked Ashley when they met up outside their motel rooms the following morning.

Although Ashley could see he was attempting to use words to make light of the situation, she sincerely hoped those words would ring true. Could she and Tim catch the person/s behind all of the shootings? Could they catch them that very day? It might seem like winning a lottery if they did, and Ashley knew how unlikely *that* was.

"We can only hope," she finally said. "Best we get moving so we definitely don't miss that flight. No time for a big breakfast today, Timmy Boy!"

Tim grinned at her, glad to hear she was at least trying to maintain some positivity. It was never easy when he saw his work partner be down on herself. While there might not be anything to smile about later in the day, he was glad that they were both able to smile in that moment. Evening out the seriousness and horrors they often had to deal with, with forced humor and smiles, was essential in their job. It helped both of them maintain a sound level of sanity, if nothing else.

"There'll be plenty of time for coffee and food at the airport, Ash, and you know it," he teased her as they both stepped quickly toward the car. "Give me your room key and I'll drop these in the box."

As Ashley watched him jog over to the drop box beside the motel office door, she took a moment to once again appreciate that he was her work partner. Even on the hardest cases - the ones that sometimes seemed to gain no or very little momentum - Tim was a rock for her, lifting her up when she needed it. She couldn't help but be grateful for all of his people skills, but especially the one centered around being able to make anyone feel at ease, and feel good about themselves. At that, she sometimes thought he was a master.

"Done," she saw him say as he climbed back into the car and secured his seatbelt. "What are we waiting for, Partner? Things to do, places to go…"

"People to catch," Ashley finished for him, chuckling before beginning to drive. "Today could certainly be the day," she added, as much to herself as to him.

"Indeed it could, Special Agent Power," said Tim. "Indeed it could."

CHAPTER 44

Sitting on the plane, Ashley's mind remained active, going over every detail that she could remember from all three of the previous situations, and from all that she'd read about Welburn and their prime suspect.

"What's currently going on in that head of yours?" she heard Tim ask.

"I'm..." Ashley started to say before wondering if she should voice what had been going through her mind a moment earlier. "I know it probably sounds stupid but..."

"Nothing ever sounds stupid, Ash," Tim reassured her. "What're you thinking?"

"Well, it's just that ... we think that all of our shooters have somehow been, I dunno, *brainwashed*, I guess."

"As weird as it sounds, it certainly has started to seem that way," said Tim.

"But then ... Tim, if someone does have that kind of power - and I'm not sure I believe anyone could, but if they *do* - how..." Ashley started to ask before feeling a shudder flow through her. "How do we know that they can't do that to *us*?"

Even as she voiced the question, she felt silly. The whole idea seemed ridiculous, and yet, the more they got into the case, and the more victims they were alerted to, the more it did seem a possibility.

"I think that what you're asking is..." Tim began to say.

"Insane."

"Not quite," Tim said, smiling. "I mean, sure, in a regular case, maybe this would all seem insane, but I don't think we can rule out that something *is* happening here that isn't normal. Is it brainwashing? I don't know, and I don't know if that's even possible, but until we figure this all out, we just have to maintain that it *could* be."

"That doesn't actually answer my question, Timmy Boy," Ashley said when she'd waited long enough in the hope of him continuing his speech.

"I know," Tim said. "And I wish I *could* answer it, but you know I can't. We don't know how the person behind all of this does what they do and, even if we did, how could we know how to not let ourselves be influenced by them? I think we just have to try and keep an eye out for the guy we're on the tail of, and hope that we can somehow creep up on him before he sees us."

"But even then he could still alter our thinking," Ashley suggested.

"I think it'd be best we don't dwell on that…"

"But we *have* to!" Ashley exclaimed. "If we don't, he has the upper hand."

"Ash, if this is what's really going on - someone is manipulating people's thinking and actions - I'd say he's *always* going to have the upper hand," Tim replied. "We need to focus on finding him. That's it. Whatever else happens, we'll deal with it. We know that nobody in law enforcement has ever been … *recruited* … to do these killings. All of the shooters have been ordinary people who happened to own a gun. That, in itself, makes me believe that you and I are going to be fine, even after we come face to face with this person."

"I hope you're right," Ashley said, fighting to stay positive about whatever lay ahead for the two of them.

"Now, Ash, that is one thing that you and I absolutely *do* know, and most certainly can agree on," said Tim, grinning. "I'm *always* right."

Seeing her laugh in response to his words, Tim forced himself to relax. He was also nervous. He didn't need to show his work partner that.

CHAPTER 45

As soon as the agents landed and disembarked their flight in Welburn, they were alerted to someone from the Sheriff's office waiting for them.

"Special Agents Power and Moore," Tim read aloud to Ash as they entered the arrivals area and saw the large sign being held up. "I'm guessing that's us."

Despite feeling her heart beating faster in anticipation of the day ahead, Ashley smiled at Tim before they reached the woman waiting for them.

"Welcome," the officer said when they approached her. "Sheriff Simons has asked me to meet you and take you to the station."

"Thank you, um…?" Ashley asked.

"Oh, sorry. Pleased to meet you. I'm Stacey Biggalo, but everyone calls me Biggs," the officer said as she held out her hand to each agent. "Good flight?"

"Not too bad, thanks, Biggs," Tim replied, prompting Ashley to give him a teasing glance. When off the job, she knew he was a bit of a player. Even so, she equally knew he never was when he was *on* the job, although certainly his good looks and charm had come in handy plenty of times when attempting to find something out.

For the short time they were driven from the airport to the local law enforcement premises, Ashley and Tim were provided with a running commentary of all that Biggs seemed to deem important for them to know about the small town of Welburn.

By the end of the journey, Ashley couldn't help but wonder if the officer had any idea about why they were there. During the drive, there had been no mention of the case, or any questions about anything that might have been considered important.

"Welcome," Ashley saw a man in his mid-30s say as he held out his hand to her upon entering the station. "Sheriff Glen Simons. I am very pleased to make your acquaintance."

"Hello Sheriff, I'm Ashley Power and this is Tim Moore," Ashley said as they entered the small office and the sheriff closed the door behind them. "We understand our supervisor has explained the full situation to you?"

"She did," the sheriff confirmed. "Since I got the phone call yesterday afternoon, I've had various officers of mine remain out and about, just in their civvies and plain cars, keeping an eye out. As yet, there's been no sign of the person we were provided a photo of."

"We were hoping he might be bold enough to not be difficult to find," Ashley said.

"The staff at the Bureau are monitoring his phone's movements, I understand," Sheriff Simons said. "I'm sure it won't be hard to find him…"

"Yes, so long as he doesn't suspect any of us are looking for him," said Tim.

"But if you know where he is right at this very moment, why not go and arrest him, no matter how far away from town he is?" the sheriff asked.

"Yes, we're hoping it'll be that easy," Ashley replied. "We're not entirely sure what kind of person we're dealing with - or, to be honest, if this *is* the right person. At this point, he's our main suspect, but there's a lot of unknowns and uncertainties in this case. It's difficult to tell where it will lead in the end."

As she spoke, she watched the face of the sheriff change from that of a man in charge, to one that reminded her of her late grandfather.

"I've been in this job for a very long time," Sheriff Simons said. "One thing I've learned over my career is that some cases take longer than others to solve, and some criminals are far more adept at escaping notice than others are. One thing to keep in the forefront of your mind is that you are great at what you do. If you weren't, you wouldn't have been an agent with the Bureau for this long, so don't worry. With your intel, plus my team who are all hard working and dedicated to making this world a better place, we will get this guy. No matter where he's hiding, if he's coming into my town, we'll get him before he can do any harm. I'll make sure of it."

Ashley smiled at the man's passion for his work and his job. She'd met many members of the law enforcement society over the years she'd been working. As dismaying as Ashley had always found it, not all had seemed to have entirely pure intentions. As she studied the face of the man in front of her, she felt more positive just from knowing where his morals and enthusiasm lay.

"I'm sure you will," she said.

"Do you know where he was last seen on your tracker?" the sheriff asked. "I haven't been asked to move any of my staff to any location, so I'm not sure what's been happening since I spoke to your supervisor - Sarah, is it? Do you know if there's been any update at all?"

"No," said Tim. "I talked to Sarah when we first landed. As far as our tech guys know, the phone being tracked hasn't moved from a point just outside of town. Here," he added as he walked around the desk and showed the map on his phone. "Looks like it might be a forest area? Do you know it?"

"Hmm," the sheriff said. "Yes, that's forest, alright. Often used for camping and bush walking. If he was that close and was making his way into town, he certainly should already be here unless he's camped up out there."

"Unfortunately we can only track him if his phone is turned on," said Ashley. "That's the issue now. When the tech guys were watching the phone, it was moving, so they knew it was turned on. Now that there hasn't been any update to its location, it could be that either he's now remained stopped at that spot, or the phone has been turned off..."

"Or it's been tossed," Tim surmised. "So, none of your team have been out to this location?"

"No, your supervisor hinted that she thought it best we don't make our awareness known too much. The roads in and out of here are usually pretty quiet, so I've asked my guys to remain closer to town," the sheriff said. "Someone being seen on the outskirts would definitely be noticed. I wasn't sure how noticed - or not noticed - you wanted us to be, so I've erred on the side of caution."

"Right," said Ashley. "Yes, if he's here, and he's planning to do what he's already done in three other towns, we certainly don't want him to be alerted to the fact that we're wanting to keep an eye on him."

"Just keep an eye on him? Is that the plan?" the sheriff asked. "If you're sure this guy has killed all those people..."

"It is a little bit more complicated than that, Sheriff," said Tim.

"Your supervisor said it was the person behind the attacks in Seaview, Leefton and Kildare," Sheriff Simons replied. "In my books, that certainly makes him a murderer."

Ashley sighed. How could they describe to anyone what they thought had been happening? It still seemed unbelievable, even to them.

"Have you ever worked on a case where the suspect couldn't remember what they'd done, Sheriff?" she asked, feeling bold.

"Couldn't remember? Or *said* they couldn't remember?" the sheriff asked.

"In this case, there has been one shooter for each of

the victims," said Tim.

"Yes, I heard that," said the sheriff.

"Every one of those shooters has undergone multiple polygraph tests, all of which have shown the shooters to be telling the truth," Tim said. "The tests show that the people who we know fired the guns, didn't shoot anyone, and they weren't even anywhere near the crime scenes on those nights."

"*Not* the right people then?" the sheriff asked. "You got the wrong guys."

"No," said Ashley. "The thing is that every one of those shooters thinks they were in a specific place, where we know they weren't. They weren't there, but the tests show that every one of them truly *believes* they were."

Tim watched the sheriff's face as Ashley spoke. Both agents knew that their boss, Sarah, had explained it all to the sheriff the day before, but of course it was crazy enough for someone to not believe.

"Hypnotized?" the sheriff asked.

"Perhaps," said Tim.

"Reminds me of a case I worked on in my first position," the sheriff said, leaning forward, looking from one agent to the other. "A guy in Hastings went on a killing rampage, stabbing almost thirty people before he was finally stopped."

"What happened then?" Ashley asked.

"He argued black and blue that he didn't do what he'd done, and then the same thing as you're talking about happened as well - polygraph showed that he wasn't lying," the sheriff said. "In that case, we doubted our own evidence for a while. Then we doubted the test."

"And … then?" Tim asked, intrigued.

"He asked for a second polygraph so eventually we granted it," Sheriff Simons said. "He didn't pass that one. Are you sure the people you've questioned under polygraph conditions didn't also have a bad test?"

"No, they've all been tested by multiple testers, with multiple machines, just in case," Tim replied. "I think we could have accepted one or two people beating the machines - maybe even a handful - but there are too many now. I've never heard of that many people being able to be successful in that. Have you?"

"You're talking about hundreds of people?"

"Over a thousand now," said Ashley.

Both agents watched as the sheriff shook his head and sat back in his chair.

"*That* is a mystery, I must admit," he finally said. "Certainly it's not impossible to fool a polygraph - we see that more often than people would think - but that many people fooling it, and fooling several different tests too. That ... yeah, that's new to me."

"To us, as well," said Tim. "We don't know how the people are passing the tests, but we are leaning towards them somehow being brainwashed..."

"Is that a real thing?" the sheriff asked. "In reality? I think I'd lean towards them being hypnotized, before I'd go down the brainwashing route. Personally, I'm not even sure about hypnotism, but at least it's considered more common."

"Yes, all possibilities point to something we don't understand," Ashley replied. "But given that all suspects have passed these tests, we can't deny that they do all seem to believe they were somewhere else, doing something different, other than their actions of going and shooting someone."

"And how does this guy fit into all of this?" Sheriff Simons asked. "The one we're on a manhunt for."

"We don't know how, but we do think he might be behind it all, or at least have some major part in it," said Tim.

"And you think this because?"

"It's our belief that he dressed up as a security guard and inserted himself at one of the crime scenes..." said

Ashley.

"At *least* one of the crime scenes," Tim added. "We mainly noticed him in Kildare so we're not 100% sure if he was also at any of the scenes in Seaview or Leefton."

"Right," said the sheriff. "One of those killers who likes to quietly observe what's happening after his deed is done then."

"Like Tim said, we can only know that for sure when it comes to the latest town," said Ashley. "Whether he did the same thing at the previous two towns, there's no way for us to know now. The crime scene photos that were taken in all three towns don't show him at all. He wasn't even accidentally photographed in the background."

"If he's good, he'd certainly know how to avoid that if he was the kind of criminal who likes to visit the scenes he creates," said the Sheriff. "But I'm curious. Just how do you think he does this mass killing?" asked the sheriff. "It's indicated that he gets other people to do it for him - I understand that - but how does he get them to do it? Even with hypnotism, or brainwashing as you've suggested, how could he get so many people under his influence all at once? Could it all, instead, be due to maybe something more generic like blackmail?"

"After investigations into all of the shooters, we don't think blackmail was used. The shooters are all pretty average people, with nothing hidden in their closets, so to speak, that would make them susceptible to that. No, we're pretty sure he's using some form of manipulation of the mind," said Tim. "It's an area we know nothing about so Sarah has found three professionals in the area…"

"The area of … brainwashing?" the sheriff asked, surprise evident on his face.

"We know it sounds farfetched, Sheriff, but we have to investigate all possibilities, as you know," Tim said. "The people that Sarah's got ready to come here, each claim to be experts in mind manipulation so, once we catch this guy, we hope these professionals will be able to determine what exactly has been going on, and how so many people have been manipulated to do something so horrible."

Ashley watched the face of the man facing them. It was clear to see his disbelief, and she knew exactly why that was. Even she and Tim couldn't understand any of what had been happening. Telepathy? Brainwashing? Hypnotism? Were they really real things that actually happened in the real world, or just something created for fictional stories?

"Alright, well, what do you want to do now?" the sheriff asked. "I can dispatch my team however you want them to move."

"Great. Let me do another check with the team monitoring the location of our guy," said Tim as he pulled out his phone. It took less than a minute for him to get the reply he was after. "The phone is still where it was showing up earlier. We can't pinpoint its exact location, but we know it's somewhere in that area."

"That area is up on the hills coming into town," said the sheriff as he stood up and began to move toward the door. "One of our two entry roads is on that side, so he'll probably be entering via that one. I'll get two of my plain clothes staff to head up the road to have a look."

"We don't want to startle him," Ashley said.

"I'll tell them to just do a drive by, with no interaction," the sheriff reassured her. "All we need to do at this stage is see if that phone is up there somewhere, and if the person with it is the guy in the photo. Correct?"

"Yes," replied Ashley. "We'd like to see how he does what he does - stop him before he can carry out any more destruction, but see how he goes about influencing the people who end up doing his dirty work."

"Right," the sheriff said as he nodded. "Makes

sense."

Tim and Ashley watched as the sheriff gathered his staff around him, explained the situation, and gave the command for two of the officers to do as he instructed.

"And remember - no engagement!" he added as they were about to head out the door. "No matter what you see, just cruise on by as if you're on your way out of town, and don't let him see you looking at him."

"Yep!" both officers called back before leaving the room.

"Nervous?" Tim quietly asked Ashley.

"I am, but I'm not sure what exactly I'm nervous about," Ashley admitted. "We need to catch whoever's behind this, but I don't like not knowing for sure that this is the right person."

"Once we can get him in for questioning, I'm sure all will become clearer," said Tim.

"Or foggier," Ashley quipped. "It's always daunting meeting anyone who likes killing people…"

"I don't think this guy likes killing, Ash," said Tim. "Maybe he likes to know people are being killed under his command, but as far as we know, he hasn't killed anyone himself."

"In my eyes, I still see him as a killer," Ashley whispered. "A killer on one hand, and perhaps a brainwasher on the other. I just wonder what kind of monster this guy is going to be like."

Although Tim found her choice of words interesting, he didn't respond. Someone that might be associated with everything, could be within their grasp. That was the most important thing he wanted to focus on - that and making sure nobody else was going to die under the command of whoever was behind it all.

CHAPTER 46

Sitting in the back of his RV, Jaz McMenamin put on his disposable gloves and shuffled through the latest set of invitations. Many weeks had passed since he'd done his check of the next town he was visiting. Even without having yet set foot inside the actual town, he already knew where his dance party was going to be held, who was going to be invited to attend, and where each of those people lived.

Although he'd had a moment of doubt about if he should move ahead with another event, the uncertainty had passed quickly. Scouring more newspapers and online content in the hope of seeing someone suggest a change to gun laws, and finding nothing, he couldn't see he had any other choice. Why was it taking them so long to see how dangerous guns were, and see that allowing citizens to have so many guns when they really weren't needed only lead to more deaths, not less.

In his mind, he did know that his thinking went way beyond the normal level of consideration when it came to guns. There were probably millions of people in the world who thought it would be better to get rid of guns, rather than have more of them. Those people didn't go out and kill just to make a point.

Thinking about his 'why', his thoughts drifted back to Christie once again. It was always a bittersweet exercise, letting his mind dwell there. There was extreme sadness and anger that came from thinking about her being killed. There was also extreme happiness in the memory of their time together, and the love they shared. They'd have had a wonderful life together, Jaz was sure of it. They'd spent hours talking about marriage, getting a house together, and then having kids. They'd both grown up in less than ideal circumstances, and knew how much negative influence parents could have on their kids. Christie had been as determined as Jaz was that once they became parents, they'd never treat their kids like their own parents had treated them.

His thoughts going around and around, changing from positive to negative, and from the past to the present, Jaz refocused on the invitations. This time, there were exactly three hundred and sixty seven to be delivered. That was exactly how many gun owners there were in Welburn. It wasn't as many as the first two towns Jaz had completed his experiment in, but it was more than the last town.

Over three hundred. It was going to take quite some time to deliver all of those, but he'd done more than that before. Looking outside of the RV, he could see the sun heading towards its highest point of the day, just as it always did in the approach to noon. He'd wait till the darkness of night came before he would begin his deliveries. In the meantime, he needed to check into the local campground. He could do what he needed to do from where he currently was, but it was too exposed and too likely to attract attention. In a campground, he would just be some guy in an RV, like all the other people in RVs. Nothing out of the ordinary at all.

Thinking about the deliveries he'd later make, he jumped up and checked the pushbike that was housed on its rack. Tyres were all good, and everything was sound, just as it always was.

Half an hour later, when the invitations had been sorted into logical delivery order and safely housed in the small saddle bag on the bike, Jaz switched off his phone and finally moved up front and started the engine. First stop - as only a tourist of course - was to view in person the place he'd considered would be perfect for his dance party. With no desolate buildings to be seen online in the area, he'd had to get creative in his choice of location for the upcoming event, but as he stopped the van and saw his chosen place, he grinned. It wasn't conventional, or anywhere like he'd used before, but as far as isolated went, it was *perfect*.

After a quick stop to walk inside and note the size of the interior, and the way the sound would be amazing inside but yet be shielded from the outside by the thick stone walls, he grinned to himself. It was different, and it was new - and that made it all the more exciting

Satisfied with his choice of location and how his latest plans were soon going to flow into fruition, he jumped back into the RV. Grinning, he started the engine with one thought on his mind as he whistled a happy tune.

'Welburn, here I come.'

CHAPTER 47

"I wish we could be the ones going to look for this guy," Ashley said as she and Tim exited the station and began to walk toward their car. "It feels like we've just placed all of our cards into someone else's hands."

Tim looked at her in surprise.

"Ash, you know that this guy saw you at that scene - probably saw both of us for that matter," he said. "If he sees you or me, there's too much of a strong possibility he'll recognize not only that we're here, before anything has happened, but that we're here for a *reason*."

"For him, you mean," Ashley said as she started the car. "Yeah, I know. Let's get settled into our motel and get the laptops set up. At least then we can connect with the tech guys and see what they're seeing."

"You're not missing out on anything, Partner," Tim reassured her in a teasing tone. "Once we know where he is, and that it definitely *is* the right guy, don't worry. You'll get your moment to talk to him."

"Hopefully before he mind-warps me into doing something I don't later remember," said Ashley, shuddering at the thought.

"Worry not, fair maiden," Tim said, grinning. "I will gladly protect you and your honor."

"Ha!" Ashley scoffed. "As if."

Happy to see her look more relaxed, Tim laughed. At that moment, he knew there was little more he and his work partner could do.

CHAPTER 48

Heading into the small town, Jaz smiled to himself. It was odd how often he found his emotions moving to all the extremes of happiness, sadness, anger, and then back to happiness again. Odd? Or normal? To that question, he didn't know the answer, but he'd long ago accepted he did sometimes feel like he was on an emotional roller coaster.

As he drove through the quiet streets, taking the most direct route to the campground he'd already booked into under one of his many alias names, he found his mind wandering back to his parents. Both had long since passed and, in truth, he rarely gave thought to them these days, but always before one of his dance parties - *always* - they entered his mind.

So many unhappy memories flowed over him when he thought about his mother and father. In truth, the only good thing that came out of them being his parents, that he could see, was that after they'd both passed, he'd inherited the family home. While Jaz could have held onto that and been well set up for life, when things had changed him and he'd lost Christie, he knew what he wanted to do, and selling that big old house was just what he needed in order to get the funds to live as he did.

What would his mother and father think about him having sold the home to pay for what he was currently doing? What would they think about the entire plan he'd started to put into effect? Would they chastise him for his logic, and for his actions? Would they do what they'd done to him thousands of times when he'd been a kid, and tell him how stupid and useless he was?

Stupid. Useless. They were the two strongest words that he knew he'd never say to a child. They were also the two words that he and Christie had often talked about. She'd been as familiar with them as Jaz had, from the years of growing up. When Jaz thought about that - someone calling Christie stupid - he felt his anger increase once again. There had been nothing stupid about her. She'd been beautiful, strong, intelligent, and incredibly kind. How anyone could ever have called her stupid, was stupid in itself.

Aware that his emotions were heightening again, he forced himself to toss those thoughts aside. He was in the zone where he had to focus on the job at hand, and nothing else. Not only was getting sidetracked dangerous, but it was also likely to get him noticed. No, he had a job to do, and he had to maintain the strongest focus to not only get it done, but get it done right so that he…

So that he could what? Do it again? As he thought about that, he wondered how long he *could* keep doing what he was doing. Sure, he maintained hope that at some point someone would stand up and suggest something was done about the gun laws that he thought were far too relaxed. Even so, just how long could he keep fighting that fight? Every round of trying to get attention meant that more people had to die. Usually he didn't let himself think too much about the death toll he'd already contributed to, or to the people who were now sitting somewhere, guilty of killing someone they otherwise wouldn't have wanted to hurt.

Pulling into the campground, he forced his mind to become quiet once again. He'd timed his arrival so that he wouldn't have to interact with anyone. Strict instructions had been provided about where he could go and park, and what facilities he could use. Not that he *would* use any campground facilities. To everyone else staying at the campground for that week, they wouldn't know he was inside, doing what it was that he was going to do. They wouldn't see him, and they wouldn't even really know he was there.

That was the way he liked to live his life - just like a ghost.

Often around but rarely seen.

CHAPTER 49

"Where's this phone gone?" Tim asked one of the tech guys over the phone after the agents' laptops were set up and they had the tracking software open on their screens.

"Looks like it's been turned off," came the reply. "We can't be absolutely certain but it certainly looks that way."

"No way to find it when it's off?" Tim asked, sure it sounded like a stupid question but he felt he had to ask it anyway.

"No," the tech officer replied. "As soon as it's switched on, it'll ping a cell tower and we'll be closer to knowing where he is."

"Not *exactly* where he is, right?" Ashley checked.

"Actually, Welburn has three cell towers so, between them, we will have a better chance of isolating fairly close to where he is when that phone pings," the voice said. "It might not be *precisely* where he is, but we're hopeful it'll be a lot closer than we'd otherwise be able to calculate."

"Okay, well, he's in some kind of vehicle and we're guessing it might be a truck or a caravan or an RV since he must have his gear in it," said Tim.

"The town isn't that big," said the tech guy. "If he's there, you're probably going to find him even before that phone gives us anything. I mean, that's what you guys do, right?" he added with a tone of cheekiness in his voice.

"Yeah, thanks," Tim replied before hanging up the call and turning to look at Ashley. "I love those guys but

I do feel extremely unintelligent whenever I talk to them. And right now, I wish we could go out for a walk at least."

"Got itchy feet, Timmy Boy?" Ashley teased him. "Yeah, I know what you mean. I want to find this guy too."

"I know it's not investigative science, but let's at least try and figure out where he might go, based on what we do know about him," said Tim, refocusing on the screen in front of him.

"Well, if he *is* the guy we think he is - and that's a big *if* since we don't know for sure..." Ashley began.

"Yeah, yeah, this is all hypothetical. Let's still get into it," Tim said, encouraging her to continue.

"Well, we think he's a DJ. That much must be true if we're to believe what Kane Garmin told us," Ashley continued. "He does set up dance parties, and he does provide the music when there..."

"Yep - and it's live music, Kane said, with a keyboard, not just a digital recording, so he has to have that - a keyboard - at the very least," said Tim. "Plus Kane said there were a couple of decent sized speakers at that venue, which weren't still there when we saw it."

"Right," Ashley agreed. "And we know from our contact with hire companies in the three previous towns that nobody hired any gear like that from them around the times of each of the shootings, so we can assume he owns the speakers as well."

"And our chats with the local music shop showed that nobody had purchased any new equipment in the weeks leading up to the shootings, making us sure this guy isn't buying new stuff and just dumping it somewhere as he moves on," Tim surmised.

"Right. So I'm thinking he has to have with him some kind of fairly large vehicle that he takes from town to town with all his gear in it," Ashley said. "He must have it all with him, but I suppose a keyboard and some speakers *could* fit into a regular car, at a stretch," said Ashley. "But the way he gets people *to* the events, with those invitations … where does he get those printed, and when? When we talked to the local printers in Seaview and Welburn, none of them had ever seen anything like those invitations…"

"But then, what we don't know, Ash, is if this guy did use those printing firms, but the firms just *forgot* they printed the invitations off," Tim said.

"And that's the biggest issue we're always going to have on this case, isn't it," said Ashley. "This person could have used lots of people to help him on this entire … *quest* … of his, and they just might not remember. How are we going to ever prove anything if that's the case? Even if he's the right person and we catch him, how can we *prove* anything if nobody he interacted with remembers him?"

"But someone already *does* remember him," said Tim. "Kane Garmin clearly remembers…"

"If he's telling us the truth," said Ashley, cutting his words short. "I'm not ready to rule him out as being a part of this yet."

"If he was a part of it, why would he tell us about the DJ in the first place?" Tim asked. "That would make no sense."

"I *know!*" Ashley exclaimed as she felt her body give in to the deflation she felt. "Ugh, let's move forward in this hypothetical situation. It does me no good to keep thinking like this."

"Right," Tim agreed. "Okay, well he's coming to Welburn because it's the fourth densely populated town with registered gun owners. He's coming into town with the gear needed to set up and hold a dance party. We know that, in order to do that and successfully keep it a secret, he needs security personnel to help him. Where is he getting those people from?"

"Maybe he has his own crew that go with him from

town to town?" Ashley suggested. "But in that case, there would be a whole procession of vehicles entering each town before the dance party, and that would surely get noticed."

"Plus the firms that were hired for Seaview, Leefton and Kildare were all local firms," said Tim. "We've looked into all of them and although the staff haven't remembered the jobs they did, the tech guys have found evidence in each of the computer systems that they *did* do those events on the nights of each shooting spree."

"Yes, that shows how he can have so many people help him in his quest - not only the shooters themselves, but also the security guys who check everyone entering the event premises," Ashley said. "And the premises, themselves, that are being used for these 'dance parties'..."

"Have all been places that have been unused for a long time," said Tim. "I think that needs to be our first place to look here too.'

"The premises that he'd likely use..." Ashley pondered as her thoughts aligned with her work partner's.

"Yes!" Tim exclaimed as he delved into what showed on his computer screen again. "This isn't a large area..."

"The town itself isn't, but, Tim, that site we visited in Kildare was *miles* away from the town - like, in the middle of nowhere," Ashley said. "Whatever he's aiming to use this time ... it could be *anywhere* in the desert areas around the outskirts."

"True," said Tim. "But if we look at the map online, and if we specifically hone in on this satellite image..."

"Which might have been taken years ago," Ashley suggested.

"True, it might," Tim said. "But even if it was, the worst case is that if we can see a building fit for purpose, it might not be there now, and that's okay. But if we can find *something*..."

Both agents sat at their respective laptops and began scouring the satellite image maps before them. North, south, east and west of the town, they widened their search, hopeful.

"I don't see anything like what we saw in Kildare," Ashley finally said. "That building was abandoned and unused - not to mention well overdue for demolition. I can't see any buildings at all in these outlying areas - just stark desert. Can you?"

"No," Tim replied. "Maybe it's not a building he's intending to use…"

"Or maybe we're on the completely wrong path."

Tim scowled at her. He wasn't ready to give in to doubt quite so easily.

"We need to talk to the sheriff again. He'll know every inch of ground around here, surely," he said. "Why didn't I think of this before?" he added, muttering to himself.

"One thing about this case compared to most that you and I have worked on together, Timmy Boy - there's no shortage of things to think about and consider, especially in trying to get ahead of this person," Ashley said.

"You're right," said Tim. "Okay, I'll give the sheriff a call and ask him for his thoughts."

A short time later, he turned and smiled at Ashley.

"Caves."

"You must be joking," Ashley said as she saw Tim's grin widen as he shook his head. "Seriously? The sheriff thinks a DJ might use *caves* for some secret dance party?"

"Not exactly," Tim said, chuckling. "But he did say that if we're after some kind of building - or in this case, a discreet and quiet shelter that could fit a lot of people but few people ever visit anymore - there are some caves out west that would be ideal."

"What about power though?" Ashley pondered. "To run speakers, at least, he'd need some electricity, I'm guessing."

"Maybe he has solar power running off his vehicle?" Tim suggested. "Or a mobile power unit? Anyway, the sheriff is going to keep one officer out of sight of the caves, but within distance where they can monitor them, just in case this guy - or any potential security staff - go near that area over the next couple of nights."

"Yeah, I guess he can only move around at night, given that nobody remembered seeing any strangers in the other towns," Ashley said. "Although, for all we know, *everyone* has seen this guy, but just forgotten about it."

"It'll be interesting to talk to the psych professionals coming to town tomorrow," Tim said. "I'm quite curious to see what they have to say about even the possibility that people are being brainwashed into doing something, and then being further brainwashed into forgetting they'd done it."

"And if they say that none of this *can* be true?" Ashley asked. "If they confirm that this kind of thing is only the subject of fictional stories, and could never be reality?"

"Well, I doubt that'll be the case. If this entire phenomenon was a farce, how could they possibly be professionals in it? But, sure, they might say this can't be reality and, if that's the case, then we'll know for sure," Tim said, chuckling. "That you, Special Agent Ashley Power, really are crazy."

Despite her annoyance at the comment, Ashley grinned at him. He could be a jokester, and he could be a challenge to spend too much time with, but she always appreciated when he did what he did with the purpose of making her smile.

"Idiot."

CHAPTER 50

As the sun went down, the quiet alarm on Jaz's phone woke up. He'd enjoyed a late afternoon and early evening of sleep, as was often the way since he'd lost the love of his life years earlier.

Stretching under the warmth of his blankets, he thought about all that he had to do in the hours ahead. It was always the same routine, with every town that he'd chosen before on his quest. Despite the familiarity of the routine, he was always paranoid that he'd forget something, and he'd suffer a consequence of that.

Over and over in his head, he recited the order of how it all had to go. On that night, all he needed to do was quietly deliver the invitations without being seen. With the order of delivery, he anticipated it would take him two hours at most on his pushbike, silently riding the streets of the town as its residents slept.

The other consideration was a quick check in with the security firm he'd made contact with. That was always a much harder thing to do while maintaining discretion, but he'd succeeded in the past, and he could do it again. Like everything he'd ever done, it just took commitment to maintaining focus on the single job at hand. That was all.

Finally pushing aside the blankets providing him with comfort, he jumped out of bed, dropped to the floor of the RV, and immediately did his usual fifty push ups. Routine. Even though he moved around a lot, seeing different towns and cities, deep inside he knew he had a strong need for it. Having familiar things that he did each and every day was his way of having some security. Scenery might change and his plans might require different things to be done at different times, but having just those few things that he committed to doing every day was enough to help him stay on track.

And in his current pursuit, staying on track and keeping focus was paramount.

CHAPTER 51

At 2am, Ashley was woken by her mobile alerting her to a call coming in. Sitting up sharply, she grabbed the phone in anticipation of what she might be told, and in dread that the news might be that they were too late and many more people had been killed.

"He's there," she heard Sarah's voice say. "The sheriff just called me. I have no idea why me instead of you, but he did. One of his guys has just spotted someone cycling around the streets, and he's sure it's your guy."

A moment later, Ashley heard a knock on her door.

"If that's your door, it'll be Tim," Sarah said. "I called him before I called you. Grab your things, Ashley. You're on."

For a long moment, Ashley didn't respond. She was still too asleep to be able to react quickly, and too in shock to be able to say anything.

"Move, Power!" Sarah's voice then yelled, startling Ashley out of her daze.

"Going now, Boss," Ashley said before hanging up the call and rushing to the door. "Give me a couple of minutes," she said to Tim as she greeted him then rushed to the bathroom with an armful of the nearest clothing within reach.

As Tim watched her dart away, he took a moment to check in with how his body was feeling. He could feel his heart pounding - as was always the way when they thought they were about to find someone they'd been chasing for a while in an investigation.

"Ready," Ashley said as she returned to the room.

"Sarah didn't give me any details. Where are we going?"

"The officer said they saw him riding on a bike, putting something in letterboxes," Tim replied. "I suggest you and I nab one of those deliveries so we can be sure about what's happening…"

"You think it's those invitations?" Ashley asked and saw him nod.

"If our calculations and beliefs are right," Tim said. "One way to find out and see."

"Great," said Ashley. "Where are we heading then?"

Entering an address into the GPS unit on the dashboard, Tim smiled at her. Usually she was perfectly groomed and immaculately presented. Ashley, when she'd just jumped out of bed, seemed to be a creature of an entirely different nature.

"Shut up," Ashley said, sensing him looking at her. "It's far too early - or late - for your smirks, Moore."

Tim chuckled but did as he was told and didn't say any more until they reached one home they'd been provided the address of. Readying himself with gloves, Tim quietly climbed out and extracted the piece of card from the mailbox, taking a moment to look at it before carefully placing in the clear evidence bag he held.

"Is it…?" Ashley asked when he returned to the car.

"Yep," Tim replied. "It's what we were thinking it'd be, and that means, Special Agent Power, that we might just be right in our thinking after all, no matter how crazy it's been in trying to figure all of this out."

"Right," Ashley said, feeling the same unique blend of anxiety and excitement that she always felt at that moment in an investigation. "Where to now?"

In response to the question, Tim called the sheriff to get an update on what was happening. After a couple of minutes, he turned to face Ashley once again.

"Barnes Street," he said. "Another officer has just seen him there, putting more of these in mailboxes."

"He's on a bike?" Ashley asked.

"Yes, so he could easily get away if there are any alleyways or places we can't go in a car," Tim said.

"Good thing you've got your running shoes on then," Ashley said, smiling. "Come on. Let's head there. Give the go ahead to the sheriff. If his guys can nab our suspect, they should."

Several minutes later, the two agents pulled up to what looked like a crime scene. Ashley had expected that once the suspect saw a car following him, he'd at least try and get away. She was surprised that he obviously hadn't.

"Not sure what's up with your guy," the sheriff said when he approached her and Tim. "Didn't even try to get away. He hasn't even said that we've got the wrong guy, or that he's done nothing wrong, which is new. Seems to have a particular interest in you though."

On hearing the last sentence, Ashley saw the sheriff look at her and then point to the suspect sitting in the back of a cop car. Without thought she began walking in his direction.

"Whoa, Ash," Tim said when he also noticed the way the suspect was looking at her.

"This is what we're here for, Tim," Ashley replied. "If this is our guy, we're going to be questioning him."

"I know but…" Tim started to say before dismissing her previous concerns and his natural desire to protect her. "You're right. But I'm coming with you."

"Yeah, of course," Ashley said as she resumed her journey toward the police cruiser.

"Hello," she heard the velvety voice say as the suspect looked directly into her eyes. "It is nice to see you again."

"Good, because once this officer takes you to the police station, you and I will be having a good, long talk," Ashley said, aware of the shudder passing through her body.

"I look forward to it."

CHAPTER 52

Before entering the interrogation room, Ashley and Tim took some time to study the suspect through the two way mirror glass.

"Now that you can see him properly and in the flesh, it's definitely the guy you saw at the Seaview home, Ash?" Tim asked.

"No doubt about it," Ashley replied. "He might have been dressed as a security guard, but I remember those eyes perfectly."

"Okay, then. Are you ready to find out if he's the one behind all of this?" Tim asked. "If he's so willing to be pulled in by the cops, he might just be willing to give a full confession."

"If only I could believe it could ever be that easy," Ashley said. "But, yes, let's get on with this."

Sitting down at the table, facing the suspect, Ashley once again caught the way the man before her was studying her.

"You look a lot like someone I used to know," the man said, not moving his eyes from her.

Ashley took a moment before she replied. She'd read all that they knew about Jaz McMenamin.

"Someone you loved?" she dared to ask, curious to see how he'd react.

In response she saw him smile and nod, his eyes not matching the smile on his lips, but instead revealing an intense sadness.

"Very much so," Jaz replied. "Have you ever felt a love so strong that you just knew you were supposed to be with that person until the day you died?"

"I haven't," Ashley said. Most criminals, she wouldn't engage with on a personal level. With the one in front of her, she knew about his pain and loss. She was eager to encourage him to talk, purely so she could understand what she considered must be a very twisted logic.

"That saddens me," Jaz said, smiling sadly at her. "It is the most wonderful thing … until it isn't anymore."

"What happened?" Ashley asked, pretending to be ignorant.

"I think you know," said Jaz. "You brought me here, so I believe you know who I am, and what I've been through."

"What I think and believe is that I'd like to hear you tell us what's been happening in the life of Jaz McMenamin," Ashley said, quietly encouraging him to keep talking.

"She was the love of my life," Jaz said. When he'd first realized he'd caught the attention of law enforcement, he'd wanted to run, and he'd wanted to hide. Then he'd just wanted it to all be over with. "I loved her so much. Then she was taken away."

Ashley remained quiet, hopeful he'd keep telling whatever story he needed to tell before he'd then, hopefully, explain what role he'd played in the shootings across three towns.

"That day, before she went off to college, we'd agreed to have a special dinner that night," Jaz continued. He'd never said his thoughts out loud to anyone. It felt surprisingly good to talk. "I was going to propose that night. I was excited, but nervous. I'd bought the ring that I knew she'd most love - something simple but beautiful. That was what she loved in anything - simple but beautiful."

Both agents waited for the man before them to continue, seeing him rub his watering eyes before speaking again.

"Then I got the call," Jaz said. "Dead. Some ... *insane* ... person, with no right owning a gun, just ... he just ran into that college classroom and ... he just *shot* them. And for what? There was *no reason* to do that. News reports said that he didn't even go to that college, and as far as anyone could tell, he had no links at all to anyone in that room. To him, it was just ... *sport*.

"And the worst thing of all - he then shot himself," Jaz continued. "Why? If he was prepared to kill himself, why didn't he do that first, and leave all of those other people alive? What was his point? Did he just want some kind of ... *fame*?"

"We've been wondering the same thing about you," Tim said, feeling bold. While he could certainly respect the pain someone felt when they'd lost a loved one, he couldn't respect their ongoing need to cause pain in other people who had absolutely nothing to do with that. "You've been on quite a journey..."

"You have no idea," Jaz said, his tone changing from one of sadness, to very distinctly one of anger.

"No, we don't," said Ashley. "But we'd like to know."

"And what *exactly* would you like to know?" Jaz asked.

"What part you've played in all of the shootings in Seaview, Leefton and Kildare," Ashley replied. "And what you've been planning to do here in Welburn."

"But you already know," Jaz replied. "If you didn't, why else are we here? You *know* what's been going on, don't you."

"We have a theory, but I'd really love to hear your side of the story," said Ashley.

Hearing him scoff as he moved back in his chair was a surprise, but once again Ashley waited patiently for him to speak.

"I think ... I think you might have already figured me out," Jaz said as he studied her face. "You know that I've had something to do with people shooting each other.

You know that I've chosen certain towns for a very specific reason. And you know who in this town was going to be next on my list."

"Tell us," Tim prompted, eager to stop seeing the way the man in front of him was looking at Ashley.

As Ashley watched, she saw the man turn and look at Tim. The glare she saw him deliver was unlike any she'd seen before. It made her more than a little bit wary.

"Worry not," she then heard the man say as he returned his focus to her. "It would serve no purpose for me to make your partner do or say something right now."

Ashley was so surprised by the statement, and the accuracy of it representing exactly what she'd been fearful of, that she couldn't speak.

"You've been wondering if your thoughts about me could possibly be right," Jaz continued, smiling. "Could it be possible to make people do something that they then don't remember doing? You tell me. *Could* it be done, do you think? Do I have the power to do that? Does *anyone?*"

"Tell us about Christie," Tim suggested, once again determined to keep the guy talking about the crime, and not focused on Ashley.

In response, both agents saw the man's face harden again.

"I already told you," Jaz replied. "She was the love of my life."

"And she was killed in a college shooting," said Ashley.

"As I said," Jaz confirmed.

"And you haven't been able to let that go," Ashley said. "I expect that something like that happening must have instilled in you an intense ... *anger* ... at the guy who did it."

"Of course," said Jaz. "The guy who did it wasn't sane."

"But you are?" Tim asked.

"The guy who killed all of those students, did so for no reason at all," Jaz said.

"And what is your reason, Jaz??" Ashley asked, leaning forward. "What is *your* reason for killing so many innocent people?"

"I have never killed anyone," Jaz replied, leaning forward while looking directly into Ashley's eyes. "But you know that, don't you."

"Of course we don't," Ashley replied. "We know very little about you. That's why we want to hear what you have to say."

"Hmm," Jaz muttered as he settled back into his chair again. "Why do *you* think all of this has been happening?"

"We aren't here to talk about what I think," Ashley replied. "I want to hear your thoughts - and your reasons."

"Do you?" Jaz asked. "I think, more than anything, you *don't* want to know the reason for what's happened. I think you want to know not *why* I've done what I've done, but *how*. Is that right? Do you hope that I'll tell you some little secret? Reveal to you some great ...*power* that I have?"

Ashley remained quiet as she saw him scoff and shake his head.

"Such a little thing to focus on really," Jaz continued.

"Why so?" Tim asked.

"Perhaps there has never been intention to promote the question of how this was done," Jaz admitted. "Not *how*, but *why*. That question, nobody has seemed to care about, and that has saddened me."

"*I* want to know the why," Ashley said.

"Do you?" Jaz asked. "Do you really? Because no matter how many people have died through all of this, I've not seen one news report that talked about the why at all. Even all those news reports where I saw you talking about the case, asking for the public's help - not once did you talk about why it was happening."

"Tell us why," Ashley pushed him. "The only person who knows the answer to that question is you."

Jaz shook his head. He'd expected since before he'd embarked upon his journey that he'd get caught. Admittedly, he'd expected his capture would be followed up by an array of bullets hitting his body, delivered from law enforcement. It hadn't happened that way, but he didn't mind at all. He'd tried and tried to deliver a message without actually speaking. Now he could speak and tell it all. His life would effectively be over with, but perhaps he could finally say something that would get people thinking - and talking. In some ways, he wondered if someone reporting his reason behind all of the shootings might actually result in what he'd always wanted - people to start discussing the issue.

"Too many people have guns," he said simply. "They have guns in their homes. They have guns in their cars and their workplaces. Why? Why do we, as a society, think it's okay for there to be so many guns … *everywhere*?!"

"People have them for protection," Tim said.

"Do they?" Jaz challenged. "For protection, or because deep down inside, they really desire the feeling of shooting someone - causing pain, or causing death?"

"Why do you think that?" Ashley asked him.

"Why?" Jaz asked. "*Why?!*"

"Yes," said Ashley. "You think that everyone who owns a gun has this desire in them to kill? You don't see that your logic is flawed?"

"*My* logic is flawed … or *yours*?" Jaz asked. "Have you seen the figures? The numbers of people who own guns?"

"We know that you chose Seaview, Leefton and Kildare because of the gun ownership numbers in those towns," Tim replied.

"In those towns," Jaz repeated. "Those towns have hardly any population at all…"

"*Now* they have hardly any population at all," Ashley said. "And why is that? Because you picked that town - a sleepy town that'd had hardly any crime in it for decades - and you chose to not only kill hundreds of people, but also make the same number of others responsible for those deaths. But *none* of those people - not the shooters and certainly not those killed - were people *wanting* to kill. You put that idea in their heads. *You!*"

Jaz smiled at her. However they'd figured things out, he knew they already knew everything that he could tell them - everything except, perhaps, how he'd done what he'd done. In his opinion, the how was the least important aspect of it all.

"Did I? Really?" he challenged her. "*Did* I make those people take their guns and go and shoot someone who was against owning a gun? Did I *make* them, or were they all actually people who *wanted* to use their gun? Are you sure that I *made* them? Can you prove that? Because what I believe is that every one of those gun owners had been waiting for years - waiting for just the right circumstance to come along when they could use that gun sitting in their bedside cabinet, or under their bed, or wherever - patiently waiting for when they could use it to hurt someone - to let out all of whatever pain they'd each been feeling for a very long time."

"No," Ashley started to say in objection before she saw his smile. It was a weird sensation she felt at that moment, like she sincerely had started to feel sorry for him.

"People want to hurt others," Jaz continued, ignoring her response. "It is just the way of humans. We could all be living a peaceful life, just getting on and doing what we can day to day, only ever interacting with kindness, but do we? No. And why is that? Because humans *want* to hurt others. You can argue that it isn't true, but history proves that it is."

"None of the people who've died from what you've done, wanted to die *or* hurt people," Ashley argued. "They were innocent."

"Were they?" Jaz challenged her. "Well, perhaps you're right in that. Perhaps they *were* innocent. Imagine, then, if the other people in that town hadn't owned guns. If they hadn't, they wouldn't have been able to so easily kill their neighbors, their friends ... their loved ones. If there had been no gun so easily accessible to them, none of this would have happened."

"What you really mean is that if people couldn't so easily access guns, what happened to *Christie* wouldn't have happened," Tim said.

"Maybe," Jaz acknowledged.

"But like you said, humans want to hurt, and if that gunman hadn't had access to a gun that day, but wanted to hurt people, he still could have, just using another means," said Ashley. "Your logic is flawed, Mr McMenamin. You think that stopping all access to guns will stop crime, and stop people hurting each other, but would it? Or would people just find another way..."

"Other ways are *harder*," Jaz argued. "It takes far more anger and strength to kill someone with a knife than it does with a bullet."

"That is true," Ashley said. "But anyone who wants to kill, is going to kill, no matter what tools they find to do it with. What you've done has destroyed so many lives - not only the people who were killed, and not only the people who are now charged with murder even though they may not have wanted to do it, but what about all the people left behind? What about the kids who lost their parents? What about the people who lost friends and family?"

"Family," Jaz scoffed. "Family is behind everything. Don't you know that, from what you do every day? People look at families and think everything is happy and good but, behind closed doors, parents are creating future adults who want to do just as I've done - hurt others. Whether it's through overindulging kids and making them think that everyone will always give them what they want - which is never going to be the case and will only create anger in those kids when they grow up and realize it - or using words and violence to make kids think they're worth nothing - it all ends up with the same result. People grow up and when they do, they *want* to *hurt others*."

As Tim sat and listened to the entire conversation happening primarily between his work partner and the suspect, he felt mixed in his emotions. The guy before them wasn't denying he'd somehow managed to make people go out and kill others, but there was no real confession of anything. Listening to the dialogue going on, he found himself growing dismayed with the realization that somehow they were going to have to prove that what they thought had been happening *had* been happening. Even if they did indeed have the person behind it all, what were the chances that Jaz McMenamin would ever be charged with anything at all?

"How did you do it?" he asked, suspecting he wouldn't get an answer, and even if he did, sure he wouldn't understand it. "How did you get people to go get their gun and go and shoot someone?"

Jaz grinned. As he'd expected, even after all that he'd already told them, *that* was still the most important thing to law enforcement, not changing gun laws. He'd had a plan to try and make life better. As he'd suspected after the last event he'd held, nothing had changed. People just didn't care. It was that simple.

"Get people to go get their gun and shoot someone?" Jaz repeated. "Really? You tell me, officer. How could anyone get someone to do that?"

"You are the person behind all of these killings,"

Ashley said to him, sure that was the truth, especially with all that he'd said so far.

"You might believe that," Jaz said, grinning. "Now, how are you going to *prove* it?"

"You could save us time by telling us," Ashley suggested, sure it wouldn't be that easy, but fully prepared to give him a chance to explain.

In response, Jaz laughed. He knew his days of freedom were up, but he wasn't going to make it that easy for the people who were holding him. No, they weren't interested in doing what he wanted - change the gun laws - so he certainly wasn't interested in doing what *they* wanted.

In his mind, it was that easy and that was just how things were going to go.

CHAPTER 53

Packing up their things in the small motel rooms, Tim and Ashley both felt somewhat dazed by what they'd learned in their interrogation of Jaz McMenamin. When both exited their rooms and met in the motel corridor, they stood in silence, facing one another, until roused to leave.

"I feel weird," Ashley admitted as they walked toward their car.

"So do I, to be honest," said Tim. "Do you think he hypnotized us?"

"No," Ashley said, smiling and then taking a longer moment to really consider the possibility. "Do *you* think he did?"

After throwing his overnight bag into the back seat and settling in the front, Tim faced her again.

"I don't *think* so, but then what would that feel like?" he asked. "I mean, hardly anyone seems to have remembered ever meeting this guy, so I guess he *could* have done something to us in that room - made us flap our wings and run around like chickens?"

"Tim!" Ashley said, scolding him. "Of course he didn't make us do that! Besides, the camera was rolling the whole time. If he'd used his super powers to get us to do anything, it'd be on tape."

"Unless he instructed us to go over to the camera and stop the recording," Tim suggested.

Ashley looked at him, surprised. When she saw his standard teasing face, she chuckled.

"Nice try, Moore," she said as she started the engine.

"Seriously though, where is this all going to end?"

"Our job is pretty much done, as you well know," said Tim. "We have no reason at all to believe anyone else was a part of this, and although he hasn't admitted to killing anyone, his interview shows he had reason to do what he did..."

"Yes, but how can it be proven?" Ashley challenged.

"That isn't our job," Tim reminded her. "We got the guy. It's up to a prosecution team to get a jury on side to get someone put away. All of what we've learned, including our main witness, Kane Garmin - that's what will be used to try and get McMenamin convicted..."

"Of what exactly?" Ashley asked. "He didn't actually kill anyone."

"We've talked about this, Ash," Tim said. "He doesn't need to have killed anyone. He just needs to have proactively encouraged the shooters - however he did so - to go and do what *they* did."

"You really think he'll get convicted?" Ashley asked as she turned to face him.

"I have no idea," Tim admitted. "But we've got a lot of evidence pointing to him being behind it all, and now we can leave it to the prosecuting professionals to finish the job and get him put away. Plus, there are also the other professionals that the Bureau have located, who are going to be able to assess him and see if he does have any brainwashing abilities..."

"Yeah, but you know what? If I was a criminal, using brainwashing powers to get people to do crimes for me, I wouldn't be showing those powers to someone who wanted to assess my abilities. Would you?" Ashley asked.

"You and I might hide the skills, but you know how it is with these guys. There's a little part of their nature that likes to show what they can do," said Tim. "Let's hope that Jaz McMenamin falls into that category. Even though he didn't make a proper confession, he certainly spoke enough about the reasons he has for doing it all. Whatever tests the professionals throw at him, to get him to demonstrate whatever his mind control abilities are, let's hope that he stands proud and doesn't hold back. That's all we can wish for as far as proof of any mind bending goes."

Ashley knew he was right, but it was never easy for her, walking away from a case when the bad guys had been caught but never knowing if they would go on to be punished for their crimes. Most of the time they were, but sometimes they weren't. That was a cold, hard truth about the justice system worldwide.

"For now, we go home, hopeful that at least no more people will die due to this guy, and then we move on," said Tim. "And for you, of course, you get to have your few days alone..."

"Yeah, I'm *so* needing that," Ashley said, grinning. "You're such hard work to be around, Moore."

Tim couldn't help but throw his head back and laugh. It wasn't the perfect resolution to the case they'd been on, but he knew it was enough for them to be happy with, at least for the moment.

At least until their next case begun.

~~~~~~~~~~~~~~

The End
~~~~~~~~~~~~~~

OTHER BOOKS
IN THIS SERIES

A POWER MOORE INVESTIGATION TALE
CATCH A
CATFISH
KILLER
M. PRATLEY

CATCH A CATFISH KILLER

After a suspicious gas explosion wakes a usually peaceful community, what is left of the home reveals the charred remains of Bob Masters, a hospital orderly who has a solid reputation as someone good-hearted and caring. When fire scene investigators confirm their findings that the explosion was intended, so begins a murder investigation. The one question that's on everyone's mind is why? Why would anyone intentionally try to hurt such a kind and hard working man?

Called in to work out what could have gone wrong in what appears to be a simple, quiet life, and who could be behind such a horrific act, Special Agents Ashley Power and Tim Moore start to realize how much more to someone's life there can be other than what people see on the outside.

Embark on a murder mystery involving crime solving of the digital kind. Initially, through studying online actions and conversations, it becomes evident that catfishing - an unfortunate and sad aspect of modern day dating - seems to be at the root of what begins to be a pattern. Even knowing this, the journey of discovery the agents are subjected to still surprises them.

Catfishing: a deceptive activity in which a person creates a fictional persona or fake identity on a social networking service, usually targeting a specific victim. With it being such an easy way to take advantage of people in the modern age, it may take quite some detective work to solve the mystery of who is ever behind any screen, at any time.

TIGER IN OUR HOUSE

ANN M PRATLEY

TIGER IN OUR HOUSE

When Alana Templeton goes to do the simple task of hanging her laundry outdoors, she becomes aware that something is not as it should be in her yard. The sound she hears is one that many people might not recognize at first. For Alana, it is, surprisingly, a sound she's heard before.

Being in the yard, with her toddler in the doorway of their home, she knows the right thing to do is whatever she can to save him. The previous time, she succeeded, but will she this time?

A woman and her infant being put in danger of being attacked by the large animal that has escaped the local wildlife park, not once but twice, prompts an investigation into whether there might be more than just bad luck behind the two events. It seems unlikely that someone could have used such a beast for an attempt on someone's life. Then again, it seems unlikely that the animal would escape its confine and end up at the same location two times in a row.

Sent to figure out what might be behind the strange occurrences, Special Agents Ashley Power and Tim Moore begin to delve into an elaborate and rather unconventional scheme to hurt someone through an act of revenge.

A POWER MOORE INVESTIGATION TALE
HOME
BY THE
SEA
ANN M PRATLEY

HOME BY THE SEA

A decade ago, homeless people began disappearing from four neighboring towns. Day to day, the commuters making their way to and from work never took notice of the less fortunate they passed. They didn't notice as the number of homeless reduced. They didn't even notice when entire groups of homeless people vanished.

A young woman, eager to find out where her grandfather disappeared to, began trying to find him. When four police departments dismissed her, telling her that her grandfather would no doubt turn up when he wanted to, she was too young to realize she should pursue the matter further.

Now, ten years on, she's stepped up and pushed harder for something to be done to find not only her grandfather but also the countless other people who seemed to have disappeared around the same time.

Called in to investigate the disappearances, Special Agents Ashley Power and Tim Moore find themselves searching for - and finding - so much more than they thought they would.

A POWER MOORE INVESTIGATION TALE

RESOLUTION
of
HAPPINESS

ANN M PRATLEY

RESOLUTION OF HAPPINESS

Fiona Thompson - better known as Flo to everyone who knew her - took a plunge and stepped out of her comfort zone and into the world of online dating. With persistence she found her prince. He ticked all the boxes. He was handsome. He was financially secure. He loved her. He married her.

She was warned by friends and family that there was something off about him. She didn't listen.

Then she woke up cold, inside the darkness of a wooden box.

Join Special Agents Ashley Power and Tim Moore as they investigate the disappearance of Flo, going on a surprising journey that nobody in Flo's world could possibly anticipate

A POWER MOORE INVESTIGATION TALE
HOONIGAN
ANN M PRATLEY

HOONIGAN

Tristan Clarkson has woken up, over and over, bound to a chair and unable to see. He has no idea where he is, or why he's in the situation he's woken to. His memory is vague, protecting him from recent events that will eventually haunt him for the rest of his life. He wants to remember, but at the same time his mind acts as though he really, really doesn't. Initially he's confused. With each waking, his memory clears that little bit more, as do his senses. He soon becomes aware that the very person who has abducted him, is in the room with him, determined to make Tristan pay for something he cannot even remember.

Meanwhile, in a hospital nearby, a patient has been taken. With the help of Special Agents Ashley Power and Tim Moore, an investigation begins into where the man has been taken, and who would have reason to remove him. With the patient having already been weak from time in a coma, time is of the essence in finding him alive.

Hoonigan is a blend of crime and suspense, intermingled with the strength of friendship, and the awakening of one father's realization of just how much his son really means to him.

OTHER BOOKS
BY
ANN M PRATLEY

ALESSANDRA
(CHISHOLM MANOR SERIES - BOOK #1)

Passion can come from great innocence.

After receiving news from her parents of a possible
betrothal, Alessandra, an 18 year old with an ingrained
belief that no-one would ever wish to marry her, finds
herself in a love so great that at times she cannot breathe.
Married to someone as inexperienced as herself, she
finds herself on a sexual journey of learning and
exploration.

The combination of their mutual inexperience
contributes to Alessandra discovering a degree of
emotional and physical love that she has never before
realized could exist.

That love will be tested by someone from her past with
sinister intentions. Jealous of the physical love
Alessandra shares with her husband, he is set on doing
whatever it takes to have the woman he desires, no
matter the cost.

ELIZABETH
(CHISHOLM MANOR SERIES - BOOK #2)

When innocence and scoundrel collide…

When Elizabeth Chisholm visits Venice with her family, she is unexpectedly drawn to Lord Byron - a man eleven years her senior. What she sees him present to her is grace, gentlemanlike behavior, and an enthusiasm to pursue her. What she doesn't see is how much of a scoundrel he is - something he can easily hide from a mind and a heart as pure as hers.

Having grown up watching the deep and intense love of her parents - Alessandra and Edward - Elizabeth does all that is asked of her day to day but, now the age of eighteen, deeply yearns for someone to love her. The attention she receives from the handsome lord nicely fits into her desires, but where does she fit into his?

As Elizabeth is lured into the ongoing uncertainty of Lord Byron's attention, a young Scotsman wants to overcome his intense shyness. The love of art is something that he shares with Elizabeth, but he knows he can't compete with the confidence and handsomeness of the English lord.

At the request of Elizabeth's brother, Charles, the young Scotsman proves his worth by attempting to draw Elizabeth away as more things are learned about Lord Byron's actions across Europe, but is it too late? Is the reputation of Elizabeth Chisholm already sealed and irreparable, just through being associated with the scandalous English gentleman?

CHRISTIAN
(FREEDOM OF FLIGHT SERIES - BOOK #1)

Twenty four year old Christian Shaw has a good life. He's had a rocky ride with being charged for a crime he didn't commit, but he's come out on the other side, older and wiser. He has good friends who've stood by him. He has family who love him. However there's something about Christian that he's never understood. There's something about him that sets him apart. It's made him not want to get close to anyone.

Now someone's appeared unexpectedly. To his surprise, she's just like him. Even more importantly, she has the knowledge to help him understand more about the strange existence he lives. But is she as nice as she appears, or could she have a darker reason for seeking him out and devoting time to him?

Providing an insight into one man's strange journey of coming to grips with who he really is, 'Christian' tells a story of courage, friendship and crime solving intrigue.

BRANDON
(FREEDOM OF FLIGHT SERIES - BOOK #2)

For fifteen years, Brandon McStevens has held himself away from everyone he knew prior to the day he turned fourteen. That day changed his life forever. Something happened to him that he can't explain to anyone. He feels ashamed and embarrassed. The only way he's ever been able to move past that and live, has been to find somewhere else to reside.

Since leaving his family home, he has continued to live in a small cave. Nestled high above a small coastal community, he has come to spend most of his time enjoying the ocean … oh, and up in the sky. He doesn't know how it happened. He doesn't know *why* it happened. All he knows is that despite understanding how much hurt he must have caused when he left home all those years ago, he now lives the only existence he can imagine.

He's never met anyone like him. He's never *seen* anyone like him. Until that day when that woman and her dog saw him change, no-one had ever seen or heard of him doing that. To this day he regrets having shown himself like he did. But time passed and it has all been forgotten … or has it?

Certain he's the only one like himself, he's surprised when two people come looking for him … and have much to tell him. Finally the time will come when he no longer has to feel like a freak of nature … or so alone.

TRINITY
(FREEDOM OF FLIGHT SERIES - BOOK #3)

A strange series of events have been happening in cities around the southwest of the country. When one bank is robbed on a small scale, it makes the banking professionals and law enforcement curious. When a second, then a third, then a fourth are also robbed without anyone knowing how it's been done, agencies combine resources to begin the search to find out who has been doing it and how.

Trinity Love is a twenty-five-year-old woman who's been surviving week to week, doing what she can to find money for her next meal and a roof over her head. In a unique way, she needs neither. She has a level of survival instinct built into her that should enable her to live a good life on the straight and narrow. That kind of life is one that she's never wanted or sought.

Seeing the latest news broadcast about the bank thefts, Brandon McStevens notices something about it that catches his attention. Talking to his new friends, Kelly and Christian, they decide it might be worth investigating.

Embarking on their new journey of exploration to find others like them, Christian and Kelly are faced with a new type of person they've never met before. Trinity is challenging in so many ways, but is she open to meeting people like her?

FORBIDDEN CONFLICTS
SERIES
~Family Saga / Romantic Suspense~

AMETHYST OF YOUTH
(FORBIDDEN CONFLICTS SERIES - BOOK #1)

The youngest member of the Stonewarden family, Charlotte (Charlie), is 18 years old. As with everyone in her family when they reach that age, she's been told that when she turns 19, she'll be recruited into the family business. She has her warning that she has one year to do anything else she wishes to do - travel, study, work. Whatever she wants to do, she has 365 days to do it. On her next birthday, her life will effectively stop being her own.

But Charlie wants nothing to do with the business. The youngest of six, with five older brothers, she wants a different life. Maybe if the family business was something normal like a retail shop or a business centered around trade, she'd feel differently. There are people who say that her family's long term history of robbing from the rich and providing to the poor is a good thing. To her, all she can see is that they are thieves. Plain and simple.

Her view is further secured when she and her older brother, Max, are shot at in a local supermarket. Seeing Max lying in blood and later lying unmoving in hospital in a coma, pushes her further in her resolve to find a way to not take part in the activities of her father and brothers.

At the shootout she is saved by a checkout operator, Ash. Whilst building their friendship, Charlie will learn things about her family that she didn't particularly wish to know. She will hear more and more that she can't share with Ash and, the more she learns, the wider the gap will become.

In years she's young, but having lost her mother when she was only nine years old, Charlie has an older soul. The possibilities she'll be presented with during her one final year of her own, will push her in her considerations of how she really wants her life to be. She wants one thing. Her strict ex-military father wants another. The dynamics of her new friendship will pull her in a third direction.

How will she chose what's right for her? And what would she have to do to break free from the chains that she can see her father wants to place around her for the rest of her life?

REVIEWERS SAY:

"This was a good clean romance with plenty of action to further the story along ... will make you ponder about life's situations, their actions and reactions, and how the decisions of past generations can affect the current ones. You'll be glad you read it!"

"... loved this book! It took me by surprise--great from start to finish! I don't normally read crime family dramas, but I love NA/coming-of-age novels. Charlie is on the cusp of being inducted into her family's Robin Hood-esque biz, but she doesn't want that. She isn't sure what, exactly, she does want...just not THAT. Her connection with Ash furthers that disconnect, and they stumble through the beginnings of young love together. Of course, secrets and family craziness threaten their romance at every turn. ...It's an awesome start to the Forbidden Conflicts series!"

"A wonderful read. A timeless push and pull between our own wants and our family's wants. Will she follow the path her family wants or will she follow her own path? Read the book to find out."

RUBY OF LAW
(FORBIDDEN CONFLICTS SERIES - BOOK #2)

For generations the Leadbetters have lived off crime. For as long as any of them know, fathers and mothers have taught sons and daughters how to succeed in the criminal world, primarily through theft.

Phillip Leadbetter is 29 and has devoted his whole life so far to doing what his father and mother have told him to do. The sacrifice for doing that is that he still lives at home and hasn't yet met anyone who he believes could accept the man that he is because of his family.

One night a potential tragedy brings him into the path of Daisy, an up and coming professional in the legal sector. Seeing him as her knight in shining armor, she can't stop thinking about the rugged guy who saved her. She's also very pleased when fate brings their paths to cross again.

Getting to know one another, both leave out major details about who they are. She doesn't want him to know she's a lawyer because some people just don't like lawyers. He doesn't want to tell her about his family and their long history of criminal activity.

How, then, will things turn when they meet up in a courthouse, each learning in that moment who the other really is? How will they deal with the fact that she is on one side of the law, and he is very definitely on the other?

DIAMOND OF WAR
(FORBIDDEN CONFLICTS SERIES - BOOK #3)

James Stonewarden is a playboy. He has been since the moment he first started to notice girls. He loves them all, and they all love him. Why would he want to get himself into a relationship?

Sasha Leadbetter's a hot-headed young woman, known to the law for her quick temper and harsh ways. She isn't one to mess with - especially with the way she keeps a blade in her pocket. To her it's her security. It's something that makes her feel safe and comfortable. She's had it for so long that it's nothing for her to pull it out and hold it to someone's throat without any conscious thought.

Unaware of who each other are, or how their families are distantly interconnected through crime, the chance of James Stonewarden meeting Sasha Leadbetter is slim. But it happens.

A playboy and a young woman who has the mentality to kill. What kind of recipe could that result in? And what will happen when James identifies a car at Sasha's family home, that matches the description his sister Charlie gave after the supermarket shooting months earlier?

SAPPHIRE OF PREJUDICE
(FORBIDDEN CONFLICTS SERIES - BOOK #4)

Greg and Rhett. They've grown up together since they were teenagers. They've fought together. They've stolen together. They've even loved women together. But something deeper has existed in one of them for years. He's hidden it well. Being part of the great Leadbetter gang and family, the prejudice of certain situations has always been loudly expressed by many of its members - too many, and certainly enough to make anyone fearful of what would happen if feelings were revealed and brought out into the open.

A night has passed when finally, in a moment of wondering if he'd survive till morning, Rhett's taken the chance and kissed the person of his desire.
Given their circumstances, what can they do,
and where can they go?

Meanwhile, as Phillip Leadbetter continues on his path of happiness with his Daisy, someone from her past has grown obsessed with her and wants her back. To what degree will he put into effect a plan to get her back, and get Phillip out of her life forever?

~~ NOTE: This book does contain adult sexual content and LOTS of swear words.

EMERALD OF WISDOM
(FORBIDDEN CONFLICTS SERIES - BOOK #5)

When Mitchell Stonewarden lost his wife to cancer more than a decade ago, he vowed to never give his heart to anyone else. With all of his children now adults, and a new generation of Stonewardens having already begun, he's finally started to wonder - does he really want to be alone for the rest of his life? The handover of the family business to his oldest son, Vic, has seemed to be free of difficulty or issues - but has it? Mitchell knows little of his oldest son's private life away from the family. He is surprised by what is brought to his attention that he had no idea about.

While Mitchell finally starts to move on into a new chapter of his life, another of his sons - Max - is on his own path of discovery in life and in love. Previously well-known as 'Romeo' to his family and peers, he begins to wonder if Christie - a surprising addition to his life - has grown to become more important to him than any other young woman he's ever met. When her work at a homeless shelter tests the boundaries of her safety, Max's commitment to her is also tested, making him wonder if he will, indeed, end up hurting her.

Meanwhile, on the other side of town, the Leadbetter family is shattered by an unexpected turn of events that leaves Stacey wondering if she is going to lose the man she's loved for more than three decades...

PAINFUL DELIVERANCE SERIES
~Erotic Romance/Romantic Suspense~

PAINFUL DELIVERANCE
(PAINFUL DELIVERANCE SERIES - BOOK #1)

She just wasn't made to inflict pain.

She knows it is nothing abnormal. She knows others enjoy it. But with every new level of pain he directs her to deliver to him, Alexis feels another piece of her soul die. He has wealth and he has power, and she knows he won't easily let her go.

But she has to leave. Escape. Move on. Forget. She has reached her limit of what she can do. The plans are in place to get away. She just has to hope that wherever she goes - whoever she meets - she won't find herself in exactly the same situation again.

DARKNESS OF HEART
(PAINFUL DELIVERANCE SERIES - BOOK #2)

She thought he'd stopped looking. He hadn't.

She got away from him to start a new life. She moved on. But in his mind, he still loves her and needs her. He still believes that she loves him. That she is meant to be his. That he is meant to be hers.

He will not give up searching for her. He will not give up *fighting* for her. He will pursue her and stop at nothing to get her back. But it will come at a cost … a sacrifice much greater than he will see coming. A sacrifice that will finally wake him up and bring him back to stark reality.

REVIEWERS SAY:

"… author did a great job of making brief references from the first book. Lincoln, Lexi and Alexis are back, though perhaps the most complex character is Diana … definitely written for a mature audience … the author is a great storyteller and writes with an easy to read style … certainly writes a more interesting and readable story than many best-selling authors. It's very easy for me to recommend this book with 5 of 5 stars."

"This story continued the journey of Alexis, Anthony and Lincoln while giving us a new perspective into the repercussions of Lincoln and Alexis's relationship: from the POV of Lincoln's wife Diana! I loved her addition to the story's … kept the tension of the story just right, balancing the calm new life Alexis has been building and keeping the reader engaged."

"It is a book of courage, the courage to leave everything you know behind, the courage to change, the courage to face your fears, and the courage to face the unknown."

FRIENDSHIP OF DESIRE
(PAINFUL DELIVERANCE SERIES - BOOK #3)

Tom and Samantha. Feisty friends from childhood who feel like they know each other inside out, until the day comes when one of them suggests they go to a BDSM club together, and become formal play partners. Pushing the limits of what each of them can individually stand in their lifelong friendship, they attract and repel like magnets, until the time comes when they must choose how they will relate to one another - and what kind of relationship they will go on to have in the future.

Whilst on this journey of discovery, the two of them meet and make a new friend - Alexis. A young woman with a hidden and secretive past, and a mystery surrounding the relationship she has - or has had - with a renowned business entrepreneur who begins to integrate himself into Samantha's life, unknown to any of them whether he has done it for him, or for her … or for Alexis, being the mysterious link from his past.

FOUR SWORDS
SERIES
~Medieval Saga~

KNIGHT OF DESIRE

Cecily, Azura and Maynard have grown up together from childhood. In many ways they've always felt equal ... except for Maynard being a prince, that is.

After her two closest friends find each other in love and then marriage, taking on the ruling of a kingdom, Cecily finds herself questioning if love is in her future. Over time, it becomes apparent that she certainly has caught someone's eye. He is a knight and he is known to be a rogue, but can the handsome Sir Henry capture the fair heart of Cecily, and push her fears aside?

Knight of Desire is a simple old-fashioned light-hearted short-read romance. There is no adult content or violence in this story. This story is also not an essential book in the Four Swords series, being set years prior to Blade of Envy beginning.

BLADE OF ENVY
(FOUR SWORDS SERIES - BOOK #1)

They expected quite a different kind of destruction...

In the realm of the House of Mordasini, the three royal offspring of King Maynard and Queen Azura are beginning their journeys into adulthood.

As the eldest, Prince Aldin, starts to obsess about his future role as the next king, so also begins an obsession about his younger brother. Torn between wanting to be the one who rules over everyone else, but also wanting the life that is being set up for his brother, Aldin begins a journey of envy that grows darker as time passes.

Meanwhile, as one brother ruminates about the life of the other, their younger sister, Princess Semera, appears to grow ill. In the quiet of her deep slumber, something surprising begins to happen as, from a distance, she unknowingly becomes someone else's focus.

BLADE OF LOVE
(FOUR SWORDS SERIES - BOOK #2)

In the kingdom of the House of Mordasini, a future king is waiting for the day to come when his father will die. While there's nothing to suggest that King Maynard will be leaving this world anytime soon, his oldest son, Aldin, increasingly desires to be the one on the throne. With the darkness that has been residing in his soul since he was a child, ideas begin to flow inside of Aldin's mind. All around him, there are things happening that go against his idea of how the realm should be run. In particular, the realization that his father has granted permission to his brother, Prince Iztal, to wed, is something that adds to Aldin's hatred for his brother - a hatred that has grown into an intense obsession.

While brothers continue to share their volatile relationship, their sister continues to experience signs that a beast will soon arrive in the realm, eager to cause destruction. Everyone thinks they are ready for the beast's return, but are they? To stop such destruction from happening, two princes who have no time for one another must unite, but can they?

GOLDEN DESIRES
SERIES
~Time Travel / Paranormal Romance~

THE GOLDEN DESIRES
(THE GOLDEN DESIRES SERIES - BOOK #1)

He wanted to escape. They needed to survive.

When Isabella starts to dream of a stranger, she's awakened inside with feelings she has never felt before. She knows he's not someone she's ever seen before, and he is not of her village. He is a stranger, and she's desperate to determine if he is real or he is a part of her imagination.

Far away a businessman desperate to escape the noise and stress of the city, embarks on a journey to find peace and the solitude he increasingly needs and desires. But at his destination he will find much, much more.

REVIEWERS SAY:

"I found myself drawn to keep reading ... almost as if reading a compelling action/adventure because the pacing was so excellent. And... ahem... the love scenes are quite well written, too ... I look forward to reading the sequel..."

"The author paints such a vivid picture of life in this idyllic community that one begins to think it may actually exist ... extremely well-written ... perfect for anyone who is looking for a romance with a hint of paranormal mystery."

"The concept behind this story was intriguing and very sexy ... Fireworks and all out romance, followed by some interesting obstacles, but they are overcome, because well...it's love. What I loved about this read was the fairytale like narration with a sci-fi/fantasy kick; it made me feel like I was part of the story..."

"... magical quality was a nice twist, delving into the realm of fantasy romance ... the author's style was well suited to the tone of the world she has created. Did it leave me hungry for the next installment? Absolutely!"

THE GOLDEN SUPREMACY
(THE GOLDEN DESIRES SERIES - BOOK #2)

What is lying in wait, eager to destroy them?

Over distance and time they met and fell in love, choosing to live together in an ancient village of peace and harmony. And then the battle had happened. A fight between good and evil; the warmth of fire and the cold of ice. They thought they had won. But had they?

Trent and Isabella start to feel that the entity that had tried to destroy them, might not have been defeated after all. But rather, perhaps it is lying in wait for another opportunity to strike.

What is it?
And who is its puppet now?

THE GOLDEN UNITY
(GOLDEN DESIRES SERIES - BOOK #3)

Cesare is the golden child of the village. His brilliant yellow hair is unlike the color of anyone else's. He is a cheerful child who in the eyes of some, can do no wrong.

Esmeralda is the product of two biological parents who have something buried deep within them. Something that makes them easy to manipulate by the being that has not given up on wanting to destroy the ancient village. The young lass with the blue-black hair is looked upon as an alternative child. She captures attention and intrigues the villagers. When they look at her, sometimes they feel like they're looking at a puzzle that confuses them and they cannot solve. It's impossible to determine why but there's just something *different* about Esmeralda.

Despite them being opposites in nature and appearance, the two have grown up together as best friends, just as their parents did before them. The goodness of Cesare showers a level of kindness and friendship on Esmeralda that she has never been able to turn away from. The difference of Esmeralda has always held Cesare's attention. Between them they have found a balance that holds them together as friends.

But what will happen as they move into their time as young adults? They are unknowing as yet that they are meant to be paired, whilst at the same time they are meant to be adversaries.

What does the puppet master have planned now? And how will these two gifted youth react to someone trying to manipulate them against their will?

A third strike from the puppet master. Will it win in its plan of attack this time?

TOTAL FREEDOM
(TOTAL FREEDOM SERIES - BOOK #1)

For Debbie King, life began feeling like it was all too difficult - like she would never achieve, she would never have friends, and she would simply never fit in. But when she meets someone new who seems just like her, with low self-esteem and no belief in themselves and what they have to offer, Debbie finds strength to focus more on them and less on herself.

So begins an incredible journey of friendship and love that will be tested by other people entering their world, and the shared passion they have for their musical talents and career together. It is a deep friendship that will be tested over and over again by events and an ongoing uncertainty over what their relationship really should really be like.

REVIEWERS SAY:

"The overall story was great and hooked me right in. I had to stay with them for the entire journey ... you know it's a good story when you wish it didn't have to end."

"... an incredible job developing complex characters that are emotionally scarred and then allowing the reader to really understand their pain ... a terrific coming of age story surrounding a triangle of young characters, Debbie, Craig and Steven."

"Covered a lot of different things that can happen as we grow and was appealing for that reason."

TOTAL NEW BEGINNINGS
(TOTAL FREEDOM SERIES - BOOK #2)

In her early adulthood Debbie made a choice. She had
two men who loved her. She chose one. She lost the
friendship of the other.

Twenty years on, horrific tragedy strikes. Mother to
three grown children, she has to find the strength to be
there for them, while pushing her own grief aside.
Dealing with the loss of the man who has been by her
side for two decades pushes her into depression. Every
day seems harder to deal with than the last. The feeling
of loss is further heightened by finding her husband's
lifetime of journals. Hesitant at first to look inside them,
she eventually does. Almost instantly she regrets that
decision. In the years of her husband's writing she reads
things that lead her to seriously question whether she
ever really knew him at all, or if they had actually been
strangers for two decades.

The combination of the loss of her husband, and the
uncertainty about who he really was, pushes her to retire
into a dark room and have no desire to leave. She wants
to shut out the world. She wants to not believe what she
knows in her heart is reality.

With her youngest daughter, Poppy, still living at home,
Debbie is eventually pulled from the darkness by her
daughter's pleas. Finally the dark days start to fade and
Debbie can start to see the sun shining once more.
Finally she can find the strength to keep going. Finally
she can start to move into a period of recovery and
growth. Finally she can accept that it's okay to accept
help and lean on others.

As she starts rediscovering her ability to embrace life again, results appear from her daughter's determination to help her mother. Someone from her past is brought back into her life. A friendship is re-established. It's time to let go of the past and begin a new future. It's time for total new beginnings.

Did you ever hear the words in your head … 'what if'? What if you chose one path earlier in life but later had the chance to walk down the path previously unchosen? Would you?

ANN M PRATLEY
Finding
Himself
Again

FINDING HIMSELF AGAIN

In a small seaside area of Sydney, Australia, 28-year-old Tom Santini has recently returned to the outside world after ten long years in jail following an error of judgment in his youth. Readjustment hasn't been easy but luck has taken a turn for him. The woman that his brother, Graham, has been seeing is a woman with connections. Through her, Tom has finally found an employer who will give an ex-criminal a chance to start over. It hasn't been an easy six months since his release, but Tom is learning to face his situation with reality and step up to take responsibility for his decisions.

Settled in his job at Toby's Stop'n'Dine, Tom's attention is captured by a young woman who enters. She's beautiful and alluring but, seeing and talking to her, he can deeply sense her being on the run from something … or someone.

Cat is smart, sexy and a woman who will make him wonder if he does, in fact, have a chance at being happy in love, despite his past. But why does she spook so easily? What - or who - is she on the run from? Tom knows that whatever happens, he has to think before he acts. He is determined to do things differently when it comes to dealing with difficult situations. He's already missed out on so much. He cannot go back to prison.

What can he do to calm and keep safe the woman who he so recently met but already has made a difference in his life? How can he save the woman with a deep-seated passion that drives him crazy…

THANK YOU!

Writing is something that I love to do, whether in romance, crime solving, paranormal, time travel, or something far more spicier, and I do appreciate the time you've invested into reading this story.

Every second month, I send out a newsletter to my subscribed readers, enabling them to learn about new releases and freebies, and take part in the odd opportunity to win items such as books, Amazon gift cards, and Kindle e-readers. If this sounds like something you might be interested in, you can SIGN UP HERE.

~~~~~

If you would like to make contact with me, please:
Follow me on Bookbub
https://www.bookbub.com/authors/ann-m-pratley

Follow Me On Twitter
https://twitter.com/runkiwiwriter

Thank you,
Ann M Pratley
~~~~~